A QUESTION OF BELIEF

Donna Leon has lived in Venice for many years and previously lived in Switzerland, Saudi Arabia, Iran and China, where she worked as a teacher. Her previous novels featuring Commissario Brunetti have all been highly acclaimed; including *Friends in High Places*, which won the CWA Macallan Silver Dagger for Fiction, *Through a Glass, Darkly*, *Suffer the Little Children*, *The Girl of His Dreams* and, most recently, *About Face*.

Praise for *A Question of Belief*

'Leon's books are a joy, and the 19th Venice-based Commissario Brunetti novel is well up to her consistently high standard . . . All the Leon hallmarks are here: clear, unshowy writing, atmosphere, humanity and believable characters.' *Guardian*

'To read a Donna Leon novel is to have an armchair holiday in her lovingly described Venice, in the company of an old friend – the amiable Commissario Brunetti . . . Leon never fails to impress with her carefully wrought plots and believable characters.' *Daily Mail*

'Knowingness, or an illusion of knowingness, is essential to successful crime-writing . . . Donna Leon has mastered this technique perfectly.' *Times Literary Supplement*

'Fans of Donna Leon, whose number deservedly grows each year, will need no encouragement to devour this atmospheric and amusing story.' *Evening Standard*

'[an] elegant crime novel . . . it also obliquely addresses the issues of legal gerrymandering, faith and corruption that bedevil Leon's adopted country.' *Independent*

Donna Leon

A QUESTION OF BELIEF

arrow books

Published by Arrow Books 2011

1 3 5 7 9 10 8 6 4 2

Copyright © Donna Leon and Diogenes Verlag AG Zurich 2010

Map © ML Design

Donna Leon has asserted her right under the Copyright, Designs and Patents
Act, 1988 to be identified as the author of this work.

First published in Great Britain in 2010 by William Heinemann

Arrow Books
The Random House Group Limited
20 Vauxhall Bridge Road, London, SW1V 2SA

www.rbooks.co.uk

Addresses for companies within The Random House Group Limited can be
found at: www.randomhouse.co.uk/offices.htm

The Random House Group Limited Reg. No. 954009

A CIP catalogue record for this book
is available from the British Library

ISBN 9780099547624

The Random House Group Limited supports The Forest Stewardship
Council (FSC), the leading international forest certification organisation. All
our titles that are printed on Greenpeace approved FSC certified paper carry
the FSC logo. Our paper procurement policy can be found at:
www.rbooks.co.uk/environment

Mixed Sources
Product group from well-managed
forests and other controlled sources
www.fsc.org Cert no. TT-COC-2139
© 1996 Forest Stewardship Council
FSC

Typeset by SX Composing DTP, Rayleigh, Essex
Printed and bound in Great Britain by
CPI Bookmarque Ltd, Croydon, CR0 4TD

For Joyce DiDonato

L'empio crede con tal frode
Di nasconder l'empietà

The villain believes that with fraud
He can hide his wickedness

Don Giovanni

—Mozart

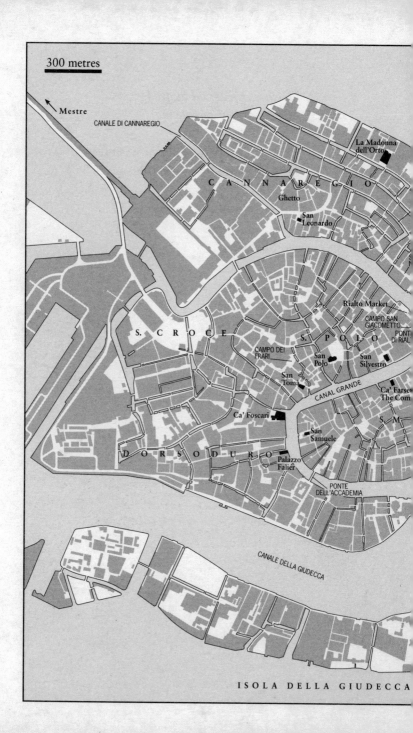

300 metres

Mestre

CANALE DI CANNAREGIO

La Madonna
dell'Orto

C A N N A R E G I O

Ghetto

San
Leonardo

Rialto Market

CAMPO SAN
GIACOMETTO

S. C R O C E

S.   P   O   L   O

PONTE
DI RIAL

CAMPO DEI
FRARI

San
Polo

San
Silvestro

San
Toma

CANAL GRANDE

Ca' Farse
The Com

Ca' Foscari

S. M

San
Samuele

D O R S O D U R O

Palazzo
Falier

PONTE
DELL'ACCADEMIA

CANALE DELLA GIUDECCA

I S O L A   D E L L A   G I U D E C C A

1

When Ispettore Vianello came into his office, Brunetti had all but exhausted the powers of will keeping him at his desk. He had read a report about gun trafficking in the Veneto, a report that had made no mention of Venice; he had read another one suggesting the transfer of two new recruits to the Squadra Mobile before realizing his name was not on the list of people who should read it; and now he had read half of a ministerial announcement about changes in the regulations concerning early retirement. That is, he had read half, if that verb could be applied to the level of attention Brunetti had devoted to the reading of the entire document. The paper lay on his desk as he stared out his window, hoping someone would come in and pour a bucket of cold water on his head or that it would rain or that he would experience the Rapture and thus escape the trapped heat of his office and the general misery of August in Venice.

Deus ex machina, therefore, could have been no more welcome than was Vianello, who came in carrying that day's *Gazzetta dello Sport*. 'What's that?' Brunetti asked, pointing to the pink newspaper and giving unnecessary emphasis to the second word. He knew what it was, of course, but he failed to understand how it could be in Vianello's possession.

The Inspector glanced at the paper, as if himself surprised to see it there, and said, 'Someone dropped it on the stairs. I thought I'd take it down and leave it in the squad room.'

'For a minute I thought it was yours,' Brunetti said, smiling.

'Don't scorn it,' Vianello said, tossing the paper on to Brunetti's desk as he sat. 'The last time I looked at it, there was a long article about the polo teams out near Verona.'

'Polo?' Brunetti asked.

'It seems. I think there are seven polo teams in this country, or maybe that's only around Verona.'

'With ponies and the white suits and hard hats?' Brunetti could not prevent himself from asking.

Vianello nodded. 'There were photos. Marchese this and Conte that, and villas and *palazzi*.'

'You sure the heat hasn't got to you and you're maybe mixing it up with something you might have read in – oh, I don't know – *Chi*?'

'I don't read *Chi*, either,' Vianello said primly.

'Nobody reads *Chi*,' Brunetti agreed, for he had never met a person who would confess to doing so. 'The information in the stories is carried by mosquitoes and seeps into your brain if you're bitten.'

'And *I'm* the one affected by the heat,' Vianello said.

They sat in limp companionship for a moment, neither

of them capable of the energy necessary to discuss the heat. Vianello leaned forward to reach behind himself and unstick his cotton shirt from his back.

'It's worse on the mainland,' Vianello said at last. 'The guys in Mestre said it was 41 degrees in the front offices yesterday afternoon.'

'I thought they had air conditioning.'

'There's some sort of directive from Rome, saying that they can't use it because of the danger of a brown-out like the one they had three years ago.' Vianello shrugged. 'So we're better off here than in some glass and cement box like they are.' He looked across at the windows of Brunetti's office, thrown open to the morning light. The curtains moved listlessly, but at least they moved.

'And they really had the air conditioning off?' Brunetti asked.

'That's what they told me.'

'I wouldn't believe them.'

'I didn't.'

They sat quietly until Vianello said, 'I wanted to ask you something.'

Brunetti looked across and nodded: it was easier than speaking.

Vianello ran his hand across the surface of the newspaper, then sat back. 'You ever,' he began, paused as if trying to find the proper wording, then went on, 'read the horoscope?'

After a moment, Brunetti answered, 'Not consciously.' Seeing Vianello's confusion, he continued, 'That is, I don't remember ever opening the newspaper to look for them. But I do glance at them if someone leaves the paper open to that page. But not actively.' He waited for some sort of explanation; when none was given, he asked, 'Why?'

Vianello shifted his weight in his chair, stood to smooth the wrinkles in his trousers, and sat down again. 'It's my aunt, my mother's sister. The last one left. Anita.

'She reads them every day. Doesn't make any difference to her if what they predict happens or not, though they never say anything much, do they? "You are going to take a trip." She goes to the Rialto Market the next day to buy vegetables: that's a trip, isn't it?'

Vianello had spoken of his aunt over the years: she was his late mother's favourite sister and his favourite aunt, as well, probably because she was the most strong-willed person in the family. Married in the fifties to an apprentice electrician, she had seen her husband go off to Torino in search of work within weeks of marrying him. She waited almost two years to see him again. Zio Franco had had good luck in finding work, most of it with Fiat, where he had been able to study and become a master electrician.

Zia Anita moved to Torino to join him and spent six years with him there; after the birth of their first son, they had moved to Mestre, where he set up his own business. The family grew, the business grew: both prospered. Franco had retired only in his late seventies and, much to the surprise of his children, all of whom had grown up on *terraferma*, moved back to Venice. When asked why none of her children had wanted to move back to Venice with them, she had said, 'They had gasoline in their veins, not salt water.'

Brunetti was content to sit and listen to whatever Vianello said about his aunt. The distraction would keep him from going to the window every few minutes to see if . . . If what? If it had started to snow?

'And she's started watching them on television,' Vianello continued.

'Horoscopes?' Brunetti asked, puzzled. He watched television infrequently, usually forced to do so by someone else in the family, and so had no idea of what sort of thing was to be found here.

'Yes. But mostly card readers and those people who say they can read your future and solve your problems.'

'Card readers?' he could only repeat. 'On television?'

'Yes. People call in and this person reads the cards for them and tells them what they should watch out for, or they promise to help them if they're sick. Well, that's what my cousins tell me.'

'Watch out not to fall down the stairs or watch out for a tall, dark-haired stranger?' Brunetti asked.

Vianello shrugged. 'I don't know. I've never watched them. It sounds ridiculous.'

'It doesn't sound ridiculous, Lorenzo,' Brunetti assured him. 'Strange, perhaps, but not ridiculous.' He added, 'And maybe not even so strange, come to think of it.'

'Why?'

'Because she's an old woman,' Brunetti said, 'and we tend to assume – and if Paola were here, or Nadia, they'd accuse me of prejudice against both women and old people for saying this – that old women will believe that sort of thing.'

'Isn't that why the witches got burnt?' Vianello asked.

Even though Brunetti had once read long passages of *Malleus Maleficarum*, he still had no idea why old women had been the specific targets of the burnings. Perhaps because many men are stupid and vicious and old women are weak and undefended.

Vianello turned his attention to the window and the light. Brunetti sensed that the Ispettore wanted no prodding; he would get to whatever it was sooner or later. For the moment, Brunetti let him study the light and used the moment to study his friend. Vianello never bore the heat well, but he seemed more oppressed by it this summer. His hair, slicked down by perspiration, was thinner than Brunetti remembered. And the skin of his face seemed puffy, especially around his eyes.Vianello broke into his observations to ask, 'But do you think old women really are more likely to believe in it?'

After considering the matter, Brunetti said, 'I've no idea. You mean any more than the rest of us?'

Vianello nodded and turned back towards the window, as if willing the curtains to increase their motion.

'From what you've said about her over the years, she doesn't sound the type,' Brunetti eventually said.

'No, she isn't. That's why it's so confusing. She was always the brains in the family. My uncle Franco's a good man, and he was a very good worker, but he never would have had the idea to go into business for himself. Or the ability to do it, come to that. But she did, and she kept the books until he retired and they moved back here.'

'Doesn't sound like the sort of person who would begin her day by checking what's new in the house of Aquarius,' Brunetti observed.

'That's what I don't understand,' Vianello said, raising his hands in a gesture of bewilderment. 'Whether she is or not. Maybe it's some sort of private ritual people have. I don't know, like not going out of the house until you've found out the temperature or wanting to know what famous people were born on your birthday. People you'd never suspect. They seem normal in everything, and then one day you discover they won't go on vacation unless their horoscope tells them it's all right to go on a journey.' Vianello shrugged, then repeated, 'I don't know.'

'I'm still not sure why you're asking me about this, Lorenzo,' Brunetti said.

'I'm not sure I know, either,' Vianello admitted with a grin. 'The last few times I've gone to see her – I try to stop in at least once a week – there were these crazy magazines lying around. No attempt to hide them or anything. *Your Horoscope. The Wisdom of the Ancients.* That sort of thing.'

'Did you ask her about them?'

Vianello shook the question away. 'I didn't know how.' He looked across at Brunetti and went on, 'And I suppose I was afraid she wouldn't like it if I did ask her.'

'Why do you say that?'

'No reason, really.' Vianello pulled out a handkerchief and wiped at his brow. 'She saw me looking at them – well, saw that I noticed them. But she didn't say anything. You know, make a joke and say one of her kids left them there or one of her friends had been to visit and had forgotten them. I mean, it would have been normal to say something about them. After all, it was like finding magazines about hunting or fishing or motorcycles. But she was almost – I don't know – almost secretive about it. I think that's what bothered me.' He gave Brunetti a long, inquisitive look and asked, 'You'd say something, wouldn't you?'

'To her, you mean?'

'Yes. If she were your aunt.'

'Maybe. Maybe not,' Brunetti said, then asked, 'What about your uncle? Can you ask him?'

'I suppose I could, but talking to Zio Franco is like

talking to any of those men of his generation: they have to make a joke about everything, slap you on the back and offer you a drink. He's the best man in the world, but he really doesn't pay much attention to anything.'

'Not even to her?'

Vianello was silent before he answered, 'Probably not.' Another silence, and then he added, 'Well, not in a way anyone would recognize. Men of his generation really didn't pay much attention to their families, I think.'

Brunetti shook his head in a mixture of agreement and regret. No, they didn't, not to their wives nor to their children, only to their friends and colleagues. He had often thought about this difference in – was it sensibility? Perhaps it was nothing more than culture: surely he knew a lot of men who still thought it a sign of weakness to display any interest in soft things like feelings.

He could not remember the first time it had occurred to him to wonder whether his father loved his mother, or loved him and his brother. Brunetti had always assumed that he had: children did. But what strange manifestations of emotion there had been: days of complete silence; occasional explosive bouts of anger; a few moments of affection and praise when his father had told his sons how much he loved them.

Surely, Brunetti's father was not the sort of man one told secrets to, or confided in about anything. A man of his time, a man of his class, and of his culture. Was it only manner? He tried to remember how his friends' fathers had behaved, but nothing came to mind.

'You think we love our kids more?' he asked Vianello.

'More than whom? And who are we?' the Inspector asked.

'Men. Our generation. Than our fathers did.'

'I don't know. Really.' Vianello twisted round and tugged repeatedly at his shirt, then used his handkerchief to mop at his neck. 'Maybe all we've done is learned new conventions. Or maybe we're expected to behave in a different way.' He leaned back. 'I don't know.'

'Why'd you tell me?' Brunetti asked. 'About your aunt, I mean.'

'I guess I wanted to hear how it sounded, whether if I listened to myself talk about it, I'd know if I should be worried about her or not.'

'I wouldn't worry until she starts reading your palm, Lorenzo,' Brunetti said, trying to lighten the mood.

Vianello shot him a stricken look. 'Might not be far off, I'm afraid,' he said, failing to make a joke of it. 'You think we should drink coffee in this heat?'

'Why not?'

2

In the bar at Ponte dei Greci, Bambola, the Senegalese helper Sergio had hired last year, was behind the bar. Both Brunetti and Vianello were accustomed to seeing Sergio there: robust, gruff Sergio, a man who had, over the decades, surely overheard – and kept to himself – enough police secrets to have kept a blackmailer in business for decades. So accustomed were the staff of the Questura to Sergio that he had achieved a state approaching invisibility.

The same could hardly be said of Bambola. The African wore a long beige djellaba and a white turban. Tall and slender, his dark face gleaming with health, Bambola stood behind the counter looking rather like a lighthouse, his turban reflecting back the light that shone in through the large windows that gave out on to the canal. He refused to wear an apron, but his djellabas never showed a spot or stain.

As the two men entered, Brunetti was struck by the increased brightness of the place and looked up to see if Bambola had turned on the lights, hardly necessary on a day that gleamed as did this one. But it was the windows. Not only were they cleaner than he had ever seen them be, but the posters and stickers for ice-cream, soft drinks and different makes of beer had all been peeled or shaved away, an innovation which redoubled the light that flooded into the bar. The windowsill had been swept clean of old magazines and newspapers, nor was there any sign of the fly-specked menus that had lain there for years. Instead, a white cloth ran from end to end, and in the middle rested a dark blue vase of pink strawflowers.

Brunetti noticed that the battered plastic display case which, for as long as he could remember, had held pastries and brioche had been replaced by a three-tier case with glass walls and shelves. He was relieved to see that the same pastries were there: Sergio might not be the most rigorous of housekeepers, but he understood pastries, and he understood *tramezzini*.

'Urban renewal?' he asked Bambola by way of greeting.

His answer was a curved gleam of teeth, like a secondary light suddenly flashing on beneath the main beam of his turban. '*Sì*, Commissario,' Bambola said. 'Sergio's down with summer flu, and he asked me to take over while he's sick.' With a cloth so white it could have been an extension of his turban, he took a swipe at the bar and asked what he could offer them.

'Two coffees, please,' Brunetti said.

The Senegalese turned away and busied himself with the machine. Unconsciously, Brunetti prepared himself for the familiar clanks and thumps of Sergio's technique as he prised loose the handle that held the used coffee grounds, banged it clean, then flipped the lever that would fill it with fresh coffee. The noises came, but muted, and when he glanced at the machine he saw that the wooden bar on which Sergio had been banging the metal cup for decades had been covered with rubber stripping that effectively buffered the noise. The name of the machine's maker, 'Gaggia', had been liberated from the accumulation of grime and coffee stains that had obscured it since Brunetti had first come to the bar.

'Will Sergio recognize the place when he comes back?' Vianello asked the barman.

'I hope so, Ispettore. And I hope he likes it.'

'The case?' Vianello asked with a nod of his chin in the direction of the pastries.

'A friend found it for me,' Bambola explained and gave it an affectionate swipe with the towel. 'Even keeps them warm.'

Brunetti and Vianello did not exchange a look, but the long silence with which they greeted the barman's explanation had the same effect. 'Bought it for me, Ispettore,' Bambola said in a more sober voice, emphasis heavy on the first word. 'I have the receipt.'

'He did you a favour, then,' Vianello said with a smile. 'It's much better than that old plastic thing with the crack on the side.'

'Sergio thought people didn't notice it,' Bambola said, his normal voice restored.

'Hah!' Vianello said. 'This one makes you want to open it and eat.' Fitting the deed to the word, he opened the case and, careful to take a napkin first, grabbed a crème-filled brioche from the top shelf. He took a bite, covering his chin and the front of his shirt with powdered sugar.

'Don't change these, Bambola,' he said as he licked away his sugar moustache.

The barman put the two coffees on the counter, setting a small ceramic plate beside Vianello's.

'No paper plates,' Vianello observed. 'Good.' He rested the remaining half of the brioche on the plate.

'It doesn't make sense, Ispettore,' Bambola said. 'Ecological sense, that is. Use all that paper, just to make a plate that gets used once and thrown away.'

'And recycled,' Brunetti offered.

Bambola shrugged the suggestion away, a response Brunetti was accustomed to. Like everyone else in the city, he had no idea what happened to the garbage they so carefully separated: he could only hope.

'You interested in that?' Vianello asked. Then, to avoid confusion, added, 'Recycling?'

'Yes,' Bambola said.

'Why?' Vianello asked. Before the barman could answer, two men came in and ordered coffee and mineral water. They took their places at the other end of the bar.

When they were served and Bambola came back, Vianello returned to his question. 'You interested because it will save Sergio money? Not using paper plates.'

Bambola removed their cups and saucers and placed them in the sink. He rinsed them quickly and set them inside the dishwasher.

'I'm an engineer, Ispettore,' he finally said. 'So it interests me professionally. In terms of cycles of consumption and production.'

'I figured you'd studied,' Vianello said. 'But I didn't know how to ask you.' After waiting a moment to see how Bambola accepted this last, he asked, 'What sort of engineer?'

13

'Hydraulic. Water purification plants. Things like that.'

'I see.' Vianello pulled some change from his pocket, sorted through it, and left the right amount on the bar.

'If you speak to Sergio,' Brunetti said as he moved towards the door, 'please say hello and tell him to get better.'

'I will, Commissario,' Bambola said and turned away towards the two men at the end of the bar. Brunetti had expected Vianello to return to the subject of his aunt, but the impulse, it seemed, had been left in the Questura and Brunetti, having no particular desire to continue that conversation, did not pursue it.

Outside, both men paused involuntarily under the whip of the sun. The Questura was less than two minutes' walk, but in the heat that appeared to have increased while they were inside, it might have been half a city away. The sun blasted down on the pavement along the canal. Tourists sat under the umbrellas in front of the trattoria on the other side of the bridge. Brunetti studied them for a moment, seeking some sign of motion. Could it be that the heat had dried them out, and they were no more than empty shells, like locusts? But then a waiter took a tall glass of some dark liquid to one of the tables, and the guest moved his head slowly to watch his arrival.

They set off. Bodies of water, Brunetti knew, were meant to cool the places where they were found, but the flat, dark green surface of the canal seemed only to reflect and redouble the light and heat. Instead of relief, it provided humidity. They trudged on.

'I had no idea he was an engineer,' Vianello said.

'Me neither.'

'Hydraulic engineer at that,' Vianello added with undisguised admiration. The door to the Questura was only a few steps away. The guard, understandably, had retreated inside.

Brunetti wiped his face with the sleeve of his shirt, marvelling that he had been so foolish as to wear a long-sleeved shirt that day. 'How long's he been around?' Brunetti asked, moving off towards the stairs.

'I'm not sure. Three, four years. I figure he was illegal for most of that, before he got his papers. He always used to disappear when I came in wearing my uniform.' Vianello smiled at the memory. 'Tall guy like that. Remarkable, he'd be there one minute, but then he simply wasn't, like he'd evaporated or something.'

'I'm going to, soon,' Brunetti said as they got to the first floor.

'What?'

'Evaporate.'

'Let's hope he doesn't,' Vianello said.

'Who? Bambola?'

'Yes. Sergio can't work all those hours. And you have to admit the place looks better. Just in a day.'

'His wife's been sick,' Brunetti said. 'Good thing he found him.'

'Lousy work, running a bar,' Vianello said. 'You're there all day, never know what sort of trouble you're going to have with the people who come in, and you always have to be polite.'

'Sounds like working here,' Brunetti said.

Vianello laughed and turned down towards the officers' squad room, leaving Brunetti to confront the second flight of steps on his own.

3

Two days later, sitting at his desk, Brunetti wondered at the possibility of making some sort of deal with the criminals in the city. Could they be induced to leave people alone until the end of this heat spell? That presupposed some sort of central organization, but Brunetti knew that crime had become too diversified and too international for any reliable agreement to be possible. Once, when crime had been an exclusively local affair, the criminals well known and part of the social fabric, it might have worked, and the criminals, as burdened by the unrelenting heat as the police, might even have been willing to cooperate. 'At least until the first of September,' he said out loud.

Too assailed by the heat to consider the papers on his desk, Brunetti allowed himself to continue his idle train of thought: how to convince the Romanians to stop picking pockets, the Gypsies to stop sending their children to break into homes? And that was only in Venice. On the mainland, the requests would have been far more serious, asking the Moldavians to stop selling thirteen-year-olds and the Albanians to stop selling drugs. He considered for a moment the possibility of persuading Italian men – men like him and Vianello – to stop wanting young prostitutes or cheap drugs.

He sat, conscious of the faint slithering sensation as perspiration moved across the skin of various parts of his body. In New Zealand, he had been told, businessmen wore shorts and short-sleeved shirts to work when it was this hot. And hadn't the Japanese decided to go jacketless during the worst of the summer heat? He took out his handkerchief and wiped the inside of his collar. This was the weather when people killed one another fighting for a parking space. Or because of an angry remark.

His thoughts drifted to the promises he had made to Paola that tonight they would discuss their own vacation. He, a Venetian, was going to turn himself and his family into tourists, but tourists going in the other direction, away from Venice, leaving room for the millions who were expected this year. Last year, twenty million. God have mercy on us all.

He heard a sound at the door and looked up to see Signorina Elettra, the light streaming in his windows illuminating her as in a spotlight. Could it be? Was it possible that, after more than a decade in which his superior's secretary had brightened his days with the flawlessness of her appearance, the heat had managed to make inroads, even here? Was that a wrinkle down the left side of her white linen shirt?

Brunetti blinked, closed his eyes for a moment, and when he opened them again, saw that it had been an illusion: the line was nothing more than the shadow created by the light coming in from his windows. Signorina Elettra paused at the door and glanced over her shoulder, and as she did another person appeared beside her.

'Good morning, Dottore,' she said. The man beside her smiled and said, '*Ciao*, Guido.'

To see Toni Brusca out of his office at the Commune during the working day was like seeing a badger out of its sett in daylight hours. Brusca had always made Brunetti think of that animal: thick dark hair with a white stripe running down one side; stocky, short-legged body, incredible tenacity once a subject took his interest.

'I met Toni on the way here,' Signorina Elettra said; Brunetti had had no idea the two were acquainted. 'So I thought I'd show him the way to your office.' She stepped back and gave what Brunetti recognized as her first-class smile to the visitor. This indicated either that Brusca was a good friend or, Signorina Elettra being a woman of endless and instinctive deceitfulness, that she knew the man was the head of the department of employment records at the Commune and thus a man of potential usefulness.

Brusca gave her a friendly nod and walked over to Brunetti's desk, gazing around the office as he did so. 'You certainly have more light than I do,' he said with open admiration. Brunetti noticed that he carried a briefcase.

Brunetti stepped around his desk and took Brusca's hand, then clapped him on the shoulder a few times. He nodded to Signorina Elettra, who smiled, though not her first-class smile, and left the office.

Brunetti showed his friend to one of the chairs in front

of his desk and sat facing him in the other. He waited for Toni to speak: surely Brusca had not come here to discuss the relative merits of their offices. Toni had never been a man to waste time or energy when he had something he wanted to do, or know: this was something Brunetti remembered from their years together in middle school. The best tactic had always been to sit and wait him out, and this is what Brunetti intended to do.

He did not have long to wait. Brusca said, 'There's something I want to ask you about, Guido.' From his briefcase he pulled out a transparent plastic folder, and from it he pulled a number of papers.

He set the briefcase back on the floor, the papers on his lap, and looked at his friend. 'A lot of people at the Commune talk to me,' he said. 'And they tell me things that sometimes make me curious, and then I ask around and people tell me more things. And because I sit in my ground floor office with only one window and because my job allows me to be curious about what people are doing – and because I am always very polite and very thorough – people tend to answer my questions.'

'Even if they really aren't about things that should concern you professionally?' Brunetti asked, beginning to suspect why Brusca might have come to see his friend the policeman.

'Exactly.'

'Is that what you have there?' Brunetti asked, nodding to the papers. Like Brusca, Brunetti was a man who preferred not to waste time.

Brusca handed the papers to Brunetti. 'Take a look,' he said.

The first paper bore the letterhead of the Tribunale di Venezia. The left side of the sheet held four vertical columns, headed: 'Case Number, Date, Judge, Courtroom Number'. After a thick vertical line appeared a single box headed 'Result'. Brunetti shifted the paper to one side and found three more like it. The quality of the reproductions varied: one was so blurred as to be barely legible. A date was stamped on the bottom right of each page with beside it a neat signature, and beside that the stamp of the Ministry of Justice. The dates differed, but the signature was the same. Twice, the seal of the Ministry of Justice was carelessly stamped and ran off the side of the page. Brunetti had spent what seemed a lifetime looking at such documents. How many had he stamped himself before consigning them to their next reader?

These were not the sort of court documents he was accustomed to reading in the course of his own investigations, not the usual transcripts of testimony or of the arguments presented at the conclusion of a trial, nor yet were they copies of the verdicts finally reached. These were for internal use only and, if he was reading them correctly, dealt with preliminary sessions. He found no pattern.

He glanced at Brusca, whose face was impassive. Brunetti returned his attention to the papers. He looked for correspondences and saw that many of the sessions listed had been adjourned or postponed without a hearing, and then he noticed that most of these cases had been heard by the same judge. He recognized the name and had no good opinion of her, though, if pressed, Brunetti could not have explained why that was. Things heard, things overheard, a certain tone of voice used when her name came up in conversation, and something, years ago, that one of his informers had said. No, not said, but implied, and not about her but about someone in her family. The name of the court functionary who had signed the papers meant nothing to him.

He looked across at his friend and said, 'My guess is that these postponements might work to the advantage of one of the two parties in each case and that Judge Coltellini is somehow involved in the delays.' Brusca gave an encouraging nod and pointed with his chin to the papers, as if to prompt a promising student. 'If that means I am to see something more here, then I'd guess that the person who signed the papers is also involved.'

'Araldo Fontana,' Brusca said. 'At the Tribunale. He started working there in 1975, was promoted to chief usher ten years later, and has been there ever since. His scheduled date of retirement is the tenth of April 2014.'

'What colour is his underwear?' asked a straight-faced Brunetti.

'Very funny, very funny, Guido.'

'All right. Forget the underwear and tell me about him.'

'As chief usher, he sees that papers are processed and delivered on time.'

'And "processed and delivered" means . . .?'

Brusca sat back and crossed his legs, then raised one hand in a gesture indicative of motion. 'There's a central deposit where all documents regarding cases are kept. When they're needed during a hearing or trial, the ushers see that they're delivered to the right courtroom so the judge can consult them if necessary. Then, when the hearing is over, the ushers take them back to the central deposit and refile them. When the next hearing is held, they're delivered again. When a verdict is reached, all of the papers in the case are moved to a permanent storage deposit.'

'But?'

'But papers sometimes go missing or aren't delivered, and when they aren't there, the judge has no choice but to postpone the hearing and set a later date. And if the hearing is anywhere near a holiday, then the judge might think it best to delay until after the holiday, but in both cases the judge has to check the docket and see when there is an opening to schedule a hearing, and then there might be long delays.'

Brunetti nodded: this had been his general understanding of how things worked. 'Then tell me,' he said, 'because to listen to you is to put my ear to the beating heart of goddess Rumour, what's going on here?'

Brusca smiled, but barely so. It was an expression not of humour or amusement but one that acknowledged human nature as it was, not as anyone would want it to be. 'Before I say anything about what might be going on here, I have to tell you one thing.' He paused long enough to be sure he had Brunetti's full attention, then continued. 'He's a decorous man, Fontana. It's an old-fashioned word, I know, but he's an old-fashioned man. Almost as if he were from our parents' generation: that's how people speak of him. He wears a suit and tie to work every day, does his job, is polite with everyone. I've never, in all these years, heard a word against him and, as you know, if there is a word to be heard against anyone at the Commune, it generally ends up being repeated to me. Sooner or later, I probably hear everything. But never a word against Fontana, save that he is tedious and shy.'

It seemed to Brunetti that Brusca had finished so he asked, 'Then why is his name on those documents? And why did you see fit to bring them to me?' It occurred to

Brunetti then to ask, 'And how did they come to you in the first place?'

Brusca looked at his lap, then at Brunetti, then at the wall, then back at Brunetti. 'Someone who works at the Tribunale gave them to me.'

'For what purpose?'

Brusca shrugged. 'Perhaps because they wanted the information to pass beyond the Tribunale.'

'That's certainly happening,' Brunetti said, but he did not smile. Then, 'Will you tell me who it was?'

Brusca shook the question away. 'It doesn't matter, and I told her I wouldn't tell anyone.'

'I understand,' said Brunetti, who did.

After waiting in vain for Brusca to say something further, Brunetti said, 'Tell me what it means. Or what you think it means.'

'You mean the delays?'

'Yes.'

Brunetti leaned back in his chair, linked his hands behind his head, and examined the ceiling.

'In the case of an acrimonious divorce, where there is a lot of money involved, it would serve the purposes of the richer party to delay things for long enough to move or hide assets.' Before Brunetti could ask, Brusca explained: 'If the papers were delivered to the wrong courtroom on the day of a hearing, or not delivered at all, then the judge would be within his or her rights in ordering a postponement until all the necessary documents were available.'

'I think I begin to understand,' Brunetti said.

'Think of the courthouses you've been in, Guido, and think of all those stacks of files lined up against the walls. You've seen them in every courthouse.'

'Isn't everything being entered into computers?' Brunetti suddenly asked, remembering the circulars distributed by the Ministry of Justice.

'All in the fullness of time, Guido.'

'Which means?'

'Which means it will take years. I work in personnel, so I know that two people have been assigned to the job: it will take them years, if not decades. Some of the files they have to transcribe go back to the fifties and sixties.'

'Is it Fontana's job to see that the papers are delivered?'

'Yes.'

'And the judge?' Brunetti asked.

'She is said to have been for some time the apple of his dull little eye.'

'But he's just a clerk, for heaven's sake. And she's a judge. Besides, he's got to be twenty years older than she is.'

'Ah, Guido,' Brusca said, leaning forward and tapping a single finger against Brunetti's knee, 'I never knew you had such a conventional mind. Guilty of class and age prejudice, all in one go. All you can think about is love, love, love. Or sex, sex, sex.'

'What should I be thinking about, instead?' Brunetti said, forcing himself to sound curious and not offended.

'In the case of Fontana,' Brusca relented, 'perhaps you could think of love, love, love, at least from what I've heard. But in the case of Her Honour, you'd be better advised to think of money, money, money.' Brusca sighed, then said in a sober voice, 'I think a great number of people are more interested in money than in love. Or even in sex.'

However interesting the thought of pursuing this thesis, Brunetti was more interested in information, and so he asked, 'And is Judge Coltellini among them?'

Jokes fled and Brusca's voice and face grew bleak. 'She comes from greedy people, Guido.' Brusca paused and then added, as if revealing a mystery he had just resolved, 'It's strange. We think that love of music can run in families, or maybe the ability to paint. So why not greed?' As Brunetti remained silent, he asked, 'You ever think about that, Guido?'

'Yes,' answered Brunetti, who had.

'Ah,' Brusca allowed himself to say and then went on, abandoning the general for the specific, 'Her grandfather was a greedy man, and her father is to this day. She learned it from them, came by it honestly, you might say. If her mother weren't dead, I'd go so far as to say the judge would consider an offer to sell her if she could.'

'Did you ever have trouble with her?'

'No, not at all,' Brusca said, looking genuinely surprised by the question. 'As I told you, I just sit there in my tiny office at the Commune and I keep track of all of the employee records: when people get hired, how much they earn, when they retire. I do my job, and people talk to me and tell me things, and occasionally I have to make a phone call and ask a question. To clarify something. And sometimes the answers people give me prompt me to be surprised, and then they tell me more about it, or they tell me other things. And over the years they've come to think it's my business to know about everything.'

'And people trust you to take things like this,' Brunetti said, 'out of the Tribunale.'

Brusca nodded, but it was such a sober nod that Brunetti asked, 'Because you are pure of heart and clean of limb?'

Brusca laughed and the mood of the room lightened.

4

Their parting was amicable, if awkward, both avoiding the fact that Brusca had never explained why he had come to Brunetti or what he wanted him to do with the information he now had. Since Brusca had made it clear that Coltellini was a woman animated by the desire for money, it was easy to conclude that she was being paid by people whose cases were being delayed. But that it was easy did not make it true, nor did it make it provable in a court of law.

What was not clear to Brunetti was the reason for any involvement on the part of Fontana. Love, love, love did not seem sufficient motive to corrupt a man described as 'decorous', but then it never did, did it?

It was seldom, after all these years, that Brunetti could be moved to indignation by some new revelation of the skill with which his fellow citizens managed to slip around the edges of the law. In some instances – though he confessed this to no one – he felt grudging admiration for the ingenuity employed, especially when it entailed getting around a law which he judged to be unjust or a situation he thought outright insane. When traffic lights were deliberately programmed to change more quickly than dictated by law so that the police could divide the extra money paid in fines with the men setting the timing devices, who but a lunatic would think bribing a policeman a crime? When scores of indicted criminals sat in Parliament, who could believe in the rule of law?

It would be difficult to say that Brunetti was shocked by the purported behaviour of Judge Coltellini, but he was certainly surprised, not least because the judge in question was a woman. Though Brunetti used statistics to support his conviction that women were less criminal than men, his belief was really based on his upbringing and experience of life. What he thought to be the right order of things – should Brusca's insinuations be true – had been doubly overturned.

With Brusca's suggestion in mind, Brunetti spread the papers on his desk and studied them anew. Centring his attention on Judge Coltellini's name, he saw that it appeared numerous times on each of the four pages, and that her name stood beside six case numbers. He opened his desk and pulled out some coloured highlighting pens. He started at the top of the first page with the green and highlighted her name the first time it appeared in the first case, then used the same colour to go through the entire list, using it to indicate all of the times she held hearings in that case. He did the same with the next case, using pink this time. The third, yellow; the fourth, orange, and then he had to circle the fifth case number with pencil, and the last with red pen.

The Greens had come before her only three times: the second appearance took place on the date listed in the 'Result' column of the first appearance, and the third on the date scheduled in the second: but still the entire process had taken two years. The Pink case respected all of the dates set for each subsequent hearing, though there had been six of them, each separated by at least half a year. Brunetti was curious to know what the case had been about; what had it taken three years to decide?

The Yellow trail was more suggestive. The first hearing, which had taken place more than two years before, ended with an unexplained six-month postponement, and when that hearing was held, a new date was set, without explanation, more than five months ahead. When the third hearing was held, the 'Results' box contained a new date, six months away, and the phrase, 'Missing documents'. The next postponement, this one for another six months, was explained by 'Illness', though whose illness was not explained. This next hearing, on the twentieth of December, appeared to have served only to postpone things a further four months, this explained by 'Holidays' in the last column. The new date, in the second half of April, convinced Brunetti that it had been scheduled during the Easter holidays, but Judge Coltellini surprised him by apparently holding a hearing and then setting a new date – seven months ahead – to allow herself to 'Question new witnesses'.

Brunetti wondered what new witnesses there could be in a case that had been moving – though he immediately chided himself for having so precipitously chosen that verb – through the courts for almost three years. No wonder people dreaded being caught in the wheels of Juggernaut: it was axiomatic that the worst thing that could befall a person, short of serious illness, was to become embroiled in a court case. Indeed.

The judge managed to surprise Brunetti again by having resolved the Orange case in less than a year, though the Pencil and the Red Pen cases were still dragging their slow lengths along, each of them for more than two years.

He searched in his desk for a list of numbers and then dialled Brusca's *telefonino*.

'Yes?' Brusca inquired in a calm tone, quite as though he were still in Brunetti's office, that same tone Brunetti had heard him use in history class during their first year of middle school. In all these years, Brunetti had never known his friend to display surprise at human behaviour, no matter how base, though, God knows, working in the offices of the city administration would have exposed him to a bellyful of it.

'I've taken a closer look at those papers,' Brunetti said. 'Have you shown them to anyone else?'

'For what purpose?' Brusca asked, his tone suddenly as serious as Brunetti's.

'If it's true, then it should be stopped,' Brunetti said, knowing that the idea of retribution was absurd.

'Yes, you're right,' Brusca said, striving to sound as though they were discussing the quality of a soccer team and not the corruption of the judicial system. 'But I don't think that's likely,' he added.

'Then why did you give them to me?' Brunetti made no attempt to disguise his irritation.

For a long time, there was no response from Brusca's end of the line, and then he said, 'I thought you might be able to think of something to do. And I hoped you'd be outraged by it.'

'That's putting it a bit too strongly,' Brunetti said.

'All right, all right, not outrage. Hope, then. Perhaps that's what I admire in you, that you can still hope that things will turn right and the Augean Stables will be cleansed.'

'That's unlikely, as you say,' Brunetti agreed. Then, turning back to the original purpose of the call and with the voice of friendship restored, he asked, 'Really, why did you give them to me?'

'It's true. I hoped you'd be able to do something,' Brusca answered. Then, in a voice Brunetti suspected his friend was deliberately making sound lighter, he added, 'Besides, it's always nice to be able to cause one of them a bit of trouble.'

'I'll see what I can do,' Brunetti said, knowing as he spoke how little chance there was of that.

Brusca said a quick goodbye.

Brunetti propped his left elbow on his desk and rubbed his thumbnail back and forth along his lower lip. His shirt felt clammy under his arms and across his back. He went to the window and looked down at the water of the canal, black in the day's harsh reflection. Campo San Lorenzo had been baked free of life; even the cats who lived in the multi-storey cat condominium erected against the façade of the church had disappeared; he wondered if they had fled the city to go on vacation.

For a moment, he let himself indulge in a fantasy about cats on vacation in the mountains or at the seaside, sent there by DINGO, the city's cooperative society of animal lovers. Brunetti hated the 'animalisti', hated them for their defence of the loathsome, disease-ridden pigeons, hated them for having rounded up all of the wild cats of the city, no doubt to the delight of the ever-increasing population of rats. While on the subject of animals, he added to his list of people he hated those who did not clean up after their dogs; if he had his way, he'd slap a fine on them so strong it would . . .

'Commissario?' His attention was torn from wild speculation about the amount of the fine he'd impose and the system he'd invent to implement it.

'Yes, Signorina?' he said, turning towards her. 'What is it?'

'I saw Vianello a moment ago. I went into the squad room and he was on the phone. He didn't look at all well.'

'Is he sick?' Brunetti asked, thinking of the sudden things that could be brought on by the heat.

Signorina Elettra came a few steps into his office. 'I don't know, sir. I don't think so. He looked more worried or frightened and not wanting to show it.' Brunetti was accustomed to the fact that she looked good; today he was amazed to realize she still looked cool. Instead of asking about Vianello, Brunetti blurted out, 'Don't you find it hot?'

'Excuse me, sir?'

'The heat. The temperature? Isn't it hot? For you, I mean. Don't you think it's hot?' If he had gone on any longer, he would probably have been reduced to drawing a picture of the sun to show her.

'No, not particularly, sir. It's only 30 degrees.'

'And that's not hot?'

'Not for me, no.'

'Why?'

He watched her hesitate about what to tell him. Finally she said, 'I grew up in Sicily, sir. So I guess my body grew accustomed to the heat. Or my thermostat was programmed. Something like that.'

'In Sicily?'

'Yes.'

'How was that?'

'Oh, my father worked there for a few years,' she said, her uninterested voice telling Brunetti that he had best be equally uninterested, or at least pretend to be.

Obediently, Brunetti veered away from her private life and asked, 'Do you have any idea who he was talking to?'

'No, sir, but it was someone he knew well enough to use "*Tu*" with. And he seemed to be doing more listening than talking.'

Brunetti got to his feet. He picked up some papers she had given him earlier that morning and said, 'I wanted to show him these. I'll take them down.' He waited for her to leave, thinking it might not be a good idea for Vianello to see them coming down the stairs together, as if she had been telling tales out of school.

She smiled before turning towards the door. 'He didn't see me, Commissario.' And then she was gone. When he reached the door to his office, she had already disappeared down the steps.

Brunetti walked down slowly. In the squad room he found Vianello at his desk and still on the phone, half turned away, but Brunetti saw immediately what Signorina Elettra had meant. The Ispettore was hunched over the phone, his free hand rolling a pencil back and forth on his desk. From this distance, it looked to Brunetti as if his eyes were closed.

Again and again, the Inspector rolled the pencil across his desk, not speaking. As Brunetti watched, Vianello tightened his lips, then relaxed them. The pencil never stopped moving. Finally he pulled the phone away from his ear, slowly, with great effort, as though there were a magnetic field between the receiver and his ear. He held it in front of him for at least ten seconds, and Brunetti heard the voice coming through the line: female, old, querulous. Vianello opened his eyes and studied the surface of his desk. Then, slowly, tenderly, as though he were replacing the person from whom the voice was still coming, he set the phone down.

The Inspector sat for a long time, looking at the phone. He pulled out his handkerchief and wiped at his forehead, then returned it to his pocket and got to his feet. By the time he turned towards the door, Brunetti had removed all emotion from his face and was taking a stride towards his assistant, the sheaf of papers clutched in his hand.

Before Brunetti could mention the papers, Vianello said, 'Let's go down to the bridge. I need a drink.'

Brunetti refolded the papers, but because he wasn't wearing his jacket he folded them smaller and slipped them into the back pocket of his trousers.

They walked out on to the pavement in front of the Questura and Brunetti realized that his sunglasses were upstairs in the pocket of his jacket. He could not stop himself from raising his left hand to protect his eyes from the glare. 'I wonder if this is what it's like to be in a lineup,' he said. Squinting, he waited for his eyes to adjust to the dazzle; then, keeping his hand above his eyes, he started towards the bar.

Inside, Bambola stood behind the counter, his djellaba looking as fresh as a document just pulled from an envelope.

It was after eleven, so both men ordered a *spritz*, Vianello asking Bambola to put them in water glasses with lots of ice. When the drinks came, Vianello picked them up and headed toward the booth farthest from the door. It was an airless corner, but Brunetti had given in to the heat: nothing could make it worse, but at least there they could talk in peace.

When they were seated opposite one another, Brunetti decided to abandon all pretence that he had not understood the nature of the phone call and asked, 'Your aunt?'

Vianello sipped at his drink, took a longer swallow, and set the icy glass on the table. 'Yes.'

'You looked worried,' Brunetti prompted.

'I suppose I am,' Vianello said, wrapping both hands around his glass, a gesture more common with hot drinks than with cold. 'I'm also trapped.'

'Why?'

'Because I can't shout at her, which is what I want to do. It's a normal enough response when people do this.' He looked at Brunetti and quickly away.

'When people do what?' Brunetti asked.

Their eyes met for an instant, but then Vianello looked at his glass again and said, 'Go crazy. Take leave of their senses.' He picked up the glass with both palms and set it down on the surface a few times, creating a pattern of rings, then he slid the glass through them, erasing them all.

'What's she done?'

'She hasn't done it yet,' Vianello said. 'But she will. I told you, Zia Anita has a strong will, and when she makes up her mind there's no changing her.'

'What's she decided to do?' Brunetti asked, and finally took a sip of his drink. It was by now so watery as to be almost tasteless, but it was cold and so he drank it.

'She wants to sell the business.'

'I thought it was your uncle's.'

'It was. Well, it was his, and now it belongs to his sons. But only in name.'

'Tell me.'

'Legally it all belongs to her. When he opened it, bought the building where the workshop and offices are, his *commercialista* told him it would be better for taxes if he put it in his wife's name. Then, as time passed, they could transfer it to the boys.' Vianello sighed.

'But they didn't?'

Vianello shook his head, finished his drink, and went to get another, not bothering to ask Brunetti if he wanted one. Brunetti finished his and slid the glass over near the wall.

Vianello was quickly back, but this time the glasses contained only mineral water and ice. Brunetti took his gratefully; the melting ice had ruined the first one, diluting the Campari and rendering the prosecco flat and tasteless.

'Why does she want to sell it?' he asked.

'To get money,' Vianello said and drank some of his water.

'Come on, Lorenzo. Either tell me about this or we go back to work.'

Vianello propped his elbows on the table, his open palms pressed to either side of his mouth. Finally he said, 'I think she wants to give it to a soothsayer.'

5

'*Gesù Bambino*,' Brunetti whispered; then, remembering what Vianello had told him, asked, 'The magazines?'

'That's just a part of it,' Vianello answered, his distress audible. He put his right hand inside the open collar of his shirt and ran his hand up his neck. 'God, I hate this heat. There's no way to get away from it.'

Brunetti avoided the distraction and took another sip of his water. He and Vianello had interrogated so many witnesses and suspects together that there was no tactic they had not been exposed to. He sat back with his arms folded, the very model of patience.

Vianello leaned back, as well. 'I told you that's how it started: reading the horoscopes. And the radio programme in the morning, and then she discovered those private channels where they have the people who read the cards.' He made a fist with his right hand and banged it on the table, but lightly to show it was a gesture and not an act of rage.

'One of her friends told her about the programmes, how much help they were to the people who called.'

'What does your aunt need help with?' Brunetti could not stop himself from asking. From the way Vianello had spoken of her over the years, she had always sounded like the pillar of strength and certainty in the family.

Something flashed across Vianello's face, something Brunetti had never seen, at least never seen directed at him. 'I'm coming to that, Guido,' he said. Vianello must have been startled by his own voice because he opened his fist and spread his arm along the top of the bench, as if offering his open hand as an apology.

Brunetti smiled but said nothing.

Vianello continued. 'She liked the way the people who read the cards gave advice to everyone who called. They seemed sensible. That's what she told her children.' Vianello paused, as if to invite questions, but Brunetti had none to ask.

'That's how I learned about this,' the Inspector continued. 'A few months ago, my cousin Loredano mentioned it to me, almost as a joke: something his mother had got interested in. Like she was listening to Radio Maria or had started to read gardening magazines. He didn't think much of it, but then his sister, my cousin Marta, called me about a month after that and told me she was worried about their mother, that she talked about it all the time and really seemed to believe in all this horoscope stuff.

'She didn't know what to do, Marta.' Vianello finished his glass of water and set it on the table. 'I didn't, either. She was worried, but Loredano thought it would pass, and I guess I thought it would, too, or I wanted to believe that because it was easier.' He looked across at Brunetti and pulled up one side of his mouth in a wry grimace. 'I think we all wanted it not to be a problem. So we ignored it and pretended it wasn't happening.'

There was noise at the door as people came into the bar, but neither of them paid attention to it. Vianello continued: 'Then Loredano called me about a month ago and told me Zia Anita had taken three thousand Euros out of the company account without telling him.'

He waited for Brunetti to comment, but he did not, so the Inspector went on. 'Loredano took a look at the bank account and saw that, over the last few months, she'd been taking money from the account: five hundred, three hundred, six hundred at a time. When he asked her about it, all she said was that it was her money and she could do whatever she wanted with it, and that it was necessary and for the best of causes and that she was doing it for his father.'

Old women, Brunetti knew, often felt a need to give their money to good causes, and very often that cause proved to be the Church. Though Brunetti would hardly call that a 'good cause', he knew that many people considered it to be, just as he knew that people who gave to the Church would feel no hesitation about naming it. Vianello's aunt's failure to do so opened a Pandora's Box of possibility about the recipient of her generosity.

' "Good cause",' Brunetti repeated in a neutral voice. ' "For his father".'

'That's all she said,' Vianello replied.

'Have your cousins got any idea how much money is involved?'

'Including that three thousand, maybe seven thousand in total. But she's also got money of her own, and they've no way of knowing what she's done with that.'

'Was that what you were talking about with her now?' Brunetti asked.

'I was listening, not talking,' Vianello said tiredly. 'She called me to complain about how Loredano is bothering her.'

'*Bothering* her?'

Vianello failed to smile. 'That's how she sees it now: she's doing something she says is necessary. She thinks she has every right to do it, and she's angry because her children are trying to make her stop.'

'I've forgotten, Lorenzo. How many children are there?'

'Marta and Loredano: they're the oldest. And Luca and Paolo, the two youngest. The three boys – men, really – run the business.'

'And your uncle? Where's he in all of this?' Brunetti asked.

Vianello raised his hands involuntarily. 'I told you: he doesn't pay attention to much. Never did, and now that he's older and not in the best of health, it's even worse. Loredano said he tried to talk to him and make him understand, but all he said was that his wife had her own money and could do whatever she wanted with it. Or with his. I suppose he thinks it's some sort of proof of his masculinity that his wife can spend a lot of money: shows what a good provider he is.'

'Even if he isn't working any more?'

'Probably more important, now that he isn't and now that he can't do the things he used to do.'

'God, it's complicated, isn't it?' Brunetti said, leaning

forward and resting his elbows on the table. 'Do any of them know what she's doing with it?'

Vianello shook his head. 'Nothing they're certain of. But if she says it's for a good cause, then she's probably giving it to someone.' This time Vianello slapped the surface of the table, making no attempt to disguise his anger. 'The trouble is,' the Inspector continued, 'I agree with her. Well, partly. She does have the right to do whatever she wants to do with her money. When the business was new, she worked like a dog for years, and she never got a lira for it. Even after things got better, she stayed on in the office and ran it. And never got paid for it.'

Brunetti nodded.

'So she's entitled to as much money as she wants. Both legally and . . . and morally, if that's the right word.'

Brunetti suspected it was.

'But . . .' the Inspector began but failed to finish the sentence.

Brunetti suggested a way to do so. 'But her family has the right to know what she's doing with it?'

'I think so, yes. I don't like saying it, but I think that's the case. And it's not because it's their money. It's not. It's hers. But surely the fact that she refuses to tell them means she suspects she shouldn't be doing whatever it is she's doing with it.'

'What are your cousins going to do?' Brunetti asked.

Vianello looked at the table. 'Follow her,' he said.

'I beg your pardon.'

Vianello looked up and, entirely without humour, said, 'I think they've watched too much television or something. They've spoken to the manager of the bank. He's known the family for thirty years. He's done all their banking for them.'

Vianello stared at his hands, as if one of his fingers were the director of the bank and he wanted to see what he was going to do.

'What did they tell him?'

'About the withdrawals and how she won't tell them what she's doing with it.'

'And?'

'And he said he'd call Loredano the next time she made a withdrawal and then start talking to her and keep her in the bank for as long as he could.'

'Until someone from the family got there to see where she went?' Brunetti asked, failing to disguise his astonishment. 'Cops and robbers?'

Vianello shook his head, eyes still on his fingers. 'I wish it were that easy.'

'It's not easy,' Brunetti said. 'It's crazy.'

'I thought so, too,' Vianello said. 'That's what I told them.'

'So?'

'So they want me to do it.'

Brunetti found no words. He looked across at his friend, who continued to study his hands. Finally Brunetti said, 'That's crazier.'

'That's what I told them, too.'

'Lorenzo,' Brunetti said, 'I don't want to have to sit here and prise this out of you. What are you going to do?'

'I thought about this while I was listening to her – some way to see what she's doing – but the only idea I could come up with involves you. Sort of.'

'Involves me how?'

'I need you to let me do it.'

'Do what?'

'Ask some of the guys if they'll help me.'

'Help you follow your aunt?'

'Yes. I thought Pucetti would be willing to do it if I asked him.' Vianello looked across at Brunetti, face tense. 'If they did it in their free time, when they're not working, then there wouldn't be anything illegal about it, not really.'

'They'd just be taking a walk through the city, minding their own business,' Brunetti snapped. 'Just happening to be going in the same direction as the little old lady with all that cash in her purse.' He felt a rush of indignation. Had the police been reduced to this?

'Guido,' Vianello said, voice dead level. 'I know how it appears and what it sounds like, but it's the only way to find out what she's doing with it.'

'And if she's been lying to you all, and she ends up going down to the Casinò to lose it all in the slot machines?' Brunetti demanded.

Vianello surprised him by taking him seriously. 'Then we can get her barred from the Casinò.'

Brunetti changed his tone and asked, 'And if she goes in somewhere and comes out without the money? Then what? You and your cousins go in and beat up whoever has the money and take it back?'

'No,' Vianello said calmly. 'Then perhaps we see if there are any more little old ladies going into the same address with cash in their purses.'

Surprise stopped Brunetti from answering immediately, and when he did speak, all he could say was, 'Oh my, oh my, oh my.' And then, 'Is that what you think?'

'I don't know what I think,' Vianello answered. 'But my aunt is no fool, so whoever is convincing her to give them money – if that's what's happening, and she's not losing it all on the slot machines – is also not a fool, so it's a fair bet that she's not the only one involved in this.'

Brunetti pushed himself out of the booth and went over to the counter, where he got two more glasses of mineral water and took them back to Vianello. He set the glasses down and slipped back into his seat.

'There's a way we can do it officially,' Brunetti said.

'How?'

'Isn't Scarpa running the training classes for new officers?'

'Yes, but I don't see . . .'

'And one of the things they're supposed to learn, if they're not Venetian, is how to follow someone in the city.'

Flawlessly, Vianello picked it up and ran. 'And since Scarpa isn't Venetian, he hasn't got an idea of how to do it.'

'Which means,' Brunetti concluded, 'that he has to let the Venetians show them how to do it.'

Vianello picked up his glass and raised it to Brunetti. 'I know it's wrong to toast with water, but still . . .' He drank some and set the glass on the table.

'And so all we've got to do,' Vianello began, heartening Brunetti with his casual use of the plural, 'is ask Signorina Elettra to see that the right Venetians are assigned to lead the detail. It won't make any difference to Scarpa: he distrusts and dislikes us all equally.'

Vianello turned towards the counter and waved a hand in Bambola's direction. 'Would you bring us two glasses of prosecco, please?'

6

Not only was it too hot to think about crossing the city to go home for lunch; it was too hot to think about eating. Brunetti went back to the Questura with Vianello, saying he would speak to Signorina Elettra about the schedule for Scarpa's orientation classes, but when he got to her office, she was gone. He went back to his own and called Paola, who sounded almost relieved to learn he would not be coming home.

'I can't think about food until the sun goes down,' she said.

'Ramadan?' Brunetti inquired lightly.

She laughed. 'No! But the sun comes into the living room in the afternoon, so I have to hide in my study most of the day. It's too hot to go out, so all I can do is sit and read.'

For most of the academic year, Paola spoke longingly of the summer vacation, when she looked forward to sitting in her study and reading. 'Ah, poor you,' Brunetti said, just as if he meant it.

'Guido,' she said in her sweetest voice, 'it takes a liar to recognize another one. But thank you for the sentiment.'

'I'll be home after sunset,' he said, quite as though she had not spoken, and replaced the phone.

Talk of food had made Brunetti feel something akin to hunger but nothing strong enough to cause him to risk leaving the building to go in search of food. He opened his drawers one after another but found only half a bag of pistachios he could not remember having seen before, a packet of corn chips, and a chocolate bar, with hazelnuts, that he had brought to the office last winter.

He prised open one of the pistachios, put it in his mouth and bit down, only to make contact with something the consistency of rubber. He spat it into his palm and tossed it and the rest of the bag into the wastepaper basket. By comparison, the corn chips were excellent, and he enjoyed them. It was good, he told himself, to eat lots of salt in this heat. These would protect him, he was sure, at the Equator.

When he tore open the chocolate bar, he noticed that it was covered with a thin white haze, the chocolate equivalent of verdigris. He took out his handkerchief and rubbed the bar vigorously until it looked like chocolate again: dark chocolate with hazelnuts. His favourite. He whispered 'Dessert', and took a bite. It was perfect, as smooth and creamy as it would have been six months before. Brunetti marvelled at this fact as he finished the bar, then lowered his head to look in the back of the drawer in hope that there might be another one, but there was not.

He glanced at his watch and saw that it was still

lunchtime. That meant the squad room computer might be free for him to use. As he entered, he saw Riverre at the desk he shared with Officer Alvise, just pulling on his jacket.

'You on your way to lunch, Riverre?' Brunetti asked.

'Yes, sir,' he said, trying to salute, but with his arm caught in his sleeve, he made a mess of it.

Brunetti followed the path of habit and ignored what had just happened. 'Could you stop at Sergio's on your way back and bring me some *tramezzini*?'

Riverre smiled. 'Sure thing, Commissario. Anything special you'd like?' When Brunetti hesitated, Riverre suggested, 'Crab? Egg salad?'

In this heat, those were probably the two most likely to go off, but Brunetti said only, 'No, maybe tomato and prosciutto.'

'How many, sir? Four? Five?'

Good Lord, what did Riverre think he was? 'No, thanks, Riverre. Two ought to be enough.' He reached into his pocket for his wallet, but the officer held up both hands, like a Christian catching sight of the devil. 'No, sir. Don't even think of it. You'll insult me.' He started towards the door, calling back over his shoulder, 'I'll get you some mineral water, too, sir. Got to drink a lot in this heat.'

Brunetti called his thanks after Riverre's retreating back, then said under his breath, in English, though he was never entirely certain of the context in which this phrase was meant to be used: 'From the mouths of babes.'

Someone had left the computer with its Internet connection open, so Brunetti, using four fingers, typed in 'Oroscopo'.

When Riverre returned more than an hour later,

Brunetti was still at the computer, though it was a wiser man who sat there. One site had led to another, one reference had spurred him to think of something else, and so he had, in that brief time, taken a tour through a world of belief and faith and the sort of deception so obvious as to leave him marvelling. 'Horoscope' had led to 'Prediction', which had led to 'Card Reader', and that in its turn had led to 'Psychic Consultant', 'Palm Reader,' and an endless list of consultants who answered specific needs. He found, as well, a long list of interactive sites which, for a price, opened the portals to real-time contact with 'Astral Consultants'.

Some dedicated themselves to the solving of problems of business or finance; many others to questions of love and affection; others handled difficulties at work or with colleagues; while yet others promised help in consulting departed relatives and friends. Or pets. There were those who offered astral help in losing weight, stopping smoking, or avoiding falling in love with the wrong person. Strangely enough, and though he searched, Brunetti found no one offering astral help in stopping drug addiction, though he did find one site that promised to tell parents which of their children were most at risk of drug dependence: it was all foretold in their stars.

Brunetti's degree was in law, and though he had never taken the state exam nor practised law, he had spent decades paying close attention to language, its use and misuse. His work had presented him with countless examples of deliberately misleading statements and contracts; thus over the years he had developed the skill to spot a lie, no matter how elaborately it was disguised and no matter how successfully the language in which it was presented removed it from all liability for false claims or promises.

The information in these sites had been written by experts: they created hope without making any pledge that punctilious minds might view as legally binding; they fostered certainty with never a binding promise; they pledged calm and tranquillity in exchange for an act of faith.

And payment? Crass lucre? Ask people to pay for their services? The very question was absurd. Probably insulting as well to the people who offered their services for the good of troubled mankind. What was ninety cents a minute to a person who needed help and who could find that help at the other end of a phone line? The chance to speak directly to a professional who was trained to understand the problems and suffering of a person who was fat/thin/divorced/unmarried/in love/out of love/lonely/trapped in an unhappy relationship – was that not worth ninety cents a minute? Besides, in some cases, there was the chance that your call would be among those taken live during the television show, and thus your name and problem would be known to a broader public, and that could lead only to greater sympathy and understanding for you and your suffering.

Brunetti could but admire such ingenuity. He quickly did the maths. At ninety cents a minute, a ten-minute conversation would cost nine Euros, and an hour would cost fifty-four. Assume that there were ten people answering the calls, or twenty, or a hundred; and assume that these lines were open twenty-four hours a day. A ten-minute call? Was he mad? This was an opportunity to speak to a compassionate listener, to reveal the painful details of the injured, unappreciated self. Besides, the ads said that the people who took the calls were 'trained professionals'. Surely they had been trained to listen, though Brunetti was of a mind that the goal of their listening might be something other than the provision of aid and assistance to the low of spirit and weak of heart. Who could resist the lure to speak of the endlessly fascinating self? Who was immune to the question asked with sympathy and expressive of the desire to know the caller more deeply?

Brunetti had a reputation at the Questura as a skilled interrogator, for he often managed to enter into conversation with even the most hardened old lag. He kept to himself the truth that his goal was not conversation, but monologue. Sit, look interested, ask the occasional question but say as little as possible, be sympathetic to what is said and to the person saying it; and few detainees or suspects can resist the instinct to fill the silence with their own words. A few of his colleagues had the same skill, Vianello chief among them.

The more sympathetic the interrogator seemed, the more important it became for the person being questioned to win their goodwill, and that could be achieved most easily, many suspects believed, by making the interrogator understand their motives, and that, naturally, required a good deal of explanation. During most interrogations, Brunetti's prime interest was in discovering what the other person had done and having them admit to it, while that other person too often became fixed on earning Brunetti's comprehension and sympathy.

Just as the people who spoke to him seldom considered the legal consequences of their talk, those who spoke to the trained professionals in their various call centres would hardly consider the economic consequences of their own garrulity.

'Here are the *tramezzini*, sir,' he heard Riverre say. Brunetti turned to thank him, but before he could speak, Riverre, seeing the screen, said, 'Oh, you use them, too, Commissario?'

Not trusting himself to speak, Brunetti took the paper bag holding the sandwiches and two half-litre bottles of mineral water and set it beside the computer. 'Oh, I'm not sure I use them,' he then said casually, quite as though he did, 'but I like to check them every so often to see if there's anything new.' Deciding that instant to dine in the squad room, Brunetti opened the bag and took out one of the sandwiches. Tomato and prosciutto. He peeled back the napkin wrapping it and took a bite.

Chewing, he pointed with the *tramezzini* towards the screen and asked, 'You have any favourites, Riverre?'

Riverre removed his jacket and stepped aside to drape it over the chair at his desk, then came back to Brunetti. 'Well, I can't say it's my favourite, sir, but there's one woman – I think she's in Torino – who talks about children and the sort of problems they can have. Or that parents can have with them.'

'The way kids are today,' Brunetti agreed soberly, 'that's got to be a good thing.'

'That's what I think, sir. My wife has called her a few times to ask what we should do about Gianpaolo.'

'He must be twelve by now, isn't he?' Brunetti asked, taking a stab at the age.

'Fourteen, sir. But just turned. And he's not a little boy any more, so we can't treat him like he is.'

'Is this what she's said, the woman from Torino?' Brunetti asked, finishing the first *tramezzino* and pulling

51

out one of the bottles of mineral water. With gas. Good. He opened it and offered it to Riverre, but the policeman shook his head. 'No, sir. It's what my mother says.'

'And the woman in Torino? What does she say?'

'She's got a course we can take. Ten lessons that we can do, my wife and me together.'

'In Torino?' asked Brunetti, unable to hide his surprise.

'Oh, no, sir,' Riverre said with a gentle laugh. 'We're in the modern age now, me and my wife. We're on line, so all we have to do is sign up, and the class comes to our computer, and then we watch the lessons and take the tests. They send you everything – quizzes and tests and study aids – at your email, and you send them back, and then they send you grades and comments.'

'I see,' Brunetti said, and took a sip of water. 'It's ingenious, isn't it?'

Riverre couldn't stop himself from smiling at Brunetti's comment. 'Only thing is, sir, I don't think we can do it right now, what with the vacation to pay for: we're going to Elba next week. Camping, but it's still expensive, for the three of us.'

'Oh,' Brunetti said with mild interest, 'how much does the class cost?'

'Three hundred Euros,' Riverre answered and looked at Brunetti to see how he responded to the price. When his superior raised his eyebrows by way of answer, Riverre explained, 'That's with the tests and all the grading, you see.'

'Humm,' Brunetti said and nodded; he reached into the bag for the other sandwich. 'It's not cheap, is it?'

'No,' Riverre said with a resigned shake of his head. 'But he's our only child, and we want the best for him. I guess that's sort of natural, wouldn't you say?'

'Yes, I think it is,' Brunetti said and took a bite. 'He's a good boy, isn't he?'

Riverre smiled, frowned in thoughtful consideration, then smiled again. 'I think he is, sir. And he does well in school. No trouble.'

'Then maybe you could wait a while on that class.' He finished the second sandwich, regretted that he had asked Riverre to bring him only two, and drank the rest of the water.

Looking around, Brunetti said, 'Where does the bottle go?'

'Over there by the door, sir. The blue bin.'

Brunetti walked over to the plastic bins, put the bottle in the blue one and the paper bag and napkins in the yellow. 'I see the hand of Signorina Elettra at work here,' he said.

Riverre laughed. 'I thought she'd have to use force when she first told us about them, but we're used to it by now.' Then, as though revealing a truth he had been considering for some time, he said, 'It's really a shame she isn't in charge here, isn't it, sir?'

'You mean the Questura?' Brunetti asked. 'The whole thing?'

'Yes, sir. Don't tell me you've never thought about it?'

Brunetti opened the second bottle of water and took a long drink. 'My daughter has an Iranian classmate: sweet young girl,' he said, confusing Riverre, who had perhaps expected a response to his question.

'Whenever she wants to express happiness, the expression she uses is, "Much, much, too, very." ' He took another drink of water.

'I'm not sure I follow you, sir,' Riverre said, his words mirrored in his face.

'It's the only thing I can think of to say in response to the idea of Signorina Elettra taking over here: "Much, much, too, very." ' He twisted closed the bottle, thanked Riverre for his lunch, and went downstairs to ask Signorina Elettra to make the changes to Scarpa's staffing plans.

7

For the next few days, it appeared that some cosmic governing force had heard Brunetti's wish that a deal be made with the forces of disorder, for crime went on holiday in Venice. The Romanians who played three card monte on the bridges appeared to have gone home on vacation, or else they had moved their work site to the beaches. The number of burglaries declined. Beggars, in response to a city ordinance banning them and subjecting them to severe penalties, disappeared for at least a day or two before going back to work. Pickpockets, of course, remained at their posts: they could go on vacation only in the empty months of November and February. Though the heat often drove people to violence, that was not the case this year. Perhaps there was some point where heat and humidity made the effort to throttle or maim too exhausting to be considered.

Whatever the cause, Brunetti was glad of the lull. He

used some of his free time to consult more sites that offered spiritual or other-worldly help to those in need of it. He had read so widely in the Greek and Roman historians that he found nothing strange at all in the desire to consult the oracles or to find some way to decipher the messages of the gods. Whether it was the liver of a freshly killed chicken or the patterns made in the air by a flock of birds, the signs were there for those who could interpret them: all that was necessary was someone willing to believe the interpretation, and the deal was done. Cumae or Lourdes; Diana of Ephesus or the Virgin of Fatima: the mouth of the statue moved, and the truth came forth.

The women of Brunetti's family had told the rosary, and as a boy he had often returned home from school on a Friday afternoon to find them kneeling on the floor in the living room, reciting their incantations. The practice, and the faith that animated it, had seemed to him then, and still seemed to him now, two generations later, an ordinary and understandable part of human life. Thus, to transfer belief in the beneficent powers of the Madonna to belief in the power of a person to make contact with departed spirits seemed – at least to Brunetti – a very small step along the highway of faith.

Never having dealt with a case that involved the mis-representation of faith – if this, indeed, was what was at work in the strange behaviour of Vianello's aunt – Brunetti was uncertain about the laws that operated. Italy was a country with a state religion; thus, the law tended to take a tolerant attitude towards the Church and the behaviour of its functionaries. Charges of usury, involvement with the Mafia, the abuse of minors, fraud, and extortion: these all managed to disappear, as if waved off by the legal equivalent of aspergillum and incense.

These sites, however, represented the competition to the religion of the state, and so the law might well take a dimmer view of their activities. And if the promises made in the churches were just as valid as those made on the websites, where did truth lie? Brunetti's speculations were halted by the telephone.

Happy at the interruption, he answered with his name.

'It's me, Guido,' Vianello said. 'Loredano just called me. The bank director called him: he's got my aunt there. She just withdrew three thousand Euros. He asked her to come up to his office for a moment to sign some papers.'

'Who's on patrol?'

'Pucetti and a new recruit are on the way to Via Garibaldi.'

Brunetti sent his memory down one side of Via Garibaldi, up the other. 'Banco di Padova?'

'Yes. Next to the pharmacy.'

'Did he say how long he can keep her there?'

'Ten minutes. He said he'll ask how the family is doing: that ought to keep her talking for a while.'

'Where are you?' Brunetti asked.

'On Murano. Someone tried to grab a woman's bag, and a mob formed and threw him in a canal. We had to come over to get him out.'

'I'll go and have a look,' Brunetti said and replaced the phone, but not before he heard Vianello say, 'She's wearing a green shirt.'

He was so preoccupied with Vianello's call that he was not prepared for the heat that hit him as he emerged from the Questura. It flowed over him in a single wave, and for a moment Brunetti didn't know if the attack of sodden air would permit him to breathe. He stopped, stepped back into the miserable shadow cast by the lintel of the door, and took out his sunglasses. They cut the light, but they did nothing to help against the heat. His jacket, light-weight blue cotton, clung to him like an Icelandic sweater.

So sudden had been the assault of heat and light that it took Brunetti a moment to remember why he had come outside and then another to remember the way to Via Garibaldi.

'Lunacy,' he muttered to himself and crossed the bridge. He had no choice but to keep his eyes lowered against the glare and leave it to his feet to find the way. He wove left and right, giving no conscious thought to where he was going. His feet took him over another bridge, then to the right, and then he emerged into Via Garibaldi and wished he had not. The paving stones had had hours to bake, and the heat they sent up seemed a form of protest at their own helplessness. Caught between the unrelenting sun and the radiant heat from below, Brunetti could think of no way to protect himself. A woman brushed past him, saying 'Con permesso' more forcefully than she might have, but he was, after all, standing motionless on the pavement and blocking her exit from the calle. Her remark unblocked him and he stepped back into the entrance to the calle, which offered the minimal protection of shade.

After a moment, Brunetti mustered the courage to take a step out into Via Garibaldi and the heat. The bank stood down on the right; farther along, some tables hid under the umbrellas in front of a bar. At one of them sat Pucetti and a young woman, who was laughing at something the young officer said. She had light hair, cut boyishly short, which impression was contradicted by the tight white T-shirt she wore. Both of them wore sunglasses and Pucetti a black T-shirt that was every bit as tight as the girl's without provoking the same effect.

Brunetti retreated into the *calle*, waited what he calculated to be a minute but knew must be less, and stepped forward again. Pucetti and the girl were getting to their feet. Brunetti noticed that she wore a very short skirt that showed tanned and attractive legs; both of them wore sandals. Between him and the two young police officers, an elderly woman stood in front of the bank, caught in that characteristically Venetian moment of calculating the shortest way to get somewhere. She looked up at the sky, as if she believed the exact temperature would be written there. She wore loose cotton trousers and a light green shirt with long sleeves. Her shoes were sensible brown pumps with a low heel, and she had the sturdy body common to women who have had many children and have been active all their lives. She carried a brown leather bag on her shoulder, both hands held in a firm grip on the straps. She set off to her left, down towards the *embarcadero* and Riva degli Schiavoni. As she walked, she stooped forward a bit and seemed to favour her left leg.

Just as she turned, the attractive young couple, who were farther along toward the boat stop, turned in the same direction and started walking ahead of her. Pucetti draped his arm over his companion's shoulders, but it proved too hot, so they settled for holding hands as they walked. They paused to look into the window of a sporting goods shop, and the old woman passed them, paying no attention. They followed slowly, and Brunetti followed the three of them.

At the end of Via Garibaldi, the old woman walked on

to the *embarcadero* and took a seat facing the water. The young couple stopped at the *edicola*, and the young man bought a copy of *Men's Health*. A Number Two came from the left, and the old woman got to her feet. With no sign of haste, the young people swiped their iMOB cards and walked up into the waiting deck and on to the boat. As the boat was unmoored and starting to back away from the dock, Brunetti stepped on board just ahead of the gate the crewman was sliding closed.

The old woman sat in the cabin, in an aisle seat in the front row, closest to whatever air managed to sneak in from the open door. Pucetti had spread his magazine on the wooden counter behind the pilot's cabin and was pointing to a grey linen jacket, asking his companion what she thought of it. His back was to the passenger cabin, but she was facing him, so she could see when the old woman got to her feet.

Brunetti came and stood alongside Pucetti. The young woman looked up at him and stood a bit straighter, but Pucetti, eyes still on the jacket, said, 'I figured Vianello would call you, too, sir.'

'Yes, he did.'

'Do you want to continue the same way: we follow her and you follow us?'

'Seems best,' Brunetti said.

The boat pulled into the San Zaccharia stop, and Pucetti turned a few pages of the magazine, reaching out to draw his companion closer so that she could see something on the page. A few pages later, they passed under the Accademia Bridge, then San Samuele, and then Brunetti heard her say, 'She's getting up.'

Pucetti closed the magazine and leaned sideways to give the young woman a kiss on the side of her forehead.

She bent her head close to his and said something, then they moved apart and got off at San Tomà, a few passengers behind the old woman with the brown leather bag and a few in front of the man in the blue cotton jacket.

At the end of the *calle*, the old woman turned right and then left into the *campo*. She crossed at a diagonal, heading to the right and into a narrow *calle* that led back towards the Frari. By unspoken agreement, they divided up, Brunetti taking the *calle* to the farther right to see that they did not lose track of her in this warren of narrow and suddenly turning *calli*.

As Brunetti was about to turn into Calle Passion, he saw the old woman ahead of him, stopped in front of a building on the right, hand raised to ring the bell. He kept on directly past the entrance to the *calle*, stopped and turned around, and when he came back, he saw what could have been a foot disappearing into a doorway. He turned into the *calle* and past the door, making a note of the number as he did.

As he emerged into Campo dei Frari, the young couple were just turning into the *calle*.

'Number two thousand nine hundred and eighty-nine,' Brunetti said casually. She looked at him as though he were one of those Internet magicians whose sites he had been consulting; Pucetti smiled and said, 'I'll tell my grandchildren about this, sir.'

Brunetti was uncertain whether the remark was meant to inflate or deflate his sense of accomplishment and thus said disparagingly, 'I just happened to be the one who saw her.' Pucetti nodded, while the young woman continued to stare at him.

'Now what, sir?'

'You two go and have a drink in the *campo*, and I'll go

into San Tomà and stand in front of the estate agency and look for a new apartment.'

'Hot work, Commissario,' the girl said with sympathy.

Brunetti nodded his thanks for the thought.

Luckily, he had remembered to bring his *telefonino* with him, so they agreed to keep in contact. He went back to the *campo* and put himself in front of the window of the estate agency. By this time of the afternoon, the sun was directly behind Brunetti and starting to burn its way slowly through his clothing. It was so intense that he turned first to expose one shoulder, then the other, like San Lorenzo on the grill.

The one advantage was that the angle of light turned the agency window into a giant mirror, in which he soon saw the approaching reflection of an old woman with a brown bag over her shoulder. But her hands no longer grasped the straps and the bag hung ignored at her side. She walked towards him while Brunetti studied the photo of a mansard apartment in Santa Croce, a mere half-million Euros for sixty square metres. 'Lunacy,' he whispered.

The woman turned to the right, then left into the *calle* going down to the *embarcadero*. Brunetti dialled Pucetti's number, and when the officer answered, said, 'She's going back towards the boat stop. Why don't you and your friend stop on the doorstep of two thousand nine hundred and eighty-nine for a long embrace?'

'I'll suggest it to her this very instant, sir,' Pucetti said and hung up. Brunetti moved away from the window and into the *calle* leading towards Goldoni's house, where he could at least stand in the shade. A few minutes later, Pucetti and the young woman appeared, no longer walking hand in hand.

'S. Gorini, sir,' Pucetti said. 'There's only one name at that number.'

'Shall we go back to the Questura, then?' Brunetti suggested.

'We're still on duty, sir,' Pucetti said.

'I think we've all had enough of following people in this heat, officers,' he said. Their relief was evident in the loosening of their bodies. He smiled at the girl for the first time and said, 'So let's see if you can follow a *commissario di polizia* back to the Questura without being noticed.'

8

Perhaps encouraged by the deference showed to his powers by the young woman, whose full name turned out to be Bettina Trevisoi, Brunetti decided to see what he could find out about S. Gorini by himself. The first thing he discovered, though he had to go only as far as the phone directory, was that the S stood for Stefano. But even with the full name, all Google provided was a wide variety of products and offers to introduce him to young girls. Because he had one of his own at home, Brunetti did not feel in need of another, and so he spurned the cyber-proposals, tempting as others might have found them.

Google having failed him, Brunetti was left to think of other places where reference to a person might be found. There must be a way to discover if he were renting the apartment or if he owned it: probably in some office of the Commune. If he owned it, then he might have a mortgage, and that might lead to his bank and thus provide an idea of his finances. There must be a way to find out if the city had granted him any licences or if he had a passport. Airline files might show if he travelled within Italy or to other countries, and how frequently. If he had any of the special cards offered by the railway, there would be a list of the train tickets he purchased. Copies of his phone bills, for both home phone and *telefonino*, would give an idea of who his friends and associates were. They would also show if he were running a commercial enterprise from that address. And credit card records often proved veritable mines of information.

He sat in front of the computer, these possibilities assaulting his imagination one after the other. He marvelled at how the most basic services of modern life exposed a person to easy scrutiny and how effectively they eliminated privacy.

But, more importantly, he marvelled at how incapable he was of finding even the first of these things. He knew all of this information must be hidden inside his computer, but he lacked the skills to discover it. He turned to Pucetti; Probationer Trevisoi stood by his side. 'It's a waste of time to try to check him out ourselves,' Brunetti said, careful to use the plural.

He watched as Pucetti fought down the impulse to object. In the last years, the young officer had learned a great deal from Signorina Elettra about the ways to slip around the roadblocks on the information highway. Pucetti glanced at the young woman at his side, and Brunetti could almost hear the creaks in his masculinity as he forced himself to nod. 'Maybe we better ask Signorina Elettra to have a look,' Pucetti finally agreed.

Pleased by the young officer's response and

considering that Trevisoi was young, attractive and female, Brunetti stood and offered the chair to Pucetti. 'Better to have two people taking a look,' Brunetti said. Then, to Trevisoi, he added, 'Pucetti's one of our information-retrieval experts.'

'Information retrieval, sir?' she said so innocently that Brunetti began to suspect there was perhaps more behind those dark eyes than he had originally believed.

'Spying,' he clarified. 'Pucetti's very good at it, but Signorina Elettra's better.'

'Signorina Elettra's the best,' Pucetti said as he flicked the screen back into life.

On his way to that person's office, Brunetti decided to restrain himself from repeating Pucetti's praise. When he entered, Signorina Elettra was just emerging from the office of her superior, Vice-Questore Giuseppe Patta. Today she wore a black T-shirt and a pair of loose black linen slacks and, below them, a pair of yellow Converse sneakers, sockless. She gave a welcoming smile. 'Have a look,' she said, moving to her chair and pointing to the screen of her computer. Perhaps as a concession to the heat, her hair was tied back from her face by a green ribbon.

He came to stand behind her and looked at the screen. On it he saw what looked like a page from a catalogue of computers, neat row after neat row and all of them, to Brunetti, looking identical. Were they, he wondered, finally going to order one for him to use in his office? There was no other reason she would bother to show him such things, was there? He was touched by her thoughtfulness.

'Very nice,' he said, in a noncommittal voice from

which all trace of personal greed had been removed.

'Yes, they are, aren't they? Some of them are almost as good as mine.' Pointing to one of the computers on the screen, she said something about numbers Brunetti could understand, like '2.33' and '1333', and words like 'mega-hertz' and 'giga-bytes', that he could not.

'Now look at this,' she said and scrolled down the screen to a list of prices that were keyed to the models shown above them. 'See the price of that one?' she asked, pointing to the third number.

'One thousand, four hundred Euros,' he read. She made a noise of assent, saying nothing, so he asked, 'Is that a good price?' He was complimented by the thought that the Ministry of Justice might be willing to spend that much on him, but modesty sealed his lips.

'It's a very good price,' she said. She hit a few keys; the image disappeared from the screen and was replaced by a long list of names and numbers. 'Now look at this,' she said, pointing to one of the items on the list.

'Is that the same computer?' he asked when he read the model name and number.

'Yes.'

Brunetti ran his eyes over to the number at the right. 'Two thousand, two hundred?' he asked. She nodded but did not comment.

'Where did the first price come from?'

'An on-line company in Germany. The computers come fully programmed in Italian, with an Italian keyboard.'

'And the others?' he asked.

'The others have been ordered and paid for already,' she said. 'What I showed you is the purchase order.'

'But that's crazy,' Brunetti said, unconsciously using

the word and tone his mother habitually used to comment on the price of fish.

Saying nothing, Signorina Elettra scrolled back to the top of the list, where she arrived at the letterhead: 'Ministro del Interno'.

'They're paying eight hundred Euros more?' he asked, not sure whether to be astonished or outraged, or both.

She nodded.

'How many did they buy?'

'Four hundred.'

It took him only seconds. 'That's three hundred and twenty thousand Euros more,' he said. She said nothing. 'Haven't these people ever heard about buying in quantity? Isn't the price supposed to come down when you do?'

'If the government is doing the buying, I think the rules are different, sir,' she answered.

Brunetti took a step back from the computer and walked around to the front of her desk. 'In a case like this, who's doing the buying? Who specifically, that is?'

'Some bureaucrat in Rome, I'd assume, sir.'

'Does anyone check what he does? Compare prices or offers?'

'Oh,' she said with audible negligence, 'I'm sure someone does.'

Time passed, during which Brunetti considered the possibilities. The fact that one person could order an item that cost eight hundred Euros more than an identical item did not mean that another person would object to the higher price, especially when it was government money that was being spent, and especially when only those two people were privy to the bidding process.

'Isn't anyone concerned about this?' Brunetti heard himself asking.

'Someone must be, Commissario,' she answered. Then, with almost militant brightness, she asked, 'What was it you wanted to see me about?'

He explained quickly about Vianello's aunt and the withdrawals she had been making, then gave her the name and address of Stefano Gorini, asking her if she had time to find out something about him.

Signorina Elettra made a note of the name and address and asked, 'Is this the aunt who's married to the electrician?'

'Ex-electrician,' Brunetti corrected, then, 'Yes.'

She gave him a sober glance and shook her head. 'I think it's like being a priest or a doctor,' she said.

'Excuse me?'

'Being an electrician, sir. I think once you do it, you have a sort of moral obligation to keep on doing it.' She gave him time to consider this, and when he made no comment, she said, 'Nothing's worse than darkness.'

From long experience as a resident of a city where many houses still had wires that had been installed fifty or sixty years ago, Brunetti grasped what she meant and had no choice but to say, 'Yes. Nothing worse.'

His ready agreement seemed to cheer her, and she asked, 'Is it urgent, sir?'

Given the fact that it probably wasn't legal, either, Brunetti said, 'No, not really.'

'Then I'll have a look tomorrow, sir.'

Before he left, he said, indicating her computer, 'While you're in there, could you see what you can find out about an usher at the Courthouse, Araldo Fontana?' Brunetti did not give her the name of Judge Coltellini, not from compunction at sharing police information with a civilian employee – he had long since set aside the things of a child – but because he did not want to burden her with a third name, and Brusca's apparent defence of the man had made Brunetti more curious about him.

But he could not stop himself from asking, 'Where did you get that information about the computers, Signorina?'

'Oh, it's all in the public record, sir. You just have to know where to look.'

'And so you sort of go trolling through the files by yourself to see what you can see?'

'Yes,' she said with a smile, 'I suppose you could phrase it that way. "Trolling." I quite like that.'

'And you never know what you're going to fish up, I suppose.'

'Never,' she said. Then, pointing to the paper where she had written the names he wanted her to check, she said, 'Besides, it keeps me in training for interesting things like this.'

'Isn't the rest of your work interesting, Signorina?' he asked.

'No, I'm afraid much of it isn't, Dottore.' She propped her chin in her cupped palm and tightened her lips in a resigned grimace. 'It's hard when so many of the people I work for are so very dull.'

'It's a common enough plight, Signorina,' Brunetti said and left the office.

9

By the time he reached his office the next day, Brunetti was resigned to the fact that he was not soon going to have his own computer, though he found it more difficult to resign himself to the temperature of his office when he arrived. The family had, the night before, discussed where they were to go for their yearly vacation, Brunetti apologizing that the uncertainty of work had kept him this long without knowing when he would be free. He had quickly squashed all discussion of going to the seaside: not in August with millions of people in the water and on the roads and in the restaurants. 'I will not go to Puglia, where it is forty degrees in the shade, and where the olive oil is all fake,' he remembered saying at one point.

In retrospect, he accepted the possibility that he might have been too firm. In his defence of his own desires, he had been emboldened by the fact that Paola never much cared where they went: her only concern was what books she should take and whether wherever they went had a quiet place for her to lie in the shade and read.

Other men had wives who begged them to go out dancing, travel the world, stay up late and do irresponsible things. Brunetti had managed to marry a woman who looked forward to going to bed at ten o'clock with Henry James. Or, when driven by wild passions she was ashamed to reveal to her husband, with Henry James and his brother.

Like the president of a banana republic, Brunetti had offered democratic choice and then rammed his own proposal past all difference of opinion or opposition. A cousin of his had inherited a farmhouse in Alto Adige, above Glorenza, and had offered it to Brunetti while he and his family went to Puglia. 'In the heat, eating fake olive oil,' Brunetti muttered, though no less grateful to his cousin for the offer. And so the Brunettis were to go to the mountains for two weeks; thinking of it, Brunetti's spirit flooded with relief at the mere thought of sleeping under a quilt and having to wear a sweater in the evening.

Vianello and his family had rented a house on the beach in Croatia, where he planned to do nothing but swim and fish until the end of the month. While they were both away, their unofficial investigation into Stefano Gorini would go on vacation, as well.

Brunetti spent the first part of the morning using the computer in the officers' squad room to check the trains to Bolzano and to consult the various tourist sites in Alto Adige. Then he went back to his own office and called a few colleagues to see if they had ever come into contact with Stefano Gorini. He had more success with the train schedule.

A bit after twelve-thirty, he dialled his home number. Paola answered on the third ring, saying, 'If you can get here in fifteen minutes, there's prosciutto and figs and then pasta with fresh peppers and shrimp.'

'Twenty,' he said and hung up.

To walk it that quickly on a hot day, he feared, would kill him, so he went out to the *riva* and was lucky enough to step directly on to a Number Two. At San Tomà he caught a Number One that pulled up after two minutes, and got off at San Silvestro. It had taken longer than it would by foot, but he had been spared crossing the city in the middle of the day.

Inside the apartment, Paola and the kids sat at the table in the kitchen: the terrace was a broiler during the day and could be used only after sunset. Brunetti hung up his jacket, wondering if he should wring it out first, and took his place at the table.

He glanced at the faces and wondered if the apathy he saw there was the result of his behaviour about their vacation or merely the heat. 'How'd you spend your morning?' he asked Chiara.

'I went over to Livia's and tried on some of the new things she got to go back to school,' Chiara answered, carefully trimming the fat from her prosciutto and passing it silently to Raffi's plate, she apparently having decided that vegetarians can eat the ham but not the fat.

'Autumn things? Already?' Paola asked, putting a plate of prosciutto and black figs in front of Brunetti. She rested her hand on his shoulder when she leaned down with the plate, allowing Brunetti to believe that at least one member of the family looked forward to the vacation.

'Yes,' Chiara said, mouth full of fig. 'When we were in Milano to visit her sister last week – Marisa: she's at

Bocconi – they took me shopping with them. The stuff there is much better than what you find here. Here it's all for teenies or old ladies.'

His daughter had gone to Milano, Brunetti reflected, site of the Brera Gallery, site of Leonardo's Cenacolo, site of the greatest Gothic cathedral in Italy, and she had gone shopping. 'Did you find anything you liked?' he asked and ate half a fig. His daughter was perhaps a philistine, but the fig was sweet perfection.

'*No, Papà*, I didn't,' she said in the descending measures of tragedy. 'Everything's crazy expensive.' She trimmed another piece of prosciutto and used the point of her knife to transfer the fat to Raffi, who was busy with his lunch and apparently uninterested in tales of shopping.

'I had my own money, but *Mamma* would have gone crazy if I'd spent two hundred Euros on a pair of jeans.'

Paola glanced up from her antipasto. 'No, I wouldn't have gone crazy, but I would have sent you to a work camp for the rest of the summer.'

'How are we supposed to get out of the financial crisis if no one spends any money?' Chiara demanded, sure proof that she had spent a day in the company of a student at Italy's best business school.

'By working hard and paying our taxes,' Raffi said, thus putting an end to any lingering doubts Brunetti might have had that his son's flirtation with Marxism was at an end.

'Would that it were that easy,' Paola said.

'What do you mean?' asked Raffi.

'To work hard, you have to have a job,' Paola said, looking across the table at him and smiling. 'Right?' Raffi nodded. 'And to pay taxes, you also have to have a job. Or run a business.'

'Of course,' Raffi said. 'Any idiot knows that.'

'And how does a person find a job?' Before Raffi could answer, Paola forged ahead. 'Without knowing someone or having a father who's a lawyer or a notary who can give him a job as soon as he finishes his studies?' Again, before her son could answer, she said, 'Think about the older brothers and sisters of your friends in school. How many of them have found decent jobs? They've got all sorts of elegant degrees in I don't know what sort of elegant subjects, and they sit at home and live off their parents.' And before her son could accuse her of insensitivity, she added, 'Not necessarily because they want to but because there are no jobs for them. If they're lucky, they get some sort of temporary work, but as soon as their contract is up, they're let go, and someone else is hired for six months.'

Good Lord, Brunetti thought, who sounded like the Marxist now? 'So how are they to get jobs and pay their taxes?' he inquired mildly.

Paola started to speak but apparently decided to abandon the topic. 'I think it's ready,' she said. It was: Paola had seared off the skins of the peppers, leaving behind a sweetness and consistency reminiscent of the figs. The family, soothed by the pleasures of lunch, spent the rest of the meal in peaceful discussion of how to spend their time in the mountains.

After lunch, Brunetti sat on the sofa and leafed through *Il Gazzettino*, but even the lightness of its every word and phrase could not lift the vague uneasiness created by Paola's obvious change of subject. Retreat was not a tactic to which she was much given.

She came in with coffee, handed him his cup, and sat in an easy chair across from him. She put her feet on the low table and took a sip. 'If I ever say again, any time in my life, how nice it is to live on the top floor, under the roof, would you please stuff me in the oven and keep me there until I come to my senses?'

'We could get air conditioning,' he said, to provoke her.

'And have Chiara move out?' she asked. 'She's toxic on the subject. One of her friends' fathers had it put in, and Chiara refuses to go to her house any more.'

'You think we've created a fanatic?' Brunetti asked.

Paola finished her coffee and set the cup and saucer on the table. After some time, she said, 'If she's got to be a fanatic, I'd rather it be the ecology than anything else.'

'But don't you think her response is a bit excessive?' Brunetti asked.

Paola shrugged. 'It is now, this year, in this historical period. But ten years from now, twenty, she might be proven right, and we'll look back at the excess of our lives and see it as criminal.' She closed her eyes and let her head fall against the back of the chair.

'And then people will call her a prophet and not a fanatic?'

'Who knows?' Paola said, eyes closed. 'They're often the same thing.'

'Why'd you change the subject?' he asked.

'About jobs and taxes?' she asked.

He studied her face. She was more than twenty years older than when he had first met her, and yet he could see no difference. Blonde hair that had a will of its own, a nose that was perhaps too large for this era of female beauty, the cheekbones that had drawn his first kisses. He grunted by way of answer.

'I didn't want to talk about taxes,' she said at last.

'Why?'

'Because I think we're crazy to continue to pay them, and if I could, I'd stop.'

'Is this excessive rhetoric?' long experience prompted him to ask.

She opened her eyes and smiled across at him. 'Probably. But I was surprised to realize a few days ago that some of the things the Lega says – those same things that had me wild with anger a decade ago – they're beginning to make sense to me.'

'We become our parents,' Brunetti said, repeating something his mother had often said. 'What things?'

'That our tax money goes South and is never seen again. That the North works hard and pays its taxes and gets very little in return for it. That the Vatican tells us to be generous to immigrants but doesn't take any in.'

'You going to start talking about building a wall between the North and the South?' he asked.

She let out a snort of laughter. 'Of course not. I simply didn't want to talk like this in front of the kids.'

'You think they don't know?'

'Of course they know,' she said. 'But they know only from what we do or what their friends' parents do.'

'For example?'

'That when we eat in a restaurant where the owner is a friend, we don't get a *ricevuta fiscale*, so no tax is paid.'

Brunetti was always, and uncontrollably, defensive about any suggestion of frugality on his part and quickly jumped to his own defence. 'I don't do it to make them charge less. You know that.'

'That's just my point, Guido. That at least would make sense because it would save you money. But you do it out of principle, not greed, so that this disgusting government of ours won't get at least that little bit of money to give to their friends or put in their own pockets.'

He nodded. That was exactly the point.

'And that's why I don't want to talk about taxes in front of them. If they're going to end up feeling that way about the government, then they have to discover it themselves: they shouldn't learn it from us.'

'Even if it is, as you say, a "disgusting" government?'

'It's not as bad as some,' she temporized after a moment's reflection.

'I'm not sure that's the most eloquent defence of our government I've ever heard,' he said.

'I'm not trying to defend it,' she said angrily. 'It's disgusting, but at least it's disgusting in a non-violent way. If that makes a difference.'

After some reflection, Brunetti said, 'I suppose it does.' He pushed himself to his feet, walked around the table and bent to kiss her and said he'd be back at the usual time for dinner.

10

On his way back to the Questura, again taking the vaporetto to avoid the sun, Brunetti considered what he and Paola had said to one another and what Paola had not said to the children at lunch. How many times had he heard people use the phrase, '*Governo Ladro*'? And how many times had he agreed in silence that the government was a thief? But in the last few years, as though some previous sense of restraint or shame had been overcome, there had been less attempt on the part of their rulers to pretend that they were anything more than what they were. One of his previous superiors, the Minister of Justice, had been accused of collusion with the Mafia, but all it had taken was a change of government for that story to have drifted out of the newspapers and, for all he knew, out of the halls of justice.

Brunetti was, by disposition and then by training, a listener: people sensed that first in him and in his company spoke easily and often entirely without reserve. In the last year, what he heard more and more in the voices of people – sometimes a woman standing next to him on the vaporetto or a man in a bar – was a mounting sense of disgust at the way they were ruled and at the people who ruled them. It didn't matter if the people who spoke to him had voted for or against the politicians they reviled: they'd be happy to lock them all up in the local church and set it ablaze.

Underlying it all, and this is what troubled Brunetti, was a sense of despair. He was troubled by the help-lessness which so many people felt and their failure to understand what had happened, as if aliens had taken over and imposed this system on them. Governments came and governments went, the Left came and then gave place to the Right, and nothing changed. Though politicians often talked of it and promised it, not one of them gave evidence of having any real desire to change this system which worked so very much to their real purposes.

As the boat passed the Piazza, Brunetti saw the crowds, the queues snaking back from the entrance to the Basilica, even at three in the afternoon. What possessed people to stand in the open, under that sun, motionless? It was difficult for him to subtract his familiarity with the Basilica from his store of knowledge. He had been taken there countless times in his youth by his teachers and by his mother: the teachers took their students to show them the beauty, and his mother had taken him, he supposed, to show him the truth and power of her faith. He tried to wipe his mind clear of familiarity with the sweeping glory of the interior and wondered to what lengths he would go if he had but one chance in his lifetime to stand inside Basilica San Marco, and to do so he had to stand in a queue for an hour under the afternoon sun.

He turned to his right to consult the angel on the bell tower of San Giorgio, and together they decided. 'I'd do it,' Brunetti said and nodded in affirmation, much to the discomfiture of the two scantily clad girls who sat between him and the window of the boat.

He went directly to Signorina Elettra's office, which was, as he expected to find it, even hotter than it had been the day before. Today it was her blouse that was yellow, but she still seemed entirely untouched by the heat.

'Ah, Commissario,' she said as he came in, 'I've found your Signor Gorini.'

'Speak, Muse,' Brunetti said with a smile.

'Signor Gorini, who is forty-four, according to the information on his *carta d'identità*,' she began, sliding a sheet of paper towards him, 'was born in Salerno where, from the age of eighteen to twenty-two, he was a seminarian with the Franciscan fathers.'

She looked up, pleased. Brunetti smiled in return, equally pleased.

'Then, for a period of four years, there is no sign of him, until he reappeared in Aversa, working as a clinical psychologist.' She glanced at Brunetti to see that he was following. He nodded encouragingly.

'While he was living there, he married and had a son, Luigi, who is now sixteen.' She flicked a speck of dust from the page before consulting it again.

'After he had been in practice – though I think that word is notional – in Aversa for five years, he was discovered to have neither a licence nor a degree in psychology, nor, so far as the ULSS authorities could determine at the time, any training in psychology whatsoever.'

'What happened to him?'

'His practice was closed and he was fined three million lire. But the fine was never paid because Signor Gorini removed himself from Aversa.'

'And the wife? And the son?'

'It would seem neither of them ever heard from him again.'

'Obviously, he was better suited to the cloistered life,' Brunetti permitted himself to say.

'Clearly,' she agreed and shifted the paper aside to uncover another.

'He next came to the attention of the authorities eight years ago, when it was discovered that the centre he was running in Rapallo, which specialized in helping integrate refugees from Eastern Europe into the workforce, was merely a kind of hostel where he allowed immigrants to live while they went out to work at jobs he found for them.'

'And in exchange?'

'In exchange, they gave him 60 per cent of their salaries, but they were at least given a place to live.'

'Meals?'

'Don't be absurd, Dottore. He was also helping to introduce them to the experience of living in a capitalist society.'

'Every man for himself,' Brunetti said.

'Dog eat dog,' she replied, then added, 'Though in this case one hopes that is not true. They could cook in this place where they lived.'

'At least that,' Brunetti said. 'What happened?'

'One of the women went to the Carabinieri. She was Romanian, so she could make herself understood. She told them what was going on, and they made a visit to the centre. But Signor Gorini was not to be found.'

'Did he use his own name all this time?' Brunetti asked.

'Yes, he did,' she said. 'And apparently that was fine.'

'Lucky for you that he did use it,' he said, then, seeing her response, quickly added, 'Though I'm sure it would have made no difference to you if he'd used another one. It just would have taken longer.'

'Minimally,' she said, and Brunetti believed her.

'And since then?' he asked.

'There was no trace of him for a few years, and then five years ago he set up a practice as a homeopathic doctor, this time in Naples, but,' and here she looked up and shook her head in open astonishment, 'after two years someone checked his application file and discovered that he had never studied medicine.'

'What happened?'

'The practice was closed.' That was all she said. Perhaps it was not a crime in Naples to practise medicine without a licence.

'Two years ago,' she continued, 'he changed his residence to the address you gave me, but he is not the person in whose name the rental contract is written.'

'Who is that?'

'A woman named Elvira Montini.'

'Who is?'

'Who works as a lab technician at the Ospedale Civile.'

'Maybe he's gone straight,' Brunetti suggested.

She raised her eyebrows at this idea but said nothing.

'Have you found any indication of what he's doing?'

'For all I can find, he could be devoting himself to a life of contemplation and good works,' she said.

'Yet Vianello's aunt seems to be taking large sums of money to him at that address,' said a sceptical Brunetti.

'To one of the people at that address, at any rate,' he corrected. 'That's the only apartment that uses that entrance.'

'So that's what Vianello's been so worried about,' Signorina Elettra said, her concern and affection audible in every word.

'Yes, for some time.'

He thought about his connections at the hospital and said, 'I can ask Dottor Rizzardi. He must know the people in the lab.'

Her cough was so discreet as hardly to exist, but to Brunetti it was a clarion call. 'You spoke to him, then?'

'Yes, sir.' Before he could ask, she explained, 'I took the liberty of asking.'

'Ah,' escaped his lips. 'And?'

'And she is that one reliable person upon whom the entire enterprise depends,' she answered, and Brunetti kept his eyes from meeting hers. 'She's been there for fifteen years, never married; if anything, is married to her work.'

Impulsively, to divert them both from any reflection upon how closely this description, save for the number of years, matched Signorina Elettra herself, Brunetti asked, 'Then how explain the presence of Signor Gorini in her home?'

'Indeed,' she agreed, then continued, 'I asked the doctor if there was anything else he could tell me about her, and I sensed a certain reluctance on his part. He sounded, if anything, protective of her.'

'So what did you do?'

'I lied, of course,' she said with equanimity. 'I told him my sister knew someone who worked in the lab with her – which is true – I even gave her name. It was someone

Barbara went to medical school with but who didn't finish. I said she had spoken very well of Signorina Montini but said she thought she'd changed in the last year or so.'

Before Brunetti could ask, she explained, 'Any woman who has been living with a man like that has probably changed in the course of two years, and not for the better.'

'What did he say?'

'He said her work was still excellent, and then he changed the subject.'

'I see,' Brunetti said. 'You want to ask your sister to talk to her classmate?'

Signorina Elettra gave a sharp shake of her head and lowered her eyes to her desk. 'They don't speak,' was the only explanation she offered.

'What else?' he asked, seeing that there were still some papers she had not uncovered.

'He's got an account at the UniCredit.' She handed him a bank statement of the movements for the last six months in the account of Stefano Gorini. Brunetti studied it, looking for a pattern, but there was none. Sums, always cash and never in excess of five hundred Euros, moved in and out of the account each month. The current total was less than two thousand Euros.

'Any suggestion of how he supports himself?'

She shook her head. 'He could have generous friends, or he could be living off Signorina Montini, or he could, for all I know, be very lucky at roulette or cards. The money washes in and flows away, and there's never a deposit or withdrawal large enough to cause the least curiosity.'

'Credit card bills?' Brunetti asked.

'It would seem he doesn't have one.'

'*Mirabile dictu*,' Brunetti said. 'And this in the new millennium.'

'But he might have a *telefonino*,' Signorina Elettra said, and explained, 'I won't know until this afternoon, perhaps not until tomorrow.'

She read Brunetti's surprise and said, by way of explanation, 'Giorgio's on vacation.'

'So you have to ask someone else?'

Her expression showed her bewilderment at his failure to understand client loyalty. 'No, he'll try it from Newfoundland, but he's not sure he can get it to me today: he said it might be complicated to patch into the Telecom system from there.'

'I see,' said Brunetti, who didn't. 'I'd like to think of a way to keep an eye on his house.'

'I looked it up in *Calli, Campi, e Campielli*, sir, and it doesn't look like it would be easy. You'd need people permanently in Campo dei Frari and in San Tomà, and even then you wouldn't be sure whoever went into or came out of the *calle* had been to that address.'

'Can you think of anyone here who lives around there?' he asked.

'Let me check,' she said and turned to her computer. Brunetti assumed she was pulling up the personal files of the people who worked in the Questura. It was less than two minutes before she said, 'No, sir. No one lives within two bridges of it.

'Given his record,' Signorina Elettra added, placing her hand on the papers to call their attention back to Gorini: 'with or without Signorina Montini, it's not likely that he's living here in quiet retirement.'

'And if he's learned anything from past experiences,' continued Brunetti, 'he'll avoid hiring employees or doing anything that would open him up to licensing rules or official certification of any sort. So why not become a fortune-teller?'

'It's not far off being a psychologist, is it?' Signorina Elettra asked.

However comforting it is to have one's prejudices confirmed, Brunetti still chose to remain silent.

When he looked at her again, Signorina Elettra had her chin cupped in her left hand, the right resting on the corner of her keyboard. 'No,' she said after what seemed a long consultation with the blank screen. 'There's really no way we can watch the house. And if the Vice-Questore found out what we were doing, there'd be trouble.'

'Are you afraid of that?' he asked.

A quiet puff of dismissal escaped her lips. 'Not for me. Or you, for that matter. But he'd take it out on Vianello and on any officers involved in it, and Scarpa would join in. It's not worth it.'

She sat up straight and hit a few keys. 'Here, take a look at him.'

Brunetti moved behind her just as the photo of a man, in the classic pose of the newly arrested, came up on the screen. 'It's from the time in Aversa, so it's fifteen years old,' she said. 'I couldn't find anything more recent.'

'Didn't he renew his *carta d'identità*?' Brunetti asked.

'Yes, but in Naples, five years ago: they've lost the file.'

'Do you believe them?' he asked, made suspicious only by the location, not by the event itself, which was common enough.

'Yes,' she said. 'I asked someone I know, and I believe him. They didn't scan the photo into the computer, and then they lost the paper file.' She tapped the screen with her forefinger. 'So all we've got is this.'

The expressionless face that looked out at them, even with the long sideburns and shaggy hair Gorini had worn when the photo was taken, was well proportioned and handsome; the dark eyes tilted up above prominent cheekbones, giving the face a definite Tartar look. The nose was long, skewed a bit to one side, and there was a thickening of the bone just before the bridge. The mouth was broad and well shaped. The combination of features, Brunetti had to admit, amounted to a look of powerful masculinity. He could find no memory of having seen an older version of Gorini in the city.

He pointed to the photo. 'I'd like you to give copies of this to some of Scarpa's bloodhounds – without telling the Lieutenant.' He saw that she wanted to say something, and so added, 'Tell them it's an old photo of someone who lives in the city, and it's just part of the training to see if they can spot him.'

She smiled as she said, 'To deceive the Lieutenant – in however minor a way – is to know joy.'

11

Before he could leave her office, Signorina Elettra asked, 'Are you still curious about Signor Fontana?'

Fontana? Fontana? What did that name have to do with Vianello's aunt? Then it came back to him – that 'decorous man' – and he said, 'Ah, yes. Certainly.'

'As you told me, he's an usher at the Tribunale, so it was very easy to find him. He's worked there for thirty-five years, lives with his mother, never married. Never taken a day off sick. Only day he's ever missed work was the day of his father's funeral, thirty-four years ago.'

Brunetti stopped her there with an abruptly raised hand. 'Never missed a day of work? Well, one day, for his father's funeral. And you say this man is a civil servant?'

'Yes,' she answered. 'Should I get you a chair, Commissario?'

'Thank you, no,' he said in a very quiet voice. He placed one hand flat on her desk and made a business of supporting himself with it, head cast down limply. 'I'm sure if I just stand here quietly for a moment, I'll be all right.' After that moment had passed, he shook his head a few times and lifted his hand tentatively from her desk. 'Pucetti said yesterday that he'd seen something he would tell his grandchildren about. I think the same thing has just happened to me. Absent only once in thirty-five years.' He gazed at the far wall, as though he were watching a flaming hand write the numbers. Then, suddenly tired of foolery, he said, 'What else?'

'He and his mother rent an apartment up near San Leonardo. They lived in Castello until three years ago, when they moved into an apartment in a *palazzo* on the Misericordia.'

'Very nice,' Brunetti said, suddenly alert. 'Does the mother work?'

'No. Never.'

'Be interesting to know how he pays the rent, wouldn't it?' Brunetti asked.

'I doubt he'd have difficulty paying it,' she surprised him by saying.

'Why? Is the place small?'

'No, quite the opposite. It's a hundred and fifty square metres.'

'Then how does he manage to pay for it?'

Her small, self-satisfied smile warned him to prepare for her next remark, but even Brunetti could not have imagined what was to come. 'Because the rent's only four hundred and fifty Euros,' she said. From that, she progressed to arrant grandstanding and said, 'Or so the monthly transfers from his bank account would suggest.'

'For an apartment on the Misericordia? A hundred and fifty square metres?'

'Perhaps now you have something else to tell your grandchildren, Dottore,' she said with a smile.

His mind shot ahead, trying to find an explanation. Blackmail? A contract written with a falsely low rent so that Fontana could pay the rest in cash, letting the landlord avoid taxes? A relative?

'Who does the payment go to?' he asked.

'Marco Puntera,' she said, naming a businessman who had made a fortune in real estate in Milano and then moved back to his native Venice seven or eight years before.

A cat, Brunetti knew, could look at a king, but how on earth did an usher know a man as wealthy as Puntera was reported to be, and how was it that he was given an apartment with such a rent?

'He owns lots of apartments, doesn't he?' Brunetti asked.

'At least twelve, and all are rented out. And two *palazzi* on the Grand Canal,' she said. 'Also rented.'

'At comparable rents?' Brunetti asked.

'I haven't had time to check, sir. But I believe many of them are rented to foreigners.' She paused, as if in search of the proper phrase. Finding it, she went on, 'He is said to be an ornament to the Anglo-American community.'

'But he's neither Anglo nor American,' said Brunetti quickly, having gone to elementary school with Puntera's younger brother.

'In the sense that he is involved in their social life, sir,' she went on imperturbably. 'Membership at the Cipriani pool; Christmas carols at the English Church; Fourth of July party; first-name basis with the owners of the best restaurants.'

To Brunetti, this sounded like one of the tortures Dante

had overlooked. 'And Fontana gets a deal on his rent from a man like this?' he said, more in the sense of one repeating a wonder than asking a question about it.

'So it would seem.'

'Have you learned anything else?' he asked.

'I thought I'd speak to you first, Commissario, and see if you found their association as thought-provoking as I do.'

'I find it fascinating,' Brunetti said, always interested in the possibilities that arose from the various relationships formed among people in the city. The more unusual the couple, the more intriguing the possibilities often turned out to be.

'Good,' she said. 'I thought you might.' She paused, then said, 'But taking a closer look might require me to call in some favours, so I wanted to see if you agreed before I began to ask questions.'

He looked at Signorina Elettra and asked, 'What did you have in mind?'

Instead of answering, Signorina Elettra said, 'I'm pleased you approve of the staffing schedule, Commissario. I'll have it posted by the end of the day.'

'Good, Signorina. I appreciate it,' Brunetti replied seamlessly and turned towards the door, then gave every evidence of being surprised to discover there Vice-Questore Giuseppe Patta and, to his right, Lieutenant Scarpa, his creature.

'Ah, good morning, Vice-Questore,' Brunetti said with a pleasant smile. Then, like Copernicus recognizing a lesser planet, 'Lieutenant.'

Patta had reached the near-zenith of his summer colouring. Since May, he had been swimming daily in the pool of the Hotel Cipriani and had almost attained the colour of a horse chestnut. A few more weeks and he would have achieved that, but soon after, the days would begin to shorten and the sun's rays would lose their ferocity. And by October the Vice-Questore would resemble a *caffè macchiato* into which, as the weeks progressed, more and more milk would be added until, by December, he would be blanched to cappuccino paleness. Unless he took the expedient of using the Christmas vacation to top up his colour in the Maldives or the Seychelles, Patta ran the risk of arriving at the portals of springtime a pale shadow of his summer self.

'Signorina Elettra has just explained the new summer scheduling plan to me,' Brunetti said with an affable smile and a complimentary nod in Scarpa's direction. 'I think it's good to maximize the possibilities of force deployment with these innovations, sir.' Patta smiled, but Scarpa gave Brunetti a savage look. 'It shows creative organizational skills, really innovative planning if I might . . .' – and here he looked away, the very picture of admiring modesty – 'venture to observe.'

'I'm glad you think that way,' said an expansive Patta. 'I have to confess,' and here it was Patta who draped himself in the cloth of modesty, 'that the Lieutenant gave me the benefit of his hands-on experience with the men here.'

'Teamwork, that's the answer,' said a positively beaming Brunetti.

Signorina Elettra used this moment to interrupt. 'There was a call for you from the Cipriani while you were out, Vice-Questore. They said something about your lunch table for tomorrow and asked you to call.'

'Thank you, Signorina,' Patta said, moving towards his office door. 'I'll see to that now.' He disappeared inside, answering a Higher Call, leaving the three of them in Signorina Elettra's office.

Time passed. Signorina Elettra opened her drawer and pulled out that month's *Vogue*. She opened it and spread it on her keyboard.

Brunetti took a step towards her, glanced at the pages and asked, 'Do you really think those side vents in jackets are a good idea?'

'I haven't decided yet, Commissario. What does your wife think?'

'Well, she's always liked a jacket without vents: says it's more flattering to the figure. That might be because she's tall. But certainly that one is perfect,' he said, leaning forward and pointing to a beige jacket at the centre of the left-hand page. 'I'll ask her again tonight and see if she has any further ideas on the subject.'

She turned to the Lieutenant but he, apparently having no strong opinion to offer about vents, chose that moment to leave her office, failing to close the door behind him.

'A man without a sense of fashion is a man without a soul,' Signorina Elettra said and turned a page.

12

There was no sign that Scarpa would return and the light for Patta's phone was burning red, so Brunetti said, 'You shouldn't tempt me.'

'I shouldn't tempt myself,' she said, closing the magazine and replacing it in her drawer. 'But I can't resist the urge to goad him.'

'Did he really make out the schedule?'

'Of course not,' she snapped. 'I did it in about ten minutes this morning. It was on my desk when Scarpa came in, and he asked me what it was. I didn't say anything, but all he had to do was read the title at the top. So he picked it up and took it into Patta's office with him, and the next thing I knew, Patta was out here with it in his hand, praising the Lieutenant's initiative.' She made an angry noise and slammed her drawer shut.

'It was ever thus,' Brunetti said.

'That women do the work and men get the credit?' she asked, still angry.

'I'm afraid so.'

Brunetti noticed a stain of perspiration on the inside of the collar of her blouse. 'Patta's the only one who buys it, you know,' he said by way of consolation.

She shrugged, took a deep breath, and then said, voice much calmer, 'It's probably better that Patta shouldn't know how easy it is for me to do the work. So long as he – or his Lieutenant – continues to think he's doing it all, then I can do what I want.'

'Riverre said he thought things would be much better if you ran the place.'

'Ah, the wisdom of fools,' she said, but she smiled nevertheless.

Returning to business, Brunetti asked, 'What are you going to do about Fontana?' Translated, the question really meant: Who are you going to ask, and what is that going to cost us in terms of having to pay back favours?

'There's a clerk at the Tribunale I've known for years. I call into his office every so often when I'm over there, and occasionally we go out for a coffee, or he comes along when I buy flowers for the office. He's asked me to dinner a few times, but I've always been busy. Or said I was.' She looked at Brunetti and smiled. 'I'll wait until Tuesday and go over to the flower market. Then maybe I'll stop on the way back and see if he's free to go for a coffee.'

'What's wrong with him?'

'Oh, nothing, not really. He's honest and hard-working and quite good-looking.' From her tone, one would think she was listing his handicaps.

'And?'

'And very dull. If I make a joke, I feel like I'm hitting a

puppy. He looks at me with his big brown eyes, confused and hoping I won't be angry with him because he can't learn to do the trick.'

'But he's a clerk at the Tribunale?'

'And I am but weak human flesh,' she said with a long sigh, 'and could never resist a bargain.' Before he could ask, she went on, 'And this is the best bargain around. I have a coffee with him, and the secrets of the Tribunale are at my disposal, should I choose to ask about them.'

'Haven't you?' Brunetti asked.

'Never before,' she said. 'I've always thought I'd keep him in reserve.' She searched for the proper simile. 'Like a squirrel burying a nut, in case it turns out to be a long, hard winter.'

'To me, it sounds more like the wolf in "*Cappuccetto Rosso*",' Brunetti said, 'dressed up as the Grandmother and just waiting for the right time to gobble her up.'

'But I don't want to gobble him up,' she insisted. 'I just want to ask him some questions.'

'If Paris was worth a Mass,' Brunetti observed, 'then perhaps information about Fontana is worth a coffee.'

Primly, she said, 'It's not you who has to have it with him.'

'I know,' replied Brunetti, not at all certain how much of her tale was truth, how much art, not that one was ever sure of that with Signorina Elettra. To get her away from the subject, he asked, 'And Signor Puntera?'

'A friend of mine at the bank once worked as a consultant for him, I think. I'll see if he's still working in Venice and ask him what he knows.'

Brunetti could not remember, in all these years, that Signorina Elettra had ever used a female source. 'Is it easier to get men to talk?' he asked.

'You mean, easier than getting women to talk?'

'Yes.'

She tilted her head and looked at the closed door to Patta's office. 'I suppose it is. Women are much more discreet than men, at least when it comes to boasting. Or we boast about different things.'

'Is that why you prefer to use men?' he asked, not aware until after he had asked the question of how crass it made her sound.

'No,' she answered calmly. 'It would be more dishonest to get information from women this way.'

'Dishonest?' he repeated.

'Of course it's dishonest, what I do. I'm taking advantage of people's innocence and betraying their trust. You want that not to be dishonest?'

'Is it more dishonest than breaking into someone's computer system?' he asked, though he thought it was.

She gave him a puzzled glance, as if amazed that he could ask such an obvious question. 'Of course it is, Dottore. Information systems are built to stop you from breaking in: people know you're going to do it or try to do it. So in a sense, they're warned, and they take precautions, or they should. But when people tell you things in confidence or trust you with information they think you're not going to repeat, they have no defences.' She reached forward and touched a few keys, but nothing changed on the screen.

'So I'll go and have a coffee with him and see what he can tell me about Araldo Fontana, model worker.'

'For what it's worth,' Brunetti said, 'my source was convinced that there's nothing to tell about him. He said Fontana is a decorous man; he even seemed surprised that I should want to know anything about him.'

' "Decorous",' she repeated, savouring the word. 'How long has it been since I've heard that?' she asked with a small smile.

'Probably too long,' Brunetti said. 'It's a nice thing to say about a person.'

'Yes it is, isn't it?' Signorina Elettra agreed and then said nothing for a long time. 'I suppose it could be said about my friend at the Tribunale.'

'The clerk?'

'Yes.' Brunetti waited, but all she said was, 'I'll ask him about Fontana.'

'See if he knows anything about a Judge Coltellini, if you can,' Brunetti requested. He had hesitated before, but if Fontana was a dead end, perhaps she had best take a look at the other name that had appeared on the papers.

'Luisa?'

'Yes. Do you know her?'

'No, but I used to work with her sister. At the bank. She was one of the assistant directors. Nice person.'

'She ever have anything to say about her sister?'

'Not that I can remember,' Signorina Elettra said. 'But I suppose I can ask her. I see her once in a while on the street, and occasionally we have a coffee.'

'Does she know where you work?'

'No. I told her I got a job at the Commune: that's usually enough to kill anyone's interest.'

'From what the person I spoke to said, I gather that Fontana is interested in her sister.'

'And she's not in him?'

'No.'

'Sounds familiar,' she said and turned to her computer.

'That's very much like her,' Paola said that evening,

stretched out on the sofa and listening to him tell her about his conversation with Signorina Elettra and her remarks about dishonesty and deceit: 'that she thinks it's more dishonest to deceive a woman. I thought the days of feminine solidarity were over.'

'It wasn't exactly feminine solidarity, so far as I could tell,' Brunetti replied. 'I think it's simply that she believes dishonesty is in proportion to how much trust you're betraying, not to the lie you actually tell. And, from what she said, men are more indiscreet, more prone to boasting, and in those circumstances she thinks she's got the right to use anything they say.'

'And women?'

'She thinks they need to trust people more before they reveal things.'

'Or perhaps what women reveal is usually weakness, but what men talk about is strength,' Paola suggested. She looked at her bare feet and wiggled her toes.

'What do you mean?'

'Think about the dinners we've been to, or conversations you've had with groups of men alone. There's usually some tale of conquest: a woman, a job, a contract, even a swimming race. So it's more boasting than confession.' When he looked sceptical, she said, 'Tell me you've never listened to a man boast about how many women he's had.'

After a moment's reflection, Brunetti said, 'Of course I have,' sitting up a bit straighter as he said it.

'Women, at least women my age, would not do that in front of women they don't know.'

'And in front of the ones they do know?' asked an astonished Brunetti.

Ignoring him, she said, in a completely different tone,

'But deceit does have its uses: without it, and without betrayal, there'd be no literature.'

'I beg your pardon,' Brunetti replied, not certain how talk of Signorina Elettra's reflections on honesty had led them to the point of literature, however familiar that point was and however varied Paola's wiles in getting them to it.

'Think of it,' she said, stretching an expansive arm towards him. 'Gilgamesh is betrayed, so is Beowulf, so is Otello, someone leads the Persians around behind the Spartans . . .'

'That's history,' Brunetti interrupted.

'As you will,' Paola conceded. 'Then what about Ulysses? What is he if not the grand betrayer? And Billy Budd, and Anna Karenina, and Christ, and Isabel Archer: they're all betrayed. Even Captain Ahab . . .'

'By a *whale*?'

'No, by his megalomania and his desire for revenge. You could say by his own weaknesses.'

'Aren't you stretching things a bit, Paola?' he asked in a reasonable tone. Tired by a long day, his mind swirled off to the cases that weren't cases, where he could proceed only unofficially and where he wasn't even sure there was a crime. He had to consider two cases of what was probably human betrayal, and his wife wanted to talk about a whale.

She sobered instantly and turned to punch at the pillow lying against the arm of the sofa. 'I was trying it out. To see if it might prove an interesting idea for an article.'

'It's wide of the field of Henry James, isn't it?' he asked, not absolutely certain that she had mentioned a James character in her list.

She grew even more sober. 'I've been thinking that of late,' she said.

'Thinking what?'

'That the world of Henry James is becoming very small for me.'

Brunetti got to his feet and looked at his watch: it was after eleven. 'I think I'll go to bed now,' he said, too stunned to think of anything else to say.

13

The Ferragosto holiday seemed to expand each year, as people added days to either side of the official two-week period, in the hope of expanding their vacation as much as avoiding the traffic. The news, both radio and television, was filled with injunctions about safe driving and spoke of the twelve million cars – or fourteen, or fifteen – that were projected to be on the roads that weekend. One of the news reporters said that, if placed bumper to bumper, these cars would stretch in an unbroken line from Reggio Calabria to the Gotthard Pass. Brunetti, having no idea of the average length of an automobile, didn't even bother to check the numbers. Though he had a licence, he was in truth a non-driver and was almost entirely without interest of any sort in automobiles. They were big or small, red or white or some other colour, and far too many young people died in them every year. He had decided to travel by train:

even to discuss renting a car was to run the risk of one of Chiara's ecological denunciations. They would go to Malles, where a car would meet their train and take them to his cousin's house; there was a bus that went up and down to Glorenza twice a day.

Preparing for their holiday, each of the family had begun to pack. Paola created a pile of books on the top of their dresser, whose composition changed each day in conformity with the books she thought she would select for the class in the British Novel she was to teach during the coming term. Brunetti studied the titles every night and thus became party to the ongoing struggle: *Vanity Fair* lost place to *Great Expectations*, a substitution Brunetti attributed to weight; *The Secret Agent* lasted three days but was replaced by *Heart of Darkness*, though the weight differential seemed minimal to Brunetti; a day later, *Barchester Towers* took over from *Middlemarch*, suggesting that the weight rule was back in force. *Pride and Prejudice* appeared the first evening and stayed the course.

Three nights before their expected departure, curiosity got the better of him, and he asked, 'Why is it that all the fat books have disappeared, and *A Suitable Boy*, which is the fattest, remains?'

'Oh, I'm not going to teach that,' Paola said, as if surprised by his question. 'I've wanted to reread it for years. It's my reward book.'

'What are you being rewarded for?' Brunetti asked.

'You can ask that of a person who teaches at Cà Foscari? In the Department of English Literature?' she asked, using the voice she reserved for Expressions of Public Outrage.

Then, in a more moderate tone, she said, 'I've looked at the books you're taking.'

Brunetti had hoped she would, thinking the sobriety of his choices would set a salutary example against the vain frivolity of some of hers.

'Do I detect an unwonted modernity in your choices?' she asked.

'I've decided to read some modern history,' he asserted proudly.

'But why Russian?' she asked, pointing to a book entitled *A People's Tragedy*.

'It interests me, the Revolution,' he said.

'What interests me is the way so many of us bought it all,' she said in a voice that had suddenly grown harsh.

'We in the West, you mean?'

'We. In the West. Our generation. The workers' paradise. Brothers under Socialism. Whatever nonsense we wanted to spout to show our parents that we didn't like their choices in life.' She covered her face with her hands, and Brunetti detected nothing false in the gesture. 'To think I voted Communist. Of my own free will, I voted for them.'

The only consolation Brunetti could think of to offer her was to say, 'History swept them away.'

'But not soon enough,' she said savagely. 'You know me well enough to know I'm not much for shame or guilt, but I will forever feel guilty that I voted for those people, that I refused to listen to common sense or believe what I didn't want to believe.'

'They never had any real power here,' Brunetti said. 'You know that.'

'I'm not talking about *them*, Guido; I'm talking about *me*. That I could have been so stupid and have been so stupid for so long.' She picked up his book and flipped through it, stopped to look at some of the photos, then closed it and set it down. 'My father always hated them. But I wouldn't listen to him. What could he know?'

'You think we'll have to put up with the same thing?' he asked to change the subject. 'From our kids?'

She opened a drawer and pulled out a sweater, the very sight of which caused Brunetti to break out in a sweat. 'Raffi came to his senses quickly enough,' she said. 'I suppose we should be grateful for that. But they're sure to drag home some other ideas sooner or later.'

Brunetti moved over to the window that gave on to the north and felt the faint stirring of a breeze. 'You think the weather could be changing?' he asked.

'Getting hotter, probably,' she said and pulled out another sweater.

The next day Signorina Elettra was meant to have coffee with her admirer at the Tribunale. Brunetti assumed she would want to get the flowers early in the morning, before the heat had a chance to grab the city by the throat. Allowing time for a leisurely coffee, interspersed with interesting conversation about common acquaintances and people at the Tribunale, she would probably get to the Questura by eleven, he estimated. He was prevented from going down to see if she had arrived, however, by a long phone call from a friend who worked in the Palermo Questura, asking him if he knew anything about two new pizzerias and a hotel that had recently opened in Venice.

Brunetti had heard a number of things about them and about their ownership, both apparent and real. What his friend had to tell him concerned the real owners. Of greatest interest to Brunetti was his friend's explanation of the unwonted speed with which permits had been granted for extensive restoration of both pizzerias and the hotel.

The permits for the hotel, strangely enough, had been granted in less than two weeks. Further, permission had been granted for the crews to work round the clock, something virtually unheard of in the city. The pizzerias required less work; these permits took just under a week to be granted.

When his friend in Palermo admitted to having a special interest in the director of the office granting the permits, Brunetti could only sigh, so familiar to him was the name and so useless did he judge any attempt to investigate the methods used in conceding permissions.

With a noise that wanted to be laughter, but failed, Brunetti said, 'Once, when I was working in Naples, we parked a truck down the street from a pizzeria and left it there, filming everyone who went in and out. We even had another camera directly opposite the place, so we could film anyone who sat at the tables, until they closed.'

'How much business did they do?'

'Eight people went in and stayed long enough to eat. We filmed them waiting for their pizzas and eating them. And one man went in and took home six pizzas.'

'Let me guess,' the voice came down the line: 'the total intake for the day showed something more than fourteen pizzas.'

Brunetti could only laugh. 'They took in more than two thousand Euros.'

'What did you do?'

'We gave the film to the Guardia di Finanza.'

'And?'

'And it ended up in court, and the judge ruled that the cameras were an invasion of privacy, and the film could not be used as evidence because the people shown in it had not been warned that they were being filmed.' After a moment, Brunetti added, 'It's the same thing that happened with the baggage handlers at the airport.'

'I read about it.'

Brunetti glanced at his watch and saw that it was almost noon. Suddenly eager to speak to Signorina Elettra before she could leave for lunch, he said, 'I'll let you know if I hear anything,' and brought the conversation to a close.

To disguise, perhaps to himself, how much he wanted to speak to her, Brunetti delayed his arrival by stopping at the squad room to show Gorini's photo to some of the men on duty. Though it was a strong face, none of them could remember ever having seen him in the city. He left the photo with the request that the rest of the squad have a look and went downstairs, where he found Signorina Elettra at her desk, idly rubbing at the palm of her hand. Two bunches of flowers lay on the windowsill, half unwrapped and beginning to wilt.

'What happened?' he asked.

'A disaster. The whole thing was a disaster.'

'Tell me,' he said, pushing the flowers aside and leaning back against the windowsill, arms folded.

With a conscious effort she pressed her palms flat on either side of her keyboard. 'I got the flowers, then went over to the Tribunale and up to his office. He was there, working, so I suggested we go out for a coffee.

'We went down to Caffè del Doge, and he suggested we sit down at a table instead of standing at the bar. I said I didn't have a lot of time, but I let him persuade me to sit down, and we started talking. He told me about his job, and I listened as if I were interested.

'The only way I could think of to get him to talk about Fontana was to speak of one of the other ushers, Rizzotto, because I went to school with his daughter and I've met him in the building a few times. And then I mentioned Fontana, said I'd heard he was an excellent worker. And that started the stories about him, about how dedicated he was and how efficient, and how long he's been there, and how such men are an example to us all, and just when I thought I was going to start screaming or hit him with the flowers, he looked up and said, "Why, there he is."

'So before I could stop him, he went over and brought Fontana back with him. He was wearing a suit and tie. Would you believe it? It's 32 degrees, and he's wearing a suit and tie.' She shook her head at the memory.

To Brunetti it hardly sounded like a disaster.

'So he joined us,' she went on. 'He's a meek little man; he ordered a *macchiato* and a glass of water and said almost nothing, while Umberto kept talking and I tried to be invisible.' Brunetti doubted that.

'And then, as the three of us were sitting there all friendly, who walks in but my friend Giulia, with her sister Luisa.'

'Coltellini?' Brunetti asked, even though he knew he didn't have to.

'Yes.'

'Giulia saw me and came over and said hello, and then her sister came over, and I thought poor Fontana was going to faint. He stood up so quickly, he knocked over his coffee and got it on his trousers. It was terrible: he didn't know whether to shake Giulia's hand or not, he was so happy to see them there, but all Giulia could do was hand him a napkin. He started to wipe at the coffee. It was grotesque. Poor little man. He couldn't hide it. If he'd had a sign, we all could have read it: "I love you, I love you, I love you." '

'And the judge?'

'She said hello, and then she ignored him.'

'It doesn't sound like much of a disaster to me,' Brunetti said.

'That came when Umberto introduced us. When the judge heard my name, she couldn't hide her surprise, and then she looked at Umberto, and at Fontana, and then she shook my hand and tried to smile.'

'What did you do?'

'I pretended I hadn't noticed anything, and I don't think she saw that I did.'

'What happened?'

'She sat down with us. Before that, she looked as if all she wanted to do was run from the place rather than have to be anywhere near Fontana, but she sat down with us and started to talk.'

'About what?'

'Oh, where I worked now that I didn't work at the bank any more.'

'What did you tell her?'

'That I worked at the Commune, and when she asked more questions, I said it was all so boring I couldn't stand to talk about it, and asked her about the blouse she was wearing.'

'Did she say anything else?' Brunetti asked.

'After a while, when she realized she wasn't going to get anything out of me, she asked Fontana what we had been talking about, though she made it all sound cute and friendly: "And what interesting things have you been talking about, Araldo?" ' she said, sprinkling saccharine on her voice.

'Poor man. His face got red when she used his first name, and I thought he was going to have a seizure.'

'But he didn't?'

'No, he didn't. And he didn't answer, either, so Umberto told her we'd been talking about work at the courthouse.' She paused, shaking her head. 'Probably the worst thing he could have said.' She looked at Brunetti. 'You should have seen her face when he said that. It could have been made from ice.'

'How long did she stay after that?' Brunetti asked.

'I don't know. I picked up the flowers and said I had to get back to the office. Umberto said he'd walk me to the *traghetto*: he thinks I work in Cà Farsetti, so I had to take it across the canal and then go into the main entrance because Umberto was on the other side, waving at me.'

'But the judge doesn't think you work there?' Brunetti asked.

'Hardly. It was written all over her face. She's a *judge*, for heaven's sake: of course she'd know who works at the Questura.'

'Perhaps,' Brunetti tried to temporize.

Signorina Elettra pushed herself to her feet and came towards him so quickly that Brunetti stepped aside to avoid her. Ignoring him, she picked up the flowers and ripped the paper from them. She set them on her desk, walked over to her *armadio* and took out two large vases, then went out into the hall. Brunetti remained where he was, considering what she had just told him.

When she returned, he took one of the water-filled vases from her and set it on the windowsill. She put the other one on the small table against the wall, then went over and picked up one of the bunches of flowers. With no ceremony, she pulled the rubber bands from the stems, tossed them on her desk, and stuffed the flowers into the first vase, then repeated the process with the second bunch.

She sat back in her chair, looked at Brunetti, looked at the flowers, and said, 'Poor things. I shouldn't take it out on them.'

'I don't think you have anything to take out on anything,' he said.

'You wouldn't say that if you had seen her reaction,' she insisted.

'What are you going to do?' he asked.

'I'd like to take a look at whatever it is that aroused your curiosity about the judge.'

14

Signorina Elettra came back to his office with him, where he gave her the sheets of paper that had come to him from the Tribunale. He explained what he had made of the delays in certain cases heard by Judge Coltellini and pointed to Fontana's signature at the bottom of the papers.

'Child's play,' she said in reference to the system used by the Ministry of Justice to preserve the integrity of the judicial system. Looking at Fontana's signature, she said, 'You know, I've begun to think there's something strange about the way Fontana behaved with the judge.'

'Unrequited love is always strange to the people who don't feel it,' Brunetti observed, conscious of sounding more sententious than Polonius.

'That's just it,' Signorina Elettra said, looking at him. 'I'm not sure it *is* unrequited love.'

'Then what is it?'

'I don't know,' she answered. She crossed her arms and tapped the corner of the papers idly against her lower lip. 'I've seen unrequited love,' she said, failing to explain from which side. 'At first I thought that's what it was, but the more I think about it, the more it seems like something different. He's too abject, too servile when he speaks to her: even a man as dull as he is would realize that no one likes to be talked to that way.'

'Some people do,' Brunetti said.

'I know, I know. But she doesn't. That much is clear. One thing I didn't tell you – it's really embarrassing to talk about it – was the way he kept offering to get her things: a coffee, a glass of water, a pastry. It was as if he felt indebted to her, but in an odd way.'

'If they're in this together, then she's probably already getting the bigger share of whatever's being paid,' Brunetti said, admitting to both of them the interpretation he had made of the lists he had been sent. 'So she's the one who should be paying for the coffees.'

'No, no,' Signorina Elettra said, shaking away both his interpretation and his attempt at humour. 'It's not as if he thinks he can actually pay her back. It's as if there's some great gaping hole between them and all he can think of doing is to try to fill it up, though it's so big he knows he never can.' She thought for a moment, then added, 'No, that's not it, either. He's *grateful* to her, but grateful the way people are when the Madonna answers a prayer. It's embarrassing to see it.'

'Did your friend Umberto notice this?'

'If he did, he didn't comment. And I was so eager to get away that I didn't ask him. Besides, I dreaded the thought of standing on the *riva*, in the sun, and talking to him for a minute longer. All I wanted to do was get in the gondola and get to the other side.'

Brunetti couldn't resist asking, 'Is that how Umberto treats you – like the Madonna?'

'Oh no,' she said, without a pause. 'For him, it's unrequited love.'

Neither that day nor the next did Signorina Elettra manage to discover anything about the cause of the postponements in the law cases listed on the paper. The computer system at the Courthouse was down, and because the two people who were in charge of it were on vacation, the database would not be available for at least a week. Unfortunately, this exclusion applied equally, she discovered, to both authorized and unauthorized attempts to consult the information it contained.

Hoping for some news of success before he went on vacation, Brunetti called down to her and asked if she had had time to follow up on Fontana's landlord, Marco Puntera. She came close to apologizing for not having been able to do so, explaining that her friend no longer worked at the bank and she had been so busy drawing up Vice-Questore Patta's instructions for the holiday period that she had been too busy to see what she could find about Signor Puntera. She promised to get to it when the Vice-Questore was safely off to the island of Ponza, where he and his family were to be guests of the head of the city council of Venice, who had a summer home there.

'Yet another way to ensure the complete objectivity of the forces of order in any investigation of local politicians,' Brunetti said when he heard the name of Patta's host.

'I'm sure the Vice-Questore is resistant to blandish-ments of any kind,' Signorina Elettra said in response to

Brunetti's suggestion. 'You know how often he speaks of the need to avoid even the possibility of favouritism of any sort.'

'I know well how he speaks of it,' Brunetti said, and then they turned their attention to his absence during vacation and what needed to be done while Brunetti was gone. She wished him a *buona vacanza* and said she'd see him in two weeks.

Taking her good wishes as permission to leave, Brunetti went home and began to pack things other than books.

The next morning, the Brunettis got the 9:50 Eurostar, changed in Verona, and headed north with mounting enthusiasm. In Bolzano, they would change to a local train to Merano, and then the Vinchgau *trenino* to Malles, where the car would be waiting for them. Soon after they left Verona, they were travelling through a universe of grapevines. There was some poem that Brunetti had been forced to read in his third-year English class, something about cannon on the left and cannon on the right; only in this case it was grapevines, kilometre after kilometre of them, all pruned to an identical size; and for all he knew, the grapes as well identical in variety and size.

The time passed as time does in a train: Brunetti, happy to be in open country, looked out the window; Chiara talked to the two young people sharing the compartment with them; while Raffi, seated opposite his mother in one of the centre seats, hid under his headphones, occasionally nodding his head to the rhythm. At one point, as his head took on a particularly metronomic beat, Paola glanced up from her book and managed to confuse the five other people in the compartment by saying, in

English, 'Unheard melodies are indeed sweeter', whereupon she returned her attentions to the observations of Mr James.

Brunetti tuned in and out of the conversation taking place between his daughter and the people sitting in the window seats. He gathered that they were going to spend two weeks with friends in Bolzano, where they would listen to music and rest. Since both of them had remarked on how easy school was and how boring life in general was, Brunetti was tempted to ask them what they were going to rest *from*, but he instead devoted his attention to the grapes. Miniature tractors were patrolling the aisles between the rows of vines, spraying them. As the train began to slow for its approach into Trento, he noticed that the driver of one of the tractors was wearing the same sort of white protective suit that the crime squad wore, save that his entire head was covered with a hood and a mask.

Brunetti tapped Paola's knee to get her attention and pointed out the window. 'Looks like a Martian, doesn't he?' Brunetti asked.

Paola stared out the window for some time, then looked across at Brunetti. 'See why we eat bio fruit?' she asked.

As if the name of an edible item had penetrated his headphones and prompted an instinct never in abeyance, Raffi said in a surprisingly loud voice, 'I'm hungry.' Paola, like the cliché mother of an Italian film of the fifties, believed that food bought on a train was harmful and so had packed an enormous carrying case with sandwiches, fruit, mineral water, a half-bottle of red wine, and more sandwiches.

At a sign from his mother, Raffi got the bag down from the rack above their heads. He opened it and started handing sandwiches to everyone in the compartment, including the two young people who, after the obligatory initial refusal, accepted them gladly. There were prosciutto and tomato, prosciutto and olive, mozzarella and tomato, egg salad, tuna fish and olives, and other variations on these ingredients. Raffi filled six paper cups with water and passed them around.

Brunetti found himself suddenly overwhelmed with joy. At peace, heading north, he was surrounded by all he loved and treasured in the world. They were all healthy; they were all safe. For two weeks he could walk in the mountains, eat Speck and strudel, sleep under an eiderdown while the rest of the world broiled, and read to his heart's content. He looked out the window and saw that the grapevines had been replaced by apple trees.

Conversation among the young people grew general. The young couple were profuse in their thanks to Paola, spoke to her, and to Brunetti, with respect, addressing them as '*Lei*', though they had automatically used '*Tu*' with Chiara and Raffi. A great deal of their conversation had a hermetic quality to Brunetti, who understood almost none of their references and found that some of their adjectives made no sense to him. From context, he inferred that '*refatto*' was meant as positive praise, while nothing could be worse than to be considered '*scrauso*'.

They pulled out of Trento, still on time, and Raffi started to hand out bananas and plums.

Ten minutes later, the train now flanked by marching apple trees, Brunetti's phone rang. He toyed for an instant with letting it ring, but then pulled it out of the side pocket of Paola's bag, where he had stuffed it when they were leaving the house.

'*Pronto*,' he answered.

'Is that you, Guido?' he heard a female voice ask.

'Yes. Who's this?'

'Claudia,' she answered, and it took Brunetti a moment to place voice together with first name and realize it was Commissario Claudia Griffoni, who, as the last commissario in order of seniority, had been assigned to remain on duty during the Ferragosto vacation.

'What is it?' he asked, his imagination spared having to fear the worst by the presence of his family there with him.

'We've got a murder, Guido. It looks as if it might have been a mugging that went wrong.'

'What happened?' He saw Paola's hand on his knee and only then realized that he was looking at the floor to curtain himself off from the other people in the carriage.

There was a sudden gap on the line, and then Griffoni's voice floated back. 'He was just inside the courtyard of his house, so he might have been pushed inside after he opened the door, or someone could have been waiting for him there.'

Brunetti made an interrogative noise, and Griffoni continued. 'It looks as if someone knocked him down and then hit his head against a statue.'

'Who found him?'

'One of the men in the building, when he went downstairs to take his dog out. About seven-thirty this morning.'

'Why wasn't I called?' Brunetti demanded.

'When the call came in, the man on duty checked the roster and saw that you were on vacation. Scarpa was the only one here at the time, so he went over. He's only just called to report it.'

Brunetti glanced up then and saw that the three people

sitting opposite – his wife, his son, and the young girl near the window – were staring at him, eyes owl-open with curiosity. He got to his feet, slid the door open, and went out into the corridor, sliding the door closed behind him.

'Where is he now?'

There was another snap in the line. 'Excuse me?' Griffoni said.

'Where's the dead man now?'

'At the morgue in the hospital.'

'What's happening at the place where he was killed?'

'The crime team went over,' she began, and then her voice faded away for a few seconds. When it returned, she was saying, '. . . situation is complicated. Three families live in the building, and there's only the one door to the *calle*. Scarpa managed to keep them from coming into the courtyard until the team had gone over it, but by ten this morning he had to let them out of the building.'

Brunetti chose to make no comment on how this would contaminate the scene or at least present a legal pretext for any future defence attorney to call the evidence into question. Only on television crime shows was forensic evidence accepted without question.

'Scarpa's still there,' she said. 'He went over with a few others. He took Alvise.'

'Might as well set up a boat stop at the place where it happened,' said a disgusted Brunetti. 'Who's doing the autopsy?'

Again, the line broke up. '. . . asked for Rizzardi,' she said, showing again that her short time at the Questura had not been wasted.

'Can he do it?'

'I hope so. His name wasn't on the roster, but at least

that other idiot has been away on vacation for a week and didn't leave a contact number.'

'No way to speak of the assistant *medico legale* of the city, Commissario,' Brunetti said.

'That arrogant idiot, then, Commissario,' she corrected.

Brunetti let it pass in silent agreement. 'I'll come back.'

'I hoped you would,' she said with audible relief. 'Most people are away, and I didn't want to end up working this with Scarpa.' Then, to details. 'How? Do you want me to call Bolzano and have them send you back in one of their squad cars?'

Brunetti looked at his watch and asked,' Where are you?'

'In my office. Why?'

'Take a look at the train schedule and see when the next train going south from Bolzano leaves.'

'Don't you want a car?' she asked.

'I'd love a car, believe me. But once in a while you can see the autostrada from the train, and nothing's moving in either direction on certain parts of it. The train would be faster.'

She muttered something, and then he heard the phone being set down. He listened to the gaps, which seemed to be related to the closeness of the train to high power lines. But then he heard Griffoni say, 'The EuroCity from Munich to Venice is scheduled to leave one minute after your train gets in.'

'Good,' Brunetti said. 'Call the station in Bolzano and tell them to hold it. We should be there in twelve minutes, so I'll just get from this one to that one and be back in four hours or so.'

'Yes,' she said. 'I'll call you back.'

Brunetti broke the connection, leaned against the

window to the compartment where his family sat, and studied the mountains that soared up above the unbroken fields of apple trees.

After they had passed many fields, his phone rang and Griffoni said, 'That train's ten minutes late, so if yours is on time, you'll make it easily. It'll be on track four.'

'I have to take my family to their train, so call them and tell them to have it wait until I get there.'

'All right,' she said. 'Someone will meet you at this end.'

Brunetti pocketed his phone and turned to open the door to the compartment.

15

Later, as he sat on the train carrying him back to Venice, Brunetti reflected upon the way human nature could still surprise him: the young people had insisted on helping them carry their luggage to the connecting train, a conductor having met them and told Brunetti that the train to Venice would be delayed another ten minutes. When his family was aboard, the two young people disappeared, asking nothing about his mysterious reason for returning immediately to Venice. Brunetti kissed Paola and the children, promised he would come north again as soon as possible, and stood back from their train as it carried them off to Merano, to the mountains, and to the delights of sleeping under eiderdowns in the middle of August.

His own train back to Venice gave the same sensation, but intermittently, for the air conditioning was working only when it pleased, alternating blasts of tropical air with those more accurately described as arctic. The windows in the new trains did not open, so he and the other three people in the first-class compartment to which the conductor had taken him sat as if on some means of transport that alternated stops between Calcutta and Ulan Bator. Brunetti had sent his suitcase, and thus his sweaters, along with the family, so when the train was anywhere near Ulan Bator, he was forced to flee into the corridor, which was at least consistent in temperature, however elevated that temperature might be.

For the moment therefore, he could neither read in peace nor think calmly of the situation in Venice and what it might be necessary to do when he got there. He finally went down to the dining car, where the air conditioning was working perfectly, and sat and read the newspaper while drinking two coffees and a bottle of mineral water.

When the train pulled into Mestre, he called Griffoni's number and was glad to hear that she would meet him at the railway station with a launch.

'Vianello?' he asked, knowing his friend was on vacation but hoping that Griffoni would have thought of phoning him.

'I called him after I spoke to you. He knows someone in the Guardia Costiera, and they've got permission to enter Croatian waters to pick him up and bring him back.'

'Who does he know?' Brunetti asked.

'All he said was that it was someone he went to school with,' she explained.

'Good. Thanks.'

The train started to move out of the station, and Brunetti broke the connection. As they crossed the bridge, his attention was distracted by enormous patches of seaweed clogging the surface of the water on both sides. The higher tide of the early morning had obscured them, but there was no hiding them now. They spent minutes travelling past them, and still they did not end. A few plastic bottles bobbed in the flat green mass which spread out relentlessly on both sides and which appeared to extend beneath the bridge, as well. Boats steered clear of it. No floating water birds went anywhere near it. Like a neglected patch of eczema, it grew.

He saw the police launch moored directly in front of the station and hastened down the steps towards it. So comfortable had he become in the dining car that it took him a moment to recognize the sensation of invasive heat. His shirt was stuck to his back before he reached the boat, and he was annoyed to realize he had packed his new sunglasses and left them in the suitcase that had, by now, arrived at an altitude of 1,450 metres on the Alp above Glorenza.

He nodded to the pilot, Foa, stepped on board, and took Griffoni's hand. Her tan made her hair seem even blonder, and her short skirt showed an expanse of bronzed leg. She looked like anything but a *commissario di polizia* on duty. Foa unmoored the boat and went back into the cabin. He started the engine.

'Vianello?' Brunetti asked.

'He's back already. Waiting for us at the victim's home. It took him less than three hours.'

Brunetti smiled. Even if it ruined Vianello's vacation plans to have to return to Venice, to do so on a Coastguard patrol boat at full throttle across the Adriatic was some compensation. 'I bet he loved it.'

'Who wouldn't?' she asked and he heard the envy in her voice.

The boat turned left into the Canale di Cannaregio, passed at moderate speed under both bridges and out into the *laguna*. Griffoni explained that she had spoken with Dottor Rizzardi, who said he would try to get back from his house in the Dolomites by that evening. If he could not, then it would be the following morning.

Griffoni had not seen the body, which had been taken to the morgue before Scarpa called her to tell her about the crime. Brunetti asked carefully about Scarpa's behaviour and his response to the news that both he and Vianello were returning from vacation to take over the case.

'I didn't tell him,' Griffoni said.

'So he thinks the case is his?' Brunetti asked.

'His and mine, but since I'm only a woman, I obviously don't count.' They had chosen to stay out on the deck in the hope of catching the breeze created by their motion, so the wind carried some of their words away. Brunetti took another look at her. Though she was decidedly a woman, Brunetti would never preface that noun with the adjective 'only'. 'So my arrival will surprise him,' Brunetti said, not without satisfaction.

'I hope it upsets him, too,' she said with the sort of malice that acquaintance, however brief, with Lieutenant Scarpa so often provoked.

The water in this part of the *laguna* was surprisingly choppy, and both of them were forced to grab the railing to keep from being tossed about. Foa nevertheless put the boat to full throttle in the open water, drowning out other sound and the possibility of conversation. Brunetti glanced to the left, his eye hopping from Murano to Burano and to the bell tower of Torcello, barely visible in the muggy air.

They turned right, passed a canal and turned into the next. Brunetti saw the man leading the camel and asked, 'What are we doing in the Misericordia?'

'His home is up ahead, on the left.'

'*Oddio*,' Brunetti exclaimed. 'It's not Fontana, is it?'

'I told you his name when I called,' insisted Griffoni.

Brunetti remembered the clicks and noises on the phone line and said, 'Yes, of course.'

'You know him?' she asked, interested.

'No. But I know about him.'

'Worked at the Tribunale, didn't he?' she asked.

Feeling the boat begin to slow, Brunetti said only 'Yes', before moving forward to take the mooring rope. Foa stopped on the right side of the canal, and Brunetti stepped up to the pavement and tied the rope to a metal ring. He extended a hand to Griffoni and helped her from the boat; Foa said he would find a bar to get out of the sun and told them to call him when they were finished.

She led the way: down to the first bridge, across it and up the *calle* to the first right. Then the third house on the right: a large brown *portone* with a panel of names and bells beside it.

Griffoni had a key and let them in to what turned out to be a large courtyard filled with potted palms and bushes, the far side already shady in the late afternoon. Motion there caught his eye. A young officer, one of the new recruits, jumped to his feet and saluted the two commissari. Brunetti noticed then that scene of crime tape divided the courtyard into two parts, in the farther of which stood the young man. He and Griffoni slipped under the tape and approached. 'Where was he?' Brunetti asked.

'Over there, Commissario,' the young officer said,

pointing back towards the stairway that led up to the door to the building.

Brunetti and Griffoni walked over to the steps; Brunetti's eyes were drawn to a bloodstain on the pavement that looked as if it had been formed around three sides of a rectangle. The chalk-drawn figure of a man emerged from the stain, its feet pointing towards them. From the angle at which Brunetti saw it, the figure looked surprisingly small.

'Where's the statue?' Brunetti asked.

'Bocchese had it taken to the lab,' Griffoni said. 'It was only a nineteenth-century marble copy of a Byzantine lion.' The remark confused Brunetti, but he chose not to ask about it.

He looked back at the *portone* that opened into the *calle* and saw that the bloodstain was about fifteen metres from it, so someone could have been waiting in the courtyard. Or Fontana could have been pushed inside. Or he had gone inside with someone he knew.

'What time did it happen?' Brunetti asked Griffoni.

'No one's sure. We haven't questioned the people in the building yet, but one man told Scarpa he and his wife came home just after midnight, and didn't see anything.' Waving her arm back at the *portone* and sweeping it in a line that ended at the bloodstain, she said, 'There was no way they could not have seen him. So: some time after midnight.'

'Until seven-thirty,' Brunetti said. 'Long time.'

Griffoni nodded in agreement. 'That's one of the reasons I wanted Rizzardi to do the autopsy.'

'What did Scarpa tell you?' asked Brunetti.

'He said the wife of this couple told him Fontana lived with his mother. She's very religious, goes to Mass every day and out to the cemetery once a week to tend her husband's grave. That her son was devoted to her and it's such a pity that he should be cut off in the prime of life. Usual story: once a person is dead, people start falling over themselves saying what a fine person he was and what a loss to the world, and how wonderful his entire family is.'

'Which means, according to you?'

Griffoni smiled and answered, 'What it would mean to anyone who pays attention to what people are really saying when they're talking about how wonderful other people are: that she's a dragon and probably made her son's life a living misery.' They were some distance from the young recruit and spoke in low voices; Brunetti regretted this, for it would delay the young man's exposure to one of the basic truths his profession would eventually reveal to him: never trust anything that is said about a dead person.

Brunetti took another look at the scene of the crime, the tape, the chalked figure. He called over to the young officer, 'Did you come with Lieutenant Scarpa?'

'No, sir. I was on patrol over by San Leonardo and got a call telling me to come here.'

'Who was here when you arrived?'

'There was the Lieutenant, sir. Scarpa. And Officers Alvise and Portoghese. And three technicians from the crime squad. And the photographer.' His voice trailed off, but it was obvious that he had not finished.

'Who else?' Brunetti said in an encouraging tone.

'There were four people who lived in the building, or who acted like they did. One of them had a dog. And then some people standing over by the *portone*.'

'Did you get their names?'

'I thought about it, sir. But I figured, since there was a ranking officer and two other officers who are senior to me, well, I figured they'd already done that. And it didn't seem my place to ask if they had.'

Brunetti took a closer look at the young man. He glanced at his nametag: 'Zucchero,' he read. 'Are you Pierluigi's son?'

'Yes, sir,' he answered.

'I never met your father,' Brunetti said, 'but everyone here speaks of him with respect.'

'Thank you, sir. He was a good man.'

'Ispettore Vianello?' Brunetti asked.

'Upstairs talking to the mother, Commissario. He got here about half an hour ago.'

Brunetti stepped back from the young man and turned in a circle to study the inside of the courtyard. One wall ran along the street; opposite it, on the other side of the scene of crime tape, stood three doors made of metal grillework, all of them closed.

'What are those?' Brunetti asked, pointing to the doors.

'The storerooms for the apartments, sir.' Then Zucchero pointed to a fourth grillework door on one of the side walls, also closed, half hidden behind a line of potted palms. 'There's another one over there, sir.'

'Let's have a look,' Brunetti said.

The three of them walked over to the single door, which stood in the shade cast by two of the palms. Brunetti noticed that a metal chain had been run through the bars of the door and through a metal hasp that had been nailed into the wooden door frame. 'Lieutenant Scarpa had all the padlocks replaced, sir. But I've got the keys.' Moving past Brunetti, Zucchero stuck his hands through the bars and switched on a light which allowed them to see inside.

The room was empty, the floor swept clean, but not recently, for tiny patches of powdered stucco had fallen since the last cleaning and stood out like dusty islands in a cement sea. The walls were entirely bare, save for the occasional patch where the whitewash was flaking off.

Brunetti reached in to switch off the light, and they crossed the courtyard to the first of the other doors. The sun reached halfway up the wall and, falling through the grating at an angle, brightened the first metre of the pavement. Made from large terracotta tiles, the pavement was raised two steps above the surface of the courtyard, reducing the humidity and perhaps protecting against the risk of *acqua alta*. Zucchero opened the lock and pulled open the door. Brunetti lowered his head and stepped inside, found the light and switched it on.

In contrast to the stark emptiness of the other, this storeroom exploded with things: boxes, suitcases, knapsacks, old paint tins, plastic buckets with rags erupting from them, empty jam and pickle jars. At the end, he read the history of childhood: a collapsible wooden baby cot, its plastic bottom sheet draped across it so that only the round metal castors and the bottom of the legs were visible. A hanging mobile of animals and bells had crash-landed on a bookcase. Two cardboard boxes contained a zoo of soft animals, all the worse for wear. Two unopened boxes of Pampers stood beside the mobile, perhaps awaiting the arrival of another child.

Brunetti stepped back and bumped into Griffoni. He apologized, standing back so she could leave, then he switched off the light, and Zucchero saw to closing the door.

Griffoni chose not to go into the third storeroom when Zucchero removed the chain and opened the door. It was identical in size to the other, about three metres in width and extending at least five towards the back wall. Inside, shelves holding boxes ran from floor to ceiling on both sides. The boxes were all the same size and made of plain brown cardboard: these were boxes meant to store things, not boxes brought home from the supermarket and pressed into service. Each bore a neat hand-printed label in the centre of the side that faced out from the shelf. 'Zia Maria's Tea Set', 'Handkerchiefs', 'Winter shoes', 'Woollen scarves', 'Araldo's books'. And so it went, the detritus of life ordered and sealed in boxes and nothing to be discarded if it might some time be used or needed again.

Brunetti turned away from the room and the life it held, switched off the light, and followed Zucchero to the fourth storeroom, Griffoni again close behind them, all of them silent.

When Zucchero let them into the last, Brunetti switched on the light and saw that it was the same size as the previous storeroom and had similar shelving. It too gave evidence of many lives or, at least, that many lives had passed through the hands of the owners. Most of the shelves on the left side held empty bird cages, at least twenty of them. They were wooden and metal, all sizes, all colours. Some of them still held their water bottles, dry now, with dark stains showing the level of water when they had been placed in the storeroom. All of the doors were closed, and none of the little wooden swings moved. They had been wiped clean, but the dusty, acid smell of bird filled the space. There was one stack of boxes, these too the sort one bought to store things in. Labelled in a different hand, they contained 'Lucio's sweaters', 'Lucio's boots', and 'Eugenia's sweaters'.

The other side held wine racks; not shelves, racks that began about thirty centimetres from the ground and ran almost to the ceiling. Brunetti walked over and read the labels; he recognized and approved of some of them, saw that others had detached themselves from the bottles and hung loose. Griffoni asked, 'In this humidity, with that other smell?'

Brunetti put out a finger and rubbed one of the corks, which had herniated the metal foil. A rough white film covered the top of the cork. He pulled out the bottle. 'Nineteen eighty,' he said, and slid the bottle back, both of them wincing at the sound of glass scraping on metal.

At the far end of the room they saw a sofa and at one end a standard lamp that must have fallen victim to redecoration. Over the back of the sofa was draped a hand-knitted afghan in violent reds and greens, and at the other end stood a square table with a greying crocheted doily in the centre.

Without bothering to comment on any of the things, Brunetti said to Griffoni, 'Let's go up and see how much Vianello has got out of her so far.' This would have sounded – to anyone unfamiliar with the Ispettore's uncanny ability to lure even the most recalcitrant witness – slightly menacing; but it was merely what anyone who knew Vianello would expect him to have achieved.

Brunetti nodded to Zucchero, who saluted and moved back into the shadow.

'It's on the second floor,' Griffoni said, leading him up the stairs to the main entrance, which was open. Inside, they paused at the bottom of the oval staircase that led to the upper floors. The steps were marble, broad and low, at the top a skylight: nothing else would explain the light that flooded down, illuminating and heating the area around them.

'Were you up there before?' Brunetti asked, staring at the skylight.

'No, Scarpa went up to talk to her when he found out that Fontana lived with his mother. He didn't call me until after he'd spoken to her.'

Brunetti nodded, and the young officer left them, starting back across the courtyard. Turning to Griffoni, Brunetti asked, 'Why do you think he waited so long?'

'Power,' she answered, then more reflectively, 'So long as he can control or limit what other people know, he knows more than they do and feels as if he has power over them or what they do.' She shrugged, adding, 'It's a common enough technique.'

'I'd say in some places it's standard operating procedure,' Brunetti added and started up the stairs.

The landing of the second floor had only two doors; a policeman stood outside one of them. He saluted when he saw Brunetti and Griffoni and said, 'Ispettore Vianello is still inside.'

Brunetti indicated the other door, but the officer said, 'That side of the building's not been restored, sir. All three apartments are empty.' Then, before Brunetti could ask, he added, 'We checked them, sir.'

Brunetti nodded his thanks and tapped on the door twice, but when he saw it was ajar he pushed it open and went into the apartment. The light evaporated, and all he saw was a dim glow at the end of whát must have been a long corridor. Unconsciously, Griffoni took a step closer to him until her arm was touching his in the near-darkness. They stood still until their eyes adjusted and they could begin to make out the objects lining the corridor. Brunetti saw the outline of a door on his right and opened it, hoping to allow some light to filter into the corridor, but the room was dark, and all he could make out were four thin vertical bars of gold. It took Brunetti a moment to realize they were cracks of light at the edges of the shutters closed over two windows. Here, as well, he saw the dim shadows of objects standing about in the room, but it was impossible to distinguish what they were.

He pulled the door closed and began to pat the wall of the corridor in search of a light switch. When he found one and pressed it, the difference was minimal, for it illuminated only a single overhead light halfway down the corridor. The objects emerged closer to visibility: narrow tables, low trunks, a few standing lamps, a suitcase – all crowded back against the walls.

They heard the murmur of a voice, perhaps more than one, from the end of the corridor, and both of them set off at the same moment. They passed another door on the right and another on the left. Ordinarily the darkness would have provided some relief from the heat, but that was not the case here. If air be stagnant, then stagnant air grew in that hall. It pressed itself against them as they moved, reluctant to let them pass and interested only in adding to their discomfort. The dampness wrapped itself around them and stroked their exposed flesh.

They stopped in front of a door which was ajar, and Brunetti was about to call Vianello's name when he recalled that the woman was a widow, had lived alone with her only son, who had just been killed. 'You call him,' he told Griffoni softly.

'Ispettore Vianello?' Griffoni said into the crack between the door and the jamb.

Her voice was answered by the sound of a chair scraping on the floor, and Vianello appeared at the door and pulled it fully open. Like Brunetti, he was dressed for vacation, in jeans and a short-sleeved shirt. Whatever his clothing lacked in seriousness was more than made up for by the expression on his face and by the voice in which he said, 'Commissario Griffoni. Commissario Brunetti. I'd like to present you to Signora Fontana, the mother of the victim.' The Inspector's voice grew softer with the final word.

He stepped slowly back from the doorway and turned towards two chairs that sat in the middle of the room, both with their backs to what appeared to be a row of windows obscured by maroon velvet curtains.

The apartment had prepared Brunetti to see a woman of some austerity: he had imagined grey hair pulled tight in a small bun at the back of her head, stick-like calves under a long dark skirt. Instead, the woman sitting in the centre of the room was plump and so short that, even with her feet resting on a velvet-covered hassock, her head did not reach the top of the back of the chair. She had short curly hair, the standard dark red chosen by women of her age. She needed no make-up: her cheeks were rosy with good health, the skin as smooth and soft as that of a young woman. Her eyes, when Brunetti got close enough to see them, seemed to be the eyes of a different person entirely or to belong on a different face. Hooded, deep-set, angled down at the corners, they looked at the world, and at Brunetti, with a sharpness that was evident nowhere on her body.

He moved up behind Griffoni, who bent over the woman and said, 'Signora, I would like to extend my condolences at this terrible time.' The woman extended

136

her hand and allowed Griffoni to press hers, but she said nothing.

Brunetti bent down then and said, 'I join my colleague in extending my sympathies, Signora.' The hand she gave him was soft as a baby's, the skin smooth and unblemished by age spots. She exerted no pressure on his hand, merely allowed hers to be held for a few seconds and then removed it from his grasp.

She looked at Vianello and asked in a soft voice, 'Are these the colleagues you were telling me about, Ispettore?'

'Yes, Signora. Commissario Brunetti and I have worked together for years, and Commissario Griffoni, because of her exemplary conduct at another Questura, has been assigned here.' This was not strictly the truth. In fact, it was a lie. Claudia Griffoni, Brunetti had discovered only after she had been at the Questura for almost a year, had been sent there because she had been too active in her investigation of the business activities of one of the politicians of the party currently holding the majority in Parliament. Her questore had warned her, as had two magistrates who were working on the same investigation. Both of them had told her to be less obvious, not to speak to the press, but the press had not been able to resist a story in which the conflicting parts were played by a convicted criminal and a very attractive female police commissario, who just happened to be blonde, and whose father had been seriously wounded in a Mafia attempt on his life two decades before.

A week after a story appeared, stating that the politician was the subject of a police investigation, Griffoni had found herself transferred to Venice, a city not famed for active interference in the doings of either the members of the political class or the Mafia.

Brunetti was pulled back from these reflections by the voice of Signora Fontana, who said to Vianello, 'Ispettore, perhaps you could bring chairs for your colleagues?'

When the four of them were sitting in a rough circle, Brunetti said, 'Signora, I realize this is going to be a terribly hard time for you. Not only have you suffered an unbearable loss, but you will now have to suffer the invasion of the press and public.'

'And police,' she said instantly.

He gave an easy smile and nodded. 'And the police, Signora. But the difference is that we are interested in finding the person who did this: the press has other goals.'

Vianello sat up straighter and turned to Brunetti. 'Signora Fontana has already had an offer from a magazine. To tell her story. And her son's.'

'I see,' Brunetti said, turning to the woman. 'What did you tell them?'

'The Ispettore spoke to them for me,' she said. 'And told them I was not interested, which I am not.' She brought her lips together in an expression of prim disapproval, but her eyes were careful to watch for Brunetti's response.

He nodded in open approval, giving her what he thought she wanted.

'It won't change what they write,' Vianello interrupted to say, 'but of course they won't be able to use family photos.'

'At least not from my side of the family,' Signora Fontana said with more than a touch of asperity.

Brunetti let it pass as though he had not heard and asked, 'Have you any idea who might have wanted to hurt your son, Signora?'

She shook her head furiously, but not a single lock of her permed hair fell out of place. 'No one could want to hurt Araldo. He was such a good boy. He was always a good boy. His father raised him that way, and then when his father died, I tried to do the same.'

Griffoni placed her hand on Signora Fontana's arm and said something Brunetti could not hear, but it had no effect whatsoever on the woman. Indeed, it seemed to spur her on. 'He was hard-working and honest and devoted to his work. And to me.' She put her face in her hands and her shoulders moved convulsively, but for some reason Brunetti was not persuaded of the sincerity of her grief until she took her hands away from her face and he saw the tears. Like Saint Thomas, he was convinced then that she did mourn her son, but still he was left uneasy by the manner in which she showed it, as though the round-faced part of her was being instructed by those guarded eyes to behave in a fashion that would persuade.

When she had stopped crying and her handkerchief was clutched in her left hand, Brunetti said, 'Signora, was it unusual for your son not to return home in the evening?'

She gave him an offended look. Had not her tears washed away the possibility that she would have to answer such questions? 'I never knew when he returned home, Signore,' she said, either having forgotten, or choosing to ignore, Brunetti's rank. 'He was fifty-two years old, please remember. He had his own life, his own friends, and I tried to interfere as little as I could.'

Griffoni muttered something appreciative of suffering motherhood, and Vianello nodded in approbation of Signora Fontana's self-sacrifice.

'I see,' Brunetti said, then asked, 'Did you usually see one another in the morning, before he went to work?'

'Of course,' she insisted. 'I wouldn't let my boy go off in the morning without *caffè latte* and some bread and jam.'

'But this morning, Signora?' Vianello asked.

'The first thing I knew was Signor Marsano, banging on the door and telling me something was wrong. I was still in my nightgown so I couldn't go out, but by the time I was dressed the police were here and they wouldn't let me go down.' She glanced at the circle of sympathetic faces surrounding her and said, 'They wouldn't let a mother go to her only son', and again Brunetti had the feeling that the whole thing was being orchestrated for some purpose he could not understand.

When Signora Fontana seemed a bit calmer, Griffoni asked, 'Did he tell you where he was going last night, Signora?'

The woman looked away from the question and from the person who had asked it and addressed Brunetti. 'I go to bed early, Signore. Araldo was here when I did. We'd had dinner together.'

None of the police officers said anything, so she suggested, 'He must have gone out for a walk. Perhaps he couldn't sleep in this heat.' She glanced at their faces in turn, as if to see which one of them believed her.

'Did you hear him go out?' Griffoni asked.

Signora Fontana looked stricken. 'Why do you ask me all these things? I told you: Araldo had his own life. I don't know what he did. What else do you expect me to tell you?' Her voice had reached a point familiar to Brunetti, perhaps to all three of them, where the person being interviewed begins to see himself as a victim of persecution. It was but a step from there to anger and from anger to a truculent refusal to answer more questions.

Turning to Griffoni, Brunetti said, in a voice into which he pumped the tones of reprimand, 'I think the Signora has answered more than enough of your questions, Commissario. This is a moment of unbearable grief, and I think she should be spared more questions.'

Griffoni, no fool, lowered her head and said something contrite.

Then, quickly, before Signora Fontana could respond, Brunetti addressed her directly, saying, 'If there is anyone from your family you'd like to have here with you, Signora, please tell us and we'll do what we can to contact them for you.'

The old woman shook her head, and again her curls did not move. As if barely able to force out the words, she said, 'No one. No. I think to be alone is what I want.'

Brunetti got quickly to his feet, followed by Vianello and Griffoni. 'If there is any way we can be of help to you, Signora, you have only to call the Questura. And, speaking personally, I join my prayers to yours that *il Signore* will help you find the way to get through this terrible time.'

He led the other two – who had the good sense not to say anything – from the room and out into the corridor.

16

'That was close,' Vianello said as they walked down the stairs. Brunetti was glad the Inspector had chosen to speak: had he done so himself, it might have sounded as if he had meant his reproach to Griffoni.

'Clever of you to look so penitent, Claudia,' Vianello added.

'It's a survival skill I've developed in the job, I think,' she said.

When they stepped into the courtyard, Brunetti's heart lifted to be again in the sunlight, regardless of the residual heat of the late afternoon. 'What did you make of her answers?' he asked Griffoni.

It took her a moment to formulate an answer. 'I think she's suffering terribly. But I also think she knows more about his death than she's letting us know.'

'Or letting herself know,' continued Vianello.

'What do you mean?' Brunetti asked, remembering

that the Inspector had had time alone with the woman before their arrival.

'I don't think there's any doubt that she loved him,' the Inspector said. 'But I'd also say that she knows something she's not telling us and that she feels guilty about whatever it is.'

'But not guilty enough to tell us?' Brunetti asked.

'Quite the opposite,' Vianello answered immediately. 'I have the feeling she knows something about him that would interest us in some way.' He thought about this and continued, 'I let her talk, asked her questions about what sort of boy he'd been, how he did at school, that sort of thing. It's what mothers always want to tell you about their children.'

Brunetti, having done his fair share of it, thought it must be true of all parents, not just mothers, but he said nothing.

'Whenever I got away from that or asked about what he was doing in recent years, whether he was successful at work, she always managed to pull the conversation back into the past and talked about when he was a little boy or a student.'

'She certainly didn't want to talk about last night,' Griffoni said.

Vianello slipped a white envelope from the pocket of his shirt and opened it. He pulled out a small photo, full face, the sort of thing that would be used for a passport or *carta d'identità*, and showed it to them. A man in sober late middle age looked back at the three of them. His hair was thinning, he had a few age spots on his left cheek, and had the sort of unremarkable face that would make a viewer assume immediately that the subject was a civil servant with a long history of working at the same job. His face was expressionless, as though he'd grown tired of waiting for the picture to be taken and had forgotten about his smile.

'What a sad man,' Griffoni said with real compassion. 'To be so sad and then to die like that. God, it's unbearable.' This last she said with real passion.

'We don't know that he was sad,' Brunetti insisted.

She placed the tip of her finger on the bridge of Fontana's nose and said, 'Just look at him. Look at those eyes. And he lived with that woman for fifty-two years.' She made a motion that was halfway between a shrug and a shudder. 'Poor man,' she said.

Brunetti remembered then what Signorina Elettra had said of him: 'Poor little man.' Was he being presented, Brunetti wondered, with an example of feminine intuition, and he too dull to understand?

'She said something we need to check,' Brunetti said.

'What?' Griffoni asked.

'The family. Remember what she said, that she was sure that her side of the family wouldn't give a photo to the press?' Both of them nodded.

'I'd like to find out about her husband's family, who there is, and what they have to say about Araldo and his mother. Should be easy enough to find them,' Brunetti concluded.

'I'll see what I can find,' Vianello said.

'Zucchero,' Brunetti called over to the young man.

'Yes, Commissario?' he said, approaching.

'How much longer will you be here?'

'Until my shift finishes at eight, sir.'

'There's no reason for you to stay,' Brunetti said decisively. 'Instead, I'd like you to see if any of the people who live near here heard anything last night. After midnight. Then, when you get back to the Questura, see if you can find Alvise. Find out if they got the names of the people who were here when they arrived.' The young man nodded. 'But don't let him know that's what you want to know. Do you understand?' This time Zucchero nodded and smiled.

'You know Alvise, then?' Brunetti could not stop himself from asking.

'He was part of my orientation team, Commissario,' the young officer answered neutrally.

'I see,' Brunetti answered in the same tone.

He turned back to Griffoni and Vianello, saying, 'Let's get something to eat.'

They went into the first bar they came to and asked for a plate of *tramezzini*. When Vianello bit into the first one, he glanced at his watch and said, 'Nadia's probably just beginning to shell the shrimps.'

The others were busy eating, so he went on, 'We got them at the beach this morning, when the fishing boats came in. Two kilos. Ten Euros, and some of them were still alive.'

'Just like in the tourist brochures,' Griffoni said and took a long drink of mineral water. 'Is there traditional dancing in local costume?'

Vianello laughed and answered, 'Just about. There's a tourist village about three kilometres up the coast where they have all that.'

'But not where you are?'

'No,' he said with surprising abruptness.

'Where are you staying?' Griffoni asked with real curiosity.

'Oh, a little village to the north of Split.'

'How'd you find it?'

'A friend.' Vianello got up and went over to the bar to get three more glasses of water.

Brunetti took the opportunity to say, keeping his voice low, 'From what he told me, I'd guess it belongs to a relative of someone who . . . gives him information. He married a Croatian woman, and they rent the cottage out to friends.'

When he rejoined them, Vianello said, voice suddenly grown stern, 'Everyone's forgotten about my aunt.'

Brunetti was about to protest that they had a murder to deal with, but he was forced to admit that Vianello was right: they had forgotten about his aunt even before they left for vacation. It could be blamed on short staffing or the difficulty of staking out Gorini's house, or even on the dubious legality of what they were doing, but those were only excuses, and Brunetti knew it.

'What was your cousin going to do while you were on vacation?' he asked Vianello.

'He's taking his mother to Lignano for two weeks,' Vianello answered.

'All right. We've got two weeks, then, to see what we can find out about the way this Stefano Gorini works.'

'Even with this going on?' Vianello asked, sounding almost contrite, waving his hand in the general direction of the *palazzo* from which they had just emerged.

'Yes. But we need a woman.'

'Excuse me,' Griffoni interrupted, setting down the uneaten half of her sandwich.

'To go to him for a consultation,' Brunetti said, 'or whatever it's called.'

'Because we're more gullible?' she asked neutrally.

Brunetti took the risk of saying, 'Don't start, Claudia', hoping she would take it well.

She did, and smiled. 'Sorry. I sometimes forget who I'm with.'

'He'll be less suspicious of a woman.'

'Entrapment?' Vianello suggested, warning them both of the possibility, and the effect such an accusation could have on any case that might eventually be brought against Gorini.

'We need a woman who isn't officially connected with the police, then,' Brunetti said.

'An older woman,' Vianello added.

'Definitely,' Griffoni agreed.

'You got any ideas?' Vianello asked.

Though there were no clouds in the sky, surely they would have parted to allow the rays of Illumination to descend and encircle Brunetti's head as he said, 'My mother-in-law.'

17

'Oh, Guido, how incredibly ridiculous. I think the heat's got to you, really I do.' His mother-in-law, it seemed, was going to present obstacles to her enlistment. She sat opposite him, dressed in a white linen shirt worn over black silk slacks. She had recently had her hair cut boyishly short, and Brunetti could not shake the idea that, seen from the back, she would look like a white-haired adolescent. Her motions were still quick and decisive, definitely the gestures of a younger person. The fact that he often had trouble keeping up with her when they walked Brunetti attributed to her small size: this made it easier for her to pass through crowded streets, and there was no other kind in Venice any more.

He sat, late that same afternoon, his second *spritz* on the low table in front of him, watching the reflection of the setting sun in the windows of the *palazzo* opposite Palazzo Falier. It was the first time he had relaxed all day;

Brunetti put this down to the drinks and to the lofty ceilings that kept the rooms cool no matter what the outside temperature, and to the breeze that played perpetually through the windows. He sat and watched the curtains fluttering in and out, in and out, and thought of how he could convince her to consult Signor Gorini.

'It would help Vianello,' he said, though she had met the Ispettore only once, and then on the street for a total of two minutes.

She glanced at him but did not bother to answer. She leaned forward and sipped at her *spritz*, her first, and set the glass back on the table. Small wrinkles radiated out from her eyes, but the skin was taut over her cheekbones and under her chin. From Paola, Brunetti knew that this was the result of genes and not the surgeon's knife.

'And it might help this old woman,' he said.

'One old woman helping another?' she inquired lightly.

He laughed, knowing that her age was a subject about which she was not sensitive. 'No, not at all. It's more a case of a woman of the upper classes helping one of the worthy poor.'

'And me without my lorgnette and tiara.'

'No, I'm serious, Donatella. No one is going to help this woman. Someone's manipulating her, but she's refused to listen to her family, so they can't help her. Her banker apparently can't talk any sense into her. And if she knew we were investigating this Gorini – which is entirely against the rules, probably even illegal – I'm sure she'd break off relations with Vianello. And that would hurt him terribly, I know.'

'So it becomes the responsibility of the aristocracy to save a member of the lower orders?' she asked, her voice enclosing that last phrase in ironic quotation marks.

'Something like that, I suppose,' Brunetti said and took another sip of his drink.

'Do you have proof that this Gorini person is a charlatan?'

'He has a long record of dishonesty.'

'Ah,' she whispered, 'not unlike our own dear leaders.'

Brunetti let that pass.

'Would you like another drink?' she asked, seeing the level of his glass.

'No. I want to go home and get something to eat, call Paola, and go to bed. I spent hours on trains today.' He chose not to tell her about the murder investigation that was beginning: she could read about that tomorrow.

'Do you think this Signor Gorini is a bad man?' she asked.

He consulted the opposite windows and was relieved to see that the light had faded even more. 'To date, there's been no suggestion that he's violent,' he finally said. 'He's never been accused of that. But, yes, I do think he's a bad man. He sees where there's a weakness, and he goes for that. In the past, he's defrauded the state, but it seems he's realized it's easier to defraud people. The state will defend itself, but it has little time to defend the citizen.' He thought about stopping here but decided not to and added, 'And less interest.'

'And this from an employee of the state,' she said.

Had he been less tired, Brunetti would have been quite happy to banter with her about this, as they had countless times in the past. Paola's sardonic vision of the world had come from her father: he was sure of that. But it was her mother who had passed on the sense of irony with which she tempered what she saw.

Brunetti put his hands on the arms of his chair and was pushing himself upright when she surprised him by saying, 'All right.'

'I beg your pardon?'

'All right. I'll do it. I'll go and talk to this man and see what he's up to. But you have to find a way for me to justify my visit to him: I can't just walk in from the street and say I saw his name on the doorbell and thought perhaps he could find an astrological solution for all my problems, can I?'

'Hardly,' Brunetti agreed, lowering himself back into the chair. 'I'll have Signorina Elettra see if there is a place where he advertises or where interested people can find out more about him.'

'In the computer?' she asked, unable to disguise her astonishment.

'It's the new age, Donatella.'

The first thing he did when he got home was throw open all of the windows and step out on to the terrace where the hot air, he hoped, would follow him. The curtain brushed against his leg as it flowed outside, chasing the escaping air, a sign that his wish was coming true. After about ten minutes, Brunetti went back inside a cooler apartment.

Believing that they would be away for two weeks, Paola had cleared out the refrigerator. He opened it, found some onions in the bottom drawer. Two containers of plain yoghurt. A piece of vacuum-packed *parmigiano*. He opened a cabinet and found a small jar of pesto, a six-pack of canned tomatoes, and a jar of black olives.

He called Paola's *telefonino* number. She answered by saying, 'Fry the onions, then add the tomatoes and olives.

They don't have any pits. Make sure you put the parmigiano in a new plastic bag, one of the zip-lock ones.'

'I miss you desperately, too,' Brunetti said.

'Don't get smart with me, Guido Brunetti, or I'll tell you it's 14 degrees and I'm wearing a sweater in the house.' He started to defend himself but she added, 'And there's a fire in the stove.'

'I know a lot of lawyers who handle divorce work, you know.'

'And we went for a walk this afternoon; three hours, full sun, and the Ortler is still covered with snow.'

'All right, all right. I'll beat Patta into confessing and come up tomorrow.'

'Tell me about the phone call. Who was it that got killed?' she asked, all humour fled from her voice.

'A man who works at the Tribunale. It could have been a mugging that went wrong.'

She had been married to this man for more than twenty years and so she asked, ' "Could have been"? Does that mean that it probably was a mugging or that Patta is going to try to pass it off as one?'

'It could have been. He was killed in the courtyard of his home, and no one found him until this morning. I don't know yet what Patta will do.'

'Do you have any ideas?'

'Only vague ones,' he said. Because Paola had asked about the murder case, Brunetti felt no need to tell her that he had enlisted her mother into helping the police investigate what might be another crime. In order to stay away from that subject, he asked, 'How are the kids?'

'Tired. I've fed them and they're trying to stay awake until ten. I think they still believe it's only little kids who go to bed before that.'

'Oh, to be a little kid,' Brunetti exclaimed.

'All right. Make the sauce and eat. Then go to bed. It will be well after ten by then.'

'Thanks,' he said. 'I hope it stays sunny and cool enough to make you wear a sweater all the time.'

'How is it there?'

'Hot.'

'Go and eat, Guido.'

'I will,' he answered, said goodbye and hung up the phone.

18

The next day, if anything, was hotter, and Brunetti woke shortly after six to damp sheets and a muddled sense of having been awake often in the night. In the absence of the representatives of the Water Police, he permitted himself the luxury of a long shower, first hot and then cold and then hot again. Worse, he allowed himself to shave in the shower, an act of ecological excess which would have earned him the loud condemnation of both his children.

He didn't bother with coffee at home but stopped in the first bar he passed, then went into Ballarin for a cappuccino and a brioche. He had picked up the papers at his *edicola* and laid the second section of *Il Gazzettino* on the round table in the *pasticceria*. Sipping, he studied the headline, 'Courthouse Clerk Found Murdered'. Well, that was fair enough. The article was surprisingly clear: it gave the time of the discovery of the body and the probable cause of death.

But then it slipped into what Brunetti thought of as 'Gazzettino Mode'. The victim's fellow workers spoke of his many virtues, his seriousness, his devotion to the cause of justice, his poor mother, a widow who had now to bear the death of her only son. And then, as ever, there came the sly insinuation – oh so carefully draped in the sober garb of innocent speculation – about what might have caused this terrible crime. Could the victim have been involved in some practice that had brought his death upon him? Had his job at the Tribunale provided him with access to information that had proven dangerous? Nothing was stated, but everything was implied.

Brunetti refolded the paper, paid, and continued through the growing heat to work. When he got there, well before eight, he made a list of things he needed to check: the first was the autopsy, which should have been done the previous day. Then there was the question of the relatives on Fontana's side: perhaps Vianello had managed to find them. He also needed to know the names of the people involved in the various cases where Judge Coltellini had so long delayed her decisions. And how was it that Fontana and his mother were asked to pay Signor Puntera such a derisory rent?

He went to his open window, where the curtain hung limp, dead, and consulted with the façade of the church of San Lorenzo about how best to begin.

Suddenly overcome with impatience, Brunetti called the Ospedale Civile and learned that Dottor Rizzardi would be there all morning. He asked that the doctor be told he was on his way, and left the Questura. By the time he reached Campo SS. Giovanni e Paolo, his jacket and shirt were glued to his back, and the sides of his feet rubbed uncomfortably against the inside of his shoes. To traverse the open *campo* was to question his own sanity at having decided to walk.

He went to Rizzardi's office but was told that the doctor was still in the morgue. The very word dispersed some of the heat; the air that swirled around him when he pushed open the door drove off the rest of it. His shirt and jacket still clung to him, but the sensation was now coolly sinister instead of irritating.

Rizzardi, he was relieved to see, stood at a sink, already washing his hands. The fact that the sinks in the room were so deep and their fronts so low had always filled Brunetti with a vague uneasiness, but he had never wanted to ask about it.

'I thought I'd come over,' Brunetti said. He glanced around: three draped figures lay in a row to Rizzardi's left. 'I wanted to ask you about Fontana.'

'Yes,' Rizzardi said, wiping his hands on a thin green towel. Carefully, he wiped each finger on one hand separately, then transferred the towel to the other hand and repeated the task. 'He was killed by three blows to the head, so if anyone over there is thinking he died in a fall, they can forget about it: he didn't fall three times.' The doctor stopped drying his hands. 'There's a bruise on his left temple suggesting that he was hit there, perhaps even with a fist.'

'Was it the statue?' Brunetti asked.

'That killed him?' Rizzardi asked. When Brunetti nodded, the doctor said, 'Beyond question. There was blood and brain matter on it, and the shape of the wounds perfectly matches the configuration of the head of the statue.' Brunetti shied away from asking where the statue had ended up. Rizzardi folded the towel in half horizontally and laid it over the edge of the sink. 'One reconstruction could be that someone hit him – that would account for the bruise – and he fell against the statue.' Rizzardi bent down and held his hand about forty centimetres above the ground. 'The head of the lion is only about this high, so he would have fallen against it with some force.'

He stood up, adding, 'Then all he'd have to do is lift his head again and hit it against the statue. It would have been easy enough.'

'How long would it have taken him to die?' Brunetti asked.

'From what I saw, any of the blows could have killed him, but it would have taken some time for the blood to fill the brain and block off body function.'

'No chance at all?'

'Of what?'

'If he'd been found sooner?'

Rizzardi turned and leaned back against the sink, crossed his ankles, then folded his arms across his chest. Because Rizzardi was wearing only a light cotton shirt and trousers under his cotton gown, Brunetti, almost painfully conscious of the cold, wondered if he was trying to keep himself warm by standing like that. He watched Rizzardi process his question as if he were reviewing the information that would provide an answer.

'No,' the doctor said. 'Not likely. Not after the second, and third, blows. There are marks – really a faint bruising – on both sides of the chin and neck where he was held.' To illustrate, Rizzardi held his hands up and made as if to crush something between them. 'But either the killer was wearing gloves or he covered his hands with something, I'd say.'

'How do you know?'

'The bruises. If he'd been barehanded, the bruises would have been deeper, cleaner at the edges, but there was a kind of padding effect. If he'd been barehanded, the nails would have broken the skin, no matter how short they were.' He raised his hands, as if to repeat the gesture, but let them fall to his sides.

He pulled off his lab coat and draped it over the sink, aligning it perfectly with the towel. 'There's something else,' Rizzardi said.

His voice caught Brunetti's attention.

'Semen.' As he said this, Rizzardi turned his eyes in the direction of the three draped forms, but since it was also the same direction as the door to the refrigerated room where bodies were kept, Brunetti ignored the gesture.

He had read historic accounts of the spontaneous ejaculation of hanged men; perhaps this was a similar case. Or perhaps he had been with a woman before returning home. Given his mother's character, it would make sense that Fontana, poor thing, would keep such things far from her.

When Brunetti's silence had gone on sufficiently long, Rizzardi said, 'It was in his anus.'

'*Oddio*,' Brunetti exclaimed as the pieces of reality scrambled around in his mind and came out looking like something else entirely.

'Enough to identify the man?'

'If you find the man,' Rizzardi answered.

'Will the sample tell us anything about him?' Brunetti asked.

What does a shrug sound like, and does it sound the same when it is heard above the hum of a refrigerator? Whatever it was, that was what Brunetti thought he heard when Rizzardi raised and dropped his shoulders. 'Blood type, but for anything else, you need a sample from the other man.'

'How long will it take to know the blood type?' Brunetti asked.

'It shouldn't take long,' Rizzardi began. 'But . . .'

'But this is August,' Brunetti finished for him.

'Exactly. So it could take a week.'

'Or more?'

'Perhaps.'

'Can you hurry them up?'

'I'm sure that, even as we speak, every police officer in this country is asking the same question of every *medico legale*, and that doctor is asking it of the laboratory.'

'I suppose that means you can't?' Brunetti asked.

Rizzardi took a few steps away from the sink and stopped at the head of one of the draped figures. A sudden chill radiated out from the centre of Brunetti's still-damp back. 'I once sent DNA samples to the lab,' the doctor said. 'It was for a case in Mestre – and there were no results for two weeks.'

'I see,' Brunetti said. He turned slightly, making the gesture seem an entirely casual one, and took a few steps towards the door to the corridor. He gave a short cough that could have been brought on by the cold, and said, 'Ettore, I want to ask you something and I want you to believe I have a good reason to ask.'

Rizzardi's glance was level. 'What? Or who?'

'Signorina Montini. Elvira.'

Brunetti waited. Absently, Rizzardi reached a hand towards one end of the draped figure, and Brunetti felt his chest tighten, but all the doctor did was straighten out a wrinkle in the cloth. Keeping his eyes on the draped form, Rizzardi said, 'She's the best worker here. She's done me a lot of favours over the years. More than a decade.'

'I admire your loyalty, Ettore, but she might be involved with someone she shouldn't be involved with.'

'Who?'

Brunetti shook his head. 'I'm not sure yet.'

'But you will be?'

'I think so, yes.'

'Will you promise me something?' Rizzardi asked, finally looking at him. In all these years, Rizzardi had never asked him a favour.

'If I can.'

'Will you warn her if there's time?'

Brunetti had no idea what that might come to mean – what trimming of the law, what compromise of the rules. 'If there's time. Yes.'

'All right,' Rizzardi said, his face relaxing, but not by much. 'It's been about a year since her colleagues started to notice that something was wrong, or at least that long that they've spoken to me about it. She's moody, unhappy, or sometimes overly happy, but the mood never lasts more than a few days. In the past, her work was always perfect: she was the model the other people in the lab set their standards by.'

'And now?'

Rizzardi turned away from the draped form and, keeping it between himself and Brunetti, started to walk towards the door. Just short of it, he stopped, and turned back to meet Brunetti's glance. 'But now she comes in late, or doesn't come in at all. And she makes mistakes, mixes up samples, drops things. Nothing she's done has ever been serious enough to cause a patient harm, but people are beginning to suspect that's next. One of the men who works with her told me it's as if she doesn't have the courage to quit and wants to get herself fired.' Rizzardi stopped.

'What's she like?' Brunetti asked.

'She's a good woman. Introverted, lonely, not very attractive. But good. At least that's what I'd say. But who knows anything?'

'Indeed,' Brunetti confirmed. 'Thanks for telling me.' Then, feeling obliged to honour a promise he did not understand, he added, 'I'll do what I can.'

'Good,' Rizzardi said and opened the door. He went out, leaving the door open, and Brunetti was quick to follow him into the greater warmth of the corridor.

Brunetti walked slowly towards the exit, past the bar filled with people wearing pyjamas or street clothing. When he reached the grassy courtyard that had once been the monks' cloister, he went and sat on the low wall on the far side. Like a diver coming up to the surface, Brunetti needed to acclimatize himself to the greater temperature before daring to go out under the sun again. As he sat, his thoughts turned to the dead Fontana, recalibrating everything. He would never know the man's feelings for his mother: for any man, they were never simple. But his attentions to Judge Coltellini now had to be viewed in a different light or from a different angle. This was no case of star-crossed love, nor spurned affections. What was it Signorina Elettra had said? That he seemed grateful to her, the way a supplicant was grateful to the Madonna when his prayer was answered? But if his answered prayer had nothing to do with the magic of romance, then what did it have to do with? Brusca's words floated back to him: if you eliminate sex, sex, sex, you are left with money, money, money.

A grey cat came across the grass and jumped up beside him. He put out a hand, and the cat pressed its head against it. He rubbed it behind the ears, and the cat flopped against him. For a few minutes, he rubbed the cat's ears until it surprised him by falling asleep. Brunetti moved it gently aside, said, 'I told you not to wear your fur', and started back towards the Questura.

Signorina Elettra seemed pleased to see him, but did not smile. 'I'm sorry your vacation was cut short, Commissario,' she said as he came in.

'So am I. My family is draped in sweaters and lighting a fire at night.'

'You went to Alto Adige, didn't you?'

'Yes, but I didn't make it past Bolzano.'

She shook her head at the shame of this, then asked, 'What may I do for you?'

'Did you find the names of the people involved in the cases in those papers?' he asked.

'Not until this morning, I'm afraid,' she said, pointing to some papers on her desk. Brunetti recognized the court documents he had been sent. 'I was going to bring them up later.'

Brunetti glanced at his watch and saw that it was not yet eleven. 'Then good thing I came here.'

She slid the papers towards him. 'Two of the cases involve Signor Puntera,' she said, pointing to the ones he had circled in pencil and red pen.

'Signor Puntera,' Brunetti said. 'How very interesting.' He nodded for her to proceed.

'The first is a claim on the part of the family of a young

162

man who was injured in an accident in one of Signor Puntera's warehouses.'

'Here?'

'Yes. He's still got two warehouses, over near the Ghetto. They're used to store supplies for one of his companies that does building restoration.'

'What happened?'

'This young man – it was only his third day on the job, poor devil – was carrying bags of dry cement out to a boat in the canal behind the warehouse. Another worker was in the boat, stacking them. When the first one didn't come back for some time, the man in the boat went to look for him and found him on the floor, well, found his feet. He'd been buried under a landslide of bags of cement.'

'What happened?'

'Who knows?' she asked rhetorically. 'No one saw. The defence claims he must have yanked one out from the bottom of the pile or that he hadn't stacked them correctly in the first place. There was one of those little tractors in the warehouse, loading pallets of bags of sand, and the plaintiff's lawyer says the driver must have dislodged something from the other side of the pile. The driver denies it and says he was on the other side of the warehouse all morning.'

'What happened to him?'

'He fell on his face and was buried under the bags. Some of them opened, and sand poured around him. He broke a leg and an arm, but the lack of oxygen was much worse.'

'How bad is he?'

'His lawyer says he's like a child.'

'*Maria Vergine,*' Brunetti whispered, feeling the boy's astonishment, his terror, his awful sense of being buried.

'His lawyer,' Brunetti repeated. 'Who brought the case?'

'His parents. He's going to need lifetime care, and they don't want him to be in a state hospital.' Brunetti nodded: no parent would want this for a child. Or for themselves. Or for the man next door.

'What else?'

'His lawyer told me that, at the beginning, Puntera made the family a private offer if they'd withdraw the case. They refused, and so it went to court, but things have gone wrong with the case from the beginning. Things like delays and postponements.'

'I see,' Brunetti said. He looked at the paper and saw that the accident had taken place more than four years before. 'And until it's settled in court, where is he?'

'He's in the hospital in Mestre, but his family takes him home on weekends.'

'What will happen?' Brunetti asked, though there was no reason she should know.

She shrugged. 'Sooner or later, they'll accept his offer. There's no way of knowing when this will be settled – civil cases are backed up for eight years as it is – so eventually they'll give in. People like this can't go on paying for lawyers for years.'

'And the boy?'

'The lawyer says it will be a mercy for them all if he dies, a mercy for him, too.'

Brunetti let some time pass, then asked, 'And the other case?'

'The warehouses again. He doesn't own them: he rents them. And the landlord wants him out and the space back so that he can turn them into apartments.'

'Quickly,' Brunetti begged the surrounding air, 'please,

someone tell me a story I've never heard in Venice before.'

Ignoring him, she went on, 'So the longer the case is delayed, the longer he can continue to use the warehouses.'

'How long has *this* case been going on?'

'Three years. At one time, he had his workers go down and protest about the eviction in front of Cà Farsetti, right in front of the entrance the mayor generally uses.'

'And His Honour? What tactic did he employ with them?'

'Do you mean how did he appease the workers while making it clear that his sympathies were entirely with their employers?'

Brunetti held up his hands in awe, as if the Cumaean Sibyl herself had spoken. 'Never have I heard the man's political philosophy so accurately expressed.'

'This time our dear mayor avoided the situation,' Signorina Elettra explained. 'Someone must have told him there were only five workers outside: hardly worth his trouble.'

'What did he do?'

'He used the side entrance.'

'More proof of his genius,' Brunetti said. 'And the case?'

'It would seem that Puntera has found a larger place in Marghera and will transfer everything there next year.'

'And until then?'

'The case will probably drag its way through the courts,' she said, as though this were the most natural thing in the world.

Out of curiosity, he said, 'There were other cases listed on those papers. Did you find out anything about them?'

'No, Dottore. I haven't had the time,' she said.

'Let them go for now,' Brunetti decided. 'If you speak to your friend at the Tribunale again, would you try to find out if he knows anything about Fontana's private life?'

'From the little I saw of him in the café the other day,' she said in a serious voice, 'I'd be surprised if he had one.'

'Perhaps secret is a better word to use than private,' Brunetti said. She glanced up but said nothing, and so he continued, 'Rizzardi found evidence to suggest he was gay.'

He watched the surprise register, and then he saw her go through the same process of reassessment as she cast her memory back to her brief meeting with Fontana. '"Oh, thou who hast eyes and sees not",' she said, lowering her face into her hands and shaking her head. 'Of course, of course.'

Brunetti remained silent to allow her to run through all the possibilities. When she raised her head, he asked, 'This being the case, what do you make now of his adoration of Judge Coltellini?'

Instead of answering him, she cupped her chin in her palm and pressed her fingers against her lower lip, a habit she had when she wanted to drift off into thought. He left her to it and moved over to her window, but the air was dead there, as well.

'Either she knew something about him and wasn't telling anyone, or she had done him a favour and he wanted to pay her back in some way,' he heard her say from behind him. He said nothing, hoping she would continue.

'It seemed like some exaggerated form of gratitude,' she added.

'Could it have been mixed up with the fact that she was a judge?' Brunetti asked.

'Perhaps. He sounded like a person who had come from a simple background. So it might have been that the friendship – though I'm not sure that's the right word for it – with a judge was a sort of social promotion or proof of his status.' After a pause, she added, 'Something his mother would like.'

'Do people still think this way?' Brunetti asked, turning towards her.

'Many people think of little else, I'd say,' came her quick response.

Brunetti remembered that he still had to ask Vianello if he had had any success in finding relatives on the Fontana side of the dead man's family. Before leaving Signorina Elettra's office, though, he said, 'I'd like you to see if there's any sort of link between Judge Coltellini and Puntera.'

She looked at him with something close to admiration. 'Ah, yes, I should have thought of that. The rent. Of course.'

He turned to leave but recalled that he had to find a way for his mother-in-law to contact Gorini. 'I'd also like you to find out how people go about discovering Signor Gorini's services – whatever they may be – in the first place.'

She made a gracious waving gesture that ended with both hands indicating her computer screen, as if that would explain it all.

Brunetti was uncertain how useful this suggestion would be to his mother-in-law; nevertheless, he thanked her and went back to his office.

19

This computer stuff appeared to be catching: Brunetti found Vianello in front of the screen in the squad room, watching a man lay out cards on a table in front of him. Vianello's chair was pushed back; his arms were folded, his feet propped up on an open drawer. Slightly behind him stood Zucchero, arms similarly folded, no less intent on the screen. Brunetti came in quietly and stood next to Vianello.

The man on the screen continued to stare at the cards on the table in front of him, showing only the top of his head and a pair of thick shoulders and round torso to the camera. He rubbed at his chin like a farmer studying the barometer, unsure of what to make of it. 'You say this man has promised to marry you?' he suddenly asked, his attention still on the cards.

A woman's voice said from somewhere behind or above or below him, 'Yes, he did. Many times.'

'But he's never named a date?' The man's voice could not possibly have been more neutral.

After a long hesitation, the woman answered, 'No.'

The man raised his left hand and, with a delicate motion of a finger, shifted one of the cards a bit to the left. He raised his head and, for the first time, Brunetti saw his face. It was round, almost perfectly so, as though eyes and a nose and a mouth had been painted on a soccer ball, and then hair pasted across the forehead to make it look like a human head. Not only his head but his eyes were round, topped by thick eyebrows that were themselves perfect half-circles: the total effect was one of unvarnished innocence, as though this man had somehow just been born, perhaps just inside the entrance to the television studio, and the only thing he knew in life was how to turn over cards and stare out at his viewers, trying to help them understand what he read there.

Speaking now directly to that woman who was somewhere watching and heeding him, he asked, 'Has he ever spoken specifically about when he intends to marry you?'

This time she took even longer to answer, and when she did, she began with an 'Ummmm' that was prolonged through the space of two normal breaths. Then she said, 'He has to take care of some things first.' Brunetti had heard evasion from people he had arrested, had listened to deliberate attempts to derail a line of questioning, had heard such things from masters. The woman was an amateur, her tactic so obvious as to cause laughter, were it not that she sounded so stricken when she spoke, as though she knew no one would believe her but could still not stop herself from trying to hide the obvious.

'What things?' the man asked, his gaze straight into the

camera and, one felt, straight into the woman's lying mouth and the man's lying heart.

'His separation,' she said, her voice growing slower and softer with each syllable she pronounced.

' "His separation",' the round-faced man repeated, each syllable a slow, heavy footstep towards truth.

'It's not final,' she said. She tried to declare, but she could only implore.

The dialogue had taken place at such a slow pace that the lightning speed with which the man asked, 'Has he even asked for a separation?' startled Brunetti as it brought a gasp from the woman.

The sounds of her breathing filled the studio, filled the ears of the round-faced man, filled the airwaves. 'What do the cards say?' she asked, her voice close to a whimper.

Until now the man had sat so quietly that when he raised his hand to show the camera, and the woman, the cards that remained in his hand, the movement took Brunetti by surprise. 'Do you really want to know what the cards have to tell you, Signora?' he asked, voice far less sympathetic now.

When she finally answered, she said, 'Yes. Yes. I have to know.' After that came the continued sound of her pained breathing.

'All right, Signora, but remember: I asked you if you wanted to know.' His voice held the solemnity of a doctor asking a patient if they wanted to know the results of the laboratory tests.

'Yes, yes,' she repeated, all but pleading.

'Va bene,' he said and brought his hands together. Slowly, his right hand took the top card and slid it from the pack. The camera shifted around him, rose, and now showed, not his round face, but the top of the cards from above and behind him. He moved the card to the right, held it motionless for a few seconds, and then slowly turned it over: The Joker.

'The Deceiver, Signora,' the man said. His voice fell upon her: dead level, no emotion, no judgement. No mercy.

Vianello's feet fell to the floor, making Brunetti jump. 'God, he's a clever devil, isn't he?' the Inspector said, reaching forward to clear the screen.

It was the suddenness of Vianello's action that made Brunetti realize how enchanted – quite literally – he had been by the interchange between the two people. The weak, self-deceiving human heart had been exposed with clinical dispassion by a man who, in the process, displayed himself as an expert at seeing into its mysteries. An unreflecting viewer would surely conclude that this was a man in whose hands lay the answers to those questions they barely dared to ask themselves.

Yet what had he done? Listened to the audible hesitation and uncertainty in the woman's voice, listened to the evasions and justifications: he could have read bottle caps as well as the tarot card to have discovered the Deceiver.

Brunetti said it out loud: 'The Deceiver.'

Vianello answered with a loud guffaw. 'My mother could have told her the same thing, standing behind her in the queue at the supermarket and listening to her tell someone her story.'

Zucchero started to speak, then hesitated. Brunetti waved his hand, and the young man continued. 'But the cards help, Ispettore. They make it seem like the answer is coming from some other, mystical, place, not from common sense.'

Brunetti had had a few moments to think about parallels, and so, abandoning the comparison with bottle caps, he said, 'It's what the augurs did: they'd cut open an animal and read what was in there, but they were always careful to speak in ambiguous language. So after whatever was going to happen had happened, they could make some sort of retrospective interpretation that made it sound as if they had been right.'

'"The Deceiver",' Vianello repeated, no less contemptuously. 'And that poor woman is paying a Euro a minute to listen to him.' He looked at his watch and said, 'We were looking at it for eight minutes, more or less.' He hit a few keys and the screen came back to life. 'Let's see if he's still got her on the hook.'

But the round-faced man had moved on to different game, for this time the voice they heard when he reappeared in front of them was a man's. '. . . think it's a wise thing, but he's my brother-in-law, and my wife wants me to do it.'

'Is there a way you can turn off the sound?' Brunetti asked.

Vianello's head whipped round. 'What?'

'Turn off the sound,' Brunetti repeated.

Vianello leaned forward and turned the sound down, and then off completely, leaving them looking at the round face as it, in turn, divided its attention between the cards and the camera. A few minutes passed in silence until Brunetti said, 'I always do this on planes, if there's a film. I don't take the headset; if you don't, you see how pre-planned their gestures and reactions are: the actors in movies never behave the way people at the next table in a restaurant do. Or people walking down the street. It's never natural.'

The three men continued to watch the screen. Brunetti's observation might just as easily have been prophecy, for the gestures of the round-faced man now seemed prepared and studied. The attention he paid to the cards as he turned them over never wavered; the concentration with which he stared at the camera when he was, presumably, listening to his caller never wavered: his stare was so intense that he might as well have been observing a public execution.

As they watched, he moved his hands together and slid off another card, and the cameras moved up and behind him as they had the last time. With slowness meant to tantalize, he turned the card over and laid it beside two others. Its face was meaningless to the three men watching his performance, but Brunetti had seen enough by now to risk saying, 'When the cameras show his face, he'll look like Oedipus recognizing his mother.'

And so it proved to be. The camera cut to the man's face, where astonishment was painted with the equivalent of acrylic colours. Vianello's hand moved towards the mouse, but Brunetti put a restraining hand on his shoulder and said, 'No, give him another minute.'

They did exactly this, during which time the round face went from shock to distress. He said a few things, shook his head minimally, then closed his eyes for a long time. 'He's washing his hands of the man's decision,' Zucchero observed.

Vianello could resist no longer and raised the level of sound. '. . . nothing I can do to help. I can only show you what the cards say. What you choose to do as a result is your choice, and I can only advise you to give it enough thought.' He bowed his head like a priest about to sprinkle holy water on a coffin. Silence, and then the sound of a phone being replaced on the receiver.

'Very good, that last touch,' Vianello said with admiration he did nothing to hide. The screen changed and displayed a list of phone numbers while a woman's voice explained that professional counsellors were prepared to answer your call twenty-four hours a day. There were experts with decades of experience in reading the cards, in reading horoscopes, and in the interpretation of dreams. The screen displayed, in a red field at the bottom of the screen, the prices of the various calls.

'Isn't there any way to stop them?' asked Zucchero, and Brunetti took heart from how scandalized the young man sounded.

'The Guardia di Finanza keeps an eye on them. But so long as they don't break any laws, there's nothing that can be done about them,' Brunetti explained.

'Vanna Marchi?' the young officer asked, naming the famous television celebrity who had recently been arrested and convicted.

'She went too far,' Vianello said. Then, with a wave at the screen, he said, 'Far as I can tell, this guy is talking sense.' Before Brunetti could object, the Inspector explained, 'I've watched him a few times, and all he does is tell people what any level-headed person would tell them.'

'For one Euro a minute?' Brunetti asked.

'It's still cheaper than a psychiatrist,' Zucchero observed.

'Ah, psychiatrists,' Vianello said as one would say while knocking down a house of cards.

It occurred to Brunetti to tell Vianello that much the same could be said about the man his aunt appeared to be involved with, but he knew that this would only invite trouble. Instead, he asked Zucchero, 'You speak to the people in the neighbourhood?'

'Yes, sir.'

'And?'

'One man, who lives a few houses down, said he heard something. He thinks it might have been a little after eleven but he's not sure. He was sitting in his courtyard to get away from the heat, and he heard some noise – he said it could have been angry voices – but he said he really didn't pay much attention to it.'

'Coming from where?'

'He didn't know, sir. He said there are bars on the other side of the canal, and he thought the noise might have come from there. Or from someone's television.'

'Was he sure of the time?'

'He said he was, said he'd turned off the television and gone down to the courtyard.'

'What about Alvise? Did he give you that list?'

'Yes, sir,' the young officer said, swinging round and going over to the desk he shared with another officer. He brought back a sheet of paper and handed it to Brunetti. 'It's a list of the people who live there, sir. Alvise told me he thought it would be better if the Lieutenant spoke to the people who lived there, and when anyone in the courtyard said they didn't live there, he didn't bother to ask their names.'

In response to Brunetti's gaze, Zucchero said, 'Alvise didn't close the door to the courtyard when he went in, it seems.' There was no trace of inflection in his voice.

Brunetti allowed himself to let a soft 'Ah' escape from his lips.

'Then I think you and I should go over and talk to the people who live there,' he said to Vianello. When the

Inspector did not answer immediately, Brunetti added, 'Unless you're waiting to call in and get your horoscope read', but he said it with a laugh. Vianello closed down the screen and got to his feet.

20

Brunetti might very easily have called the other tenants in the *palazzo* in which Fontana had lived to say the police needed to talk to them, but he knew surprise gave an interviewer an added advantage. He had no idea what these people would want to reveal to – or hide from – the police, but he preferred that he and Vianello should arrive unannounced.

The heat made it impossible for them to think of walking to the Misericordia, and there was no easy way to get there by vaporetto, so Brunetti had Foa take them in a police launch. He and Vianello stayed on deck: even with the windows open, the cabin of the slow-moving launch was unbearable. Foa had raised the awning above the tiller, but it did little to help against the sun. It was minimally cooler in the open air with the breeze, and perhaps being on the water helped, but it was still so hot that none of them could bear to mention it. The only relief they found was in the occasional patches of cool air through which they passed, a phenomenon Brunetti had never understood: perhaps it seeped out of the *porte d'acque* of the *palazzi* they passed, or perhaps some system of wind and air currents trapped pockets of cooler air at random places in the canals.

When they pulled up near the *palazzo*, Brunetti told Foa to go back to the Questura, remembering Patta's morning swim. He said he'd call when they were finished or, if it took too much time, that he and Vianello would go somewhere for lunch and get back on their own.

The top bell on the panel beside the *portone* read 'Fulgoni'. Brunetti rang it.

'*Chi è?*' a woman's voice inquired.

'*Polizia*, Signora,' Brunetti answered. 'We'd like to talk to you.'

'All right,' she said after only a moment's hesitation and clicked open the entry door.

They expected the cooler air in the courtyard, and so it did not delight them the way the surprise pockets of cool air in the canals had. As they passed the place where Fontana had been killed, Brunetti noticed that the red and white tape remained, though the pavement had been wiped clean. There was still no sign of a statue.

They walked to the top floor. The door was ajar and a tall, broad-shouldered woman in her fifties stood in the doorway. Seeing her hair, Brunetti remembered having seen her on the street: it was dark as a raven's wing, brushed back from her pale face in two aerodynamic waves that created the look of a helmet, no doubt kept in place by some sort of substance known to women and hairdressers. In contrast, her face was so pale it looked as though it had been brushed with rice powder, and she wore no makeup save a light pink lipstick. She wore a dark green blouse with frills hardly suited to a woman her size. The colour, too, was inopportune and clashed with her blue skirt. Brunetti could tell the clothing was expensive and might have looked good on a person with the right colouring, but neither blouse nor skirt was in any way flattering to Signora Fulgoni.

'Signora Fulgoni?' Brunetti asked, extending his hand.

She ignored it and stepped back to wave them both inside. She led them silently down a corridor and into a small sitting room with parquet floors, a small sofa and one easy chair. The bright covers of magazines looked up happily from a low table; one wall was lined with bookcases bearing books that looked as though they had been read. Light streamed into the room through striped linen curtains drawn back from three large windows, a sharp contrast with the obscurity of the Fontanas' apartment, one floor below them. The walls were the palest of pale ivory: on one of them hung what looked like a series of Otto Dix prints; another held more than a dozen paintings that appeared all to be by the same hand: small abstracts that used only three colours – red, yellow, white – and that appeared to have been painted with a palette knife. Brunetti found them exciting and peaceful at the same time but had no idea how the artist had achieved this.

'My husband paints,' she said with careful neutrality, raising her hand to indicate the paintings and then continuing the gesture to show them the sofa. Brunetti was interested by her phrasing – not that her husband was a painter – and waited for the explanation. It came: 'He's a banker and paints when he can.' She spoke with audible pride in a voice that was calm and exact and had a very pleasing, low timbre.

'I see,' Brunetti said, sinking down beside Vianello, who had taken a notebook from the inside pocket of his jacket and was preparing to take notes. After thanking her for having agreed to speak to them, he said, 'We'd like to confirm the time you and your husband came home the other night.'

'Why is it necessary that you ask again?' She sounded honestly confused rather than irritated. 'We've already told those other officers.'

Easily, fluidly, Brunetti lied, smiling as he did so. 'There was a discrepancy of half an hour in what the Lieutenant and one of the officers remembered your saying, Signora. Only for that.'

She thought for a moment before she answered. 'It must have been five or ten minutes after midnight,' she said. 'We heard the midnight bells from La Madonna dell'Orto when we turned off from Strada Nuova, so however long it took to walk from there.'

'And you saw nothing unusual when you got back here?'

'No.'

Mildly, he asked, 'Could you tell me where you'd been, Signora?'

She was surprised by the question, which suggested to Brunetti that Alvise had not bothered to ask. She gave a small smile and said, 'After dinner, we tried to watch television, but it was too hot, and everything we looked at was too stupid, so we decided to go for a walk. Besides,' she said, her voice softening, 'it's the only time, really, that a person can walk in the city without having to dodge the tourists.'

Out of the corner of his eye, Brunetti saw Vianello nod in agreement.

'Indeed,' said Brunetti with a complicit smile. He looked around the apartment, at the high ceilings and linen curtains, suddenly struck by how very attractive it was. 'Could you tell me how long you've lived here, Signora?'

'Five years,' she answered with a smile, not unresponsive to the compliment implied in his glance.

'How did you find such a lovely place?'

The temperature of her voice lowered and she said, 'My husband knew someone who told him about it.'

'I see. Thank you,' Brunetti said, and then asked, 'How long have Signora Fontana and her son lived here?'

She glanced at one of the paintings, one that was distinguished by the thickness of the swath of yellow across its middle, then back at Brunetti, and said, 'I think three or four years.' She did not smile, but her face softened, either because she had decided she liked Brunetti or, just as easily, because he had moved away from the question of how they had found their apartment.

'Did you know either of them well?'

'Oh, no, not more than the way one knows one's neighbours,' she said. 'We'd meet on the stairs or coming into the courtyard.'

'Did you ever visit either one of them in their apartment?'

'Heavens no,' she said, obviously shocked by the very possibility. 'My husband's a bank director.'

Brunetti nodded, quite as though this were the most normal response he had ever heard to such a question.

'Has anyone in the building, perhaps someone in the neighbourhood, ever spoken to you about either of them?'

'Signora Fontana and her son?' she asked, as if they had been speaking of some other people.

'Yes.'

She glanced aside to another painting, this one with two vertical slashes of red running through a field of white, and said, 'No, not that I can remember.' She gave a small motion of her lips that was perhaps meant to serve as a smile or was perhaps the result of looking at the painting.

'I see,' Brunetti said, deciding that to continue to speak to her was to continue to go nowhere. 'Thank you for your time,' he said in a terminal voice.

She stood in a single graceful motion, while both he and a visibly surprised Vianello had to push themselves up from the sofa by using the armrests.

At the door, pleasantries were kept to a minimum; as they started down the steps, they heard the door close behind them. No sooner had it done so, than Vianello said, voice expressing shocked disapproval, ' "Heavens no. My husband's a bank director." '

'A bank director with very good taste in decorating,' added Brunetti.

'Excuse me?' came Vianello's puzzled response.

'No one who wore that blouse could have chosen those curtains,' Brunetti said, adding to Vianello's confusion.

On the first floor, he stopped at the door and rang the bell marked 'Marsano'. After a long delay, a woman's voice from inside asked who it was.

'*Polizia*,' Brunetti answered. He thought he heard footsteps moving away from the door and at last heard what sounded like a child's voice asking, 'Who is it?' From behind the door, a dog started to bark.

'It's the police,' Brunetti said in as kindly a voice as he

could muster. 'That's what I told your mother.'

'That wasn't my mother: it's Zinka.'

'And what's your name?'

'Lucia,' she said.

'Lucia, do you think you can open the door and let us in?'

'My mother says never to let anyone into the apartment,' the girl said.

'Well, that's a very good thing for her to tell you,' Brunetti admitted, 'but it's different with the police. Didn't your mother tell you that?'

It took a long time for the little girl to answer. When she did, she surprised him by asking, 'Is it because of what happened to Signor Araldo?'

'Yes, it is.'

'It's not about Zinka?' There was a note of almost adult concern in her voice.

'No, I don't even know who Zinka is,' Brunetti said, telling the truth.

At last he heard a key turn and the door opened. Standing in front of him was a girl who might have been eight or nine. She wore blue jeans and a white cotton sweater: she was barefoot. She stood a bit back from the door and looked at them with open curiosity. She was pretty in the way of little girls.

'You don't have uniforms,' was the first thing she said.

Both men laughed, which seemed to convince the girl of their good will, if not of their profession.

Brunetti saw a motion at the end of the corridor, and a woman wearing a blue apron stepped out from one of the rooms. She had the potato body of an Eastern European and the round face and wispy pale hair that often went with it. He read it in an instant: she was illegal, working there as a maid or a babysitter, but even fear of the police could not keep her from coming out to make sure the child was safe.

Brunetti took out his wallet and removed his warrant card. He held it out to the woman and said, 'Signora Zinka. I'm Commissario Brunetti, and I'm here to ask questions about Signor Fontana and his mother.' He watched to see how much she understood. She nodded but did not move. 'I am not interested in anything else, Signora. Do you understand?' Her posture seemed to grow less rigid, so he stepped aside, still outside the door, and indicated Vianello, who stood beside him, also careful to remain in the hallway. 'Nor is my assistant, Ispettore Vianello.'

Silently, she took a few hesitant steps in their direction. The child turned to her and said, 'Come on, Zinka. Come and talk to them. They won't hurt us: they're policemen.'

The word stopped the woman's forward motion, and the look that swept her face suggested that life had taught her to draw different conclusions about the behaviour of the police.

'If you don't want us to come in, Signora,' Brunetti began, speaking slowly, 'we can come back later this afternoon, or whenever you tell us Lucia's mother will be home.' She took another step closer to the child, though Brunetti had no idea of whether she was seeking or offering protection.

He looked down at the child. 'What school do you go to, Lucia?'

'Foscarini,' she said.

'Ah, that's nice. My daughter went there, too,' he lied.

'You have a daughter?' the little girl asked, as if this were not something policemen were meant to have. Then, as if this would catch him out, she asked, 'What's her name?'

'Chiara.'

'That's my best friend's name, too,' the girl said, smiling broadly, and stepped back from the door. With surprising formality, she said, 'Please come in.'

'*Permesso*,' they both said as they stepped inside. It was then that Brunetti became aware of the air conditioning, which fell on him with a sudden chill after the heat of the day.

'We can go to my father's office. That's where he always takes visitors if they're men,' she said, turning away from them and opening a door on the right. 'Come on,' she encouraged them. Vianello closed the door to the apartment, and the two men followed the child down the chilly hall. At the entrance to the office, Brunetti said to the woman, 'It would help us if we could talk to you, too, Signora, but only if you're willing. All we want to know about is Signora Fontana and her son.'

The woman took another small step towards them and said, 'Good man.'

'Signor Fontana?'

She nodded.

'You knew him?'

She nodded again.

The child went into the room and said, this time drawing the last word out, 'Come on, silly.' She crossed the room, hesitated beside a large desk, then pulled out the chair behind it and sat in it: her shoulders barely topped the desk, and Brunetti could not stop himself from smiling.

The woman saw his smile, looked across at the child, then back at Brunetti, and he watched her assess the scene and his response. 'I really do have a daughter, Signora,' he said and walked over to take one of the chairs in front of the desk. Vianello took the other one.

The woman came into the room but remained standing, halfway between the desk and the open door, a position that offered her the opportunity to try to snatch the child to safety, should that become necessary.

'Where's your Mummy?' Vianello asked.

'She works. That's why we have Zinka. She stays with me. We were supposed to go to the beach today – we have a *cabina* at the Excelsior – but *Mamma* says it's too hot today, so we stayed home. Zinka was going to let me help make lunch.'

'Good for you,' Vianello said. 'What are you going to make?'

'*Minestra di verdura*. Zinka says if I'm good, I can peel the potatoes.'

Brunetti turned his attention to the woman, who appeared to be following the conversation with no difficulty. 'Signora,' he said with real warmth. 'If I hadn't promised to ask only about Signora Fontana, I'd ask you to teach me how I could convince my daughter that I might *let* her clean her room.' He smiled to show her the joke; her face softened, and then she smiled in return.

The illegality of what he was doing suddenly descended on Brunetti, but heavier was the weight of the seaminess of it. She was just a child, for heaven's sake: how great was his need to know, if he would sink to this?

He turned to the woman. 'It's not right to ask Lucia any more questions, I think. So perhaps we should let you both get back to your *minestra*.' Vianello gave him a surprised glance, but he ignored it and said to the girl, 'I hope it cools down enough for you to go to the beach tomorrow.'

'Thank you, Signore,' she said with learned politeness, then added, 'Maybe it's not so bad if we can't go. Zinka hates the beach.' Then, turning to her, she asked, 'Don't you?'

The woman's smile reappeared, broader now. 'The beach doesn't like me, either, Lucia.'

Brunetti and Vianello stood. 'Could you tell me when I might find the Marsanos at home? We'll come back then.'

She looked at the little girl and said, 'Lucia, go down to kitchen see if I left glasses there, please?'

Happy to obey, the girl jumped down from the chair and left the room.

'Signor Marsano won't tell you things. Signora no, also.'

'Tell me what, Signora?' Brunetti asked.

'Fontana was good man. Fight with Signor Marsano, fight with upstairs people.'

She used the word for battle, so Brunetti asked, 'Word fight or hand fight, Signora?'

'Word fight, only word fight,' she said, as though the other possibility frightened her.

'What happened?'

'They call names: Signor Fontana say Signor Marsano not honest, same with man upstairs. Then Signor Marsano say he is bad man, go with men.'

'But you think he was a good man?' Brunetti asked.

'I *know*,' she said with sudden force. 'He found me lawyer. Good man at Tribunale. He help me with papers, for staying.'

'For staying in Italy?' Brunetti asked.

'They aren't there, Zinka,' the girl shouted from the

end of the corridor, then, as she approached, she asked, in that long-drawn-out voice of the impatient child, 'Can we go back to work now?'

Zinka smiled as the girl appeared at the door and said, 'One minute, then we work again.'

'Could you give me the name of the lawyer, Signora?' Brunetti asked.

'Penzo. Renato Penzo. Friend of Signor Fontana. He is good man, too.'

'And Signora Fontana,' Brunetti asked, sensitive to the child's impatience and the woman's growing uneasiness, 'is she a good woman, too?'

The woman looked at him, then down at the child. 'Our guests go now, Lucia. You open the door for them, no?'

The child, sensing the possibility of getting back to work on the potatoes, all but ran to the front door. She pulled it open and went out on the landing, where she leaned over the railing, looking down into the stairwell. Brunetti saw how nervous it made the woman to see her there and started towards the door.

He stopped just inside it. 'And Signora Fontana?' he asked.

She shook her head, saw that Brunetti accepted her reluctance to talk, and said, 'Not like son.'

Brunetti nodded in return, said goodbye to Lucia, and went down the steps, followed by Vianello.

21

Remembering the heat that awaited them outside on the embankment, Brunetti lingered in the courtyard and asked Vianello, 'You ever hear of this Penzo?'

Vianello nodded. 'I've heard his name a few times. He does a lot of *pro bono* work. Comes from a good family. Public service; all that stuff.'

'With immigrants, the *pro bono*?' Brunetti asked, remembering now what he had heard about the lawyer.

'If he's working with that woman upstairs, then it would seem so. She's certainly not being paid enough to afford a lawyer.' Vianello paused and Brunetti could almost hear him rummaging around in his memory. Finally he said, 'I can't remember anything connecting him with immigrants specifically, only that vague shadow memory that people think well of him.' Vianello waved a hand in the air, suggestive of the mystery of memory. 'You know how it is.'

'Uh-huh,' Brunetti agreed. He looked at his watch and was surprised to discover that it was not yet one-thirty. 'If I call the Tribunale and find out he's there today, do you think you have the energy to make it that far without collapsing?'

Vianello closed his eyes, and Brunetti wondered if he should prepare himself for melodrama, though Vianello had never been a source of that sort of thing. The Inspector opened his eyes and said, 'We could take the *traghetto* from Santa Sofia. It's the shortest way, and it's only on Strada Nuova and in the gondola that we'd be in the sun.'

Brunetti called the central number of the Courthouse, was passed to the secretary, and learned that Avvocato Penzo was to appear with a client in court that day. The case was scheduled for eleven, in *aula* 17 D, but things were going very slowly, so the *udienza* would probably not have begun before one, though there was no sure way of knowing that without going to the courtroom. Brunetti thanked her and broke the connection. 'Court's running late today,' he told Vianello.

Vianello opened the *portone* and took a look outside, turned back to Brunetti and said, 'Sun's in the sky.'

Twenty minutes later, they entered the Tribunale without being asked to show identification of any sort. They made their way up to the second floor, then down the corridor toward the courtrooms. From the windows on their left, they saw through offices and out the windows that gave a view to the *palazzi* on the other side of the Grand Canal.

The air was motionless, as were the people who leaned back against the walls or sat in the corridor. All of the chairs were taken; some people had turned their briefcases into chairs or hassocks and sat on them; one man perched on a pile of string-bound legal files. The doors to the offices were all open to allow air to circulate, and occasionally people emerged from them and made their slow way down the crowded hallway, stepping over feet and legs, moving around slumped bodies as best they could.

At the far end they found *aula* 17 D. Here, as well, the door stood open, and people moved in and out at will. Brunetti stopped a clerk he recognized and asked him where Avvocato Penzo was: his case was being argued now, the clerk said, then added, 'against Manfredi', a lawyer known to Brunetti. They walked inside, and in the same instant both of them removed their jackets. Not to do so was to risk their health.

At the far end of the room, the judge sat on a dais that was itself set on a raised platform. He wore his cap and robe, and Brunetti was amazed that he could endure it. He had once been told that, during the summer, some judges chose to wear nothing but their underwear under the gowns: today he believed it. The windows to the canal were open, and the few people in the room all sat in the chairs nearest to them, except for the lawyers, who stood or sat facing the judge; they too were dressed in their formal black robes. One woman lawyer sat at the end of the row of chairs farthest from the windows with her head fallen against the back of the chair. Even from a distance, Brunetti could see that her hair looked as though she had just stepped from the shower. Her eyes were closed, her mouth open: she could as easily have been unconscious as asleep, overcome by the heat as dead.

Like magnets to a file, he and Vianello moved towards

the windows and found two empty chairs. There was some sort of sound system in the room, and there were microphones in front of the judge and on the lawyers' tables, but there was something wrong with the connection, for the voices that emerged from the two speakers set high on the walls were distorted to incomprehensibility by static. The court stenographer sat just beneath the judge: she was either able to understand through the noise or close enough to the voices to hear them. She typed away at her machine as though she were on some other, cooler, planet.

Brunetti watched, familiar with the scene and the actors in it. He told himself he was on a plane and this was another scene to observe without headphones. He watched the theatrical tossing back of the sleeve of a gown, the wide arc of an arm as the speaker hammered home a conclusive argument, or chased away a fly. The other lawyer splashed a look of astonishment across his face; the first lawyer shot his hands up in the air, as if incapable of finding a better way to express his disbelief. Brunetti let himself wonder if the judges ever tuned out the sound and simply observed the gestures, if they learned to discern the truth or falsity of what was being said by the gestures that accompanied the unheeded words. Further, in a city this small, each of those lawyers had a reputation according to which his honesty could be calibrated, and so perhaps all an experienced judge needed to do was read the name of the accusing and defending lawyers to know where truth lay.

After all, much of what was being said was lies, or at least evasions and interpretations. The business of the law was not the discovery of the truth, anyway, but the imposition of the power of the state upon its citizens.

Brunetti's eyes returned to the woman lawyer, who had not moved, and then the heat overcame them, and they closed. A nudge from his left startled him awake. He looked at Vianello, who turned his eyes in the direction of the judge's table.

Two gowned figures approached the judge, who leaned forward and said a few words which did not come through, in however distorted a fashion, the loud-speakers. As if wanting to cooperate with Brunetti's conceit that this was all a mime, the judge tapped the face of his watch. The two lawyers spoke simultaneously; the judge shook his head. He reached to the left and gathered up some papers, stood, and walked from the courtroom, leaving the lawyers in front of the dais.

They turned to face one another and spoke briefly. One opened a case file and showed the other a paper. The second lawyer took it and read it, both of them undisturbed by the sound of chairs being pushed back as the spectators got to their feet and started to file out of the courtroom. Brunetti and Vianello also stood, the better to let people move past them, then sat again when their row was empty.

The second lawyer moistened his lips, then raised his eyebrows in a gesture of reluctant acceptance. He took the paper and went back to where his client was sitting. He placed the paper on the desk in front of the man and pointed to it. The other man placed a finger on the paper and moved it back and forth along the lines, as if expecting his finger to transmit the text to him. At a certain point, his finger gave up and his hand fell flat on the surface of the sheet covering – accidentally or intentionally – the text that he had just read.

He looked at his lawyer and shook his head. The

lawyer spoke, and the man glanced away. Time passed, the lawyer said something else as he grabbed up the paper and took it back to his colleague. He handed him the now-wrinkled sheet of paper, and the two lawyers turned and left the room, leaving the second lawyer's client sitting alone at the table.

Brunetti and Vianello got to their feet and moved towards the door. 'The loser was Manfredi,' said Brunetti, 'so that means Penzo won.'

'I wonder what was on the paper,' Vianello said.

'Manfredi's as crooked as they come,' Brunetti said in a voice heavy with long experience, 'so it was probably something that proved he or his client has been lying.'

'And Penzo can prove it.'

'One would like to think,' said Brunetti, reluctant to believe in the integrity of a lawyer until he had had direct experience of the person. 'Let's talk to him.' They found the lawyer at the end of the corridor, where he stood looking out of a window, his robe tossed on the windowsill, his arms lifted from his body in what Brunetti was sure was a vain attempt to find relief from the heat. Seeing Penzo from the back, Brunetti was struck by how thin the man was: hips no wider than a boy's, his shirt puffed in damp, empty folds from shoulder to waist.

'Avvocato Penzo?' Brunetti said.

Penzo turned, a look of mild inquiry on his face. Like his body, his face was narrow, an effect created by the hollows under his cheekbones, which in turn made his nose, quite a normal nose, seem disproportionately large. His eyes were the colour of milk chocolate and were encircled by the sort of small wrinkles that come from years of squinting into the sun.

'*Sì?*' he inquired, glancing from Brunetti to Vianello

and back again, recognizing them immediately as policemen. 'What is it?' the lawyer asked politely, and Brunetti liked that he did not make a joke about their being policemen, as many people would.

As if he had not noticed Penzo's expression, Brunetti said, 'I'm Commissario Guido Brunetti, and this is Ispettore Lorenzo Vianello.'

Penzo turned, retrieved his robe from the windowsill, and draped it over his arm. 'How may I help you?' he asked.

'We'd like to talk to you about a client of yours,' Brunetti said.

'Of course. Where shall we do it?' Penzo asked, glancing around the corridor. It was no longer crowded now, during lunchtime, but there were still people walking by now and again.

'We could go to Do Mori and have a drink,' Brunetti suggested. Vianello breathed an audible sigh of relief, and Penzo smiled in agreement.

'Could you give me five minutes to get rid of this,' Penzo said, raising the arm that held the robe, 'and I'll meet you at the entrance?'

It was agreed and Brunetti and Vianello turned away towards the stairs.

As they walked down, Brunetti asked, 'Who do you think he's calling?'

'His wife, probably, to say he'll be late for lunch,' Vianello said, declaring his partisanship for the lawyer.

Neither of them spoke again until they stood outside. The sun had blasted all life from Campo San Giacometto. The florist's and the two stands that sold dried fruit were closed; even the water trickling from the fountain looked beaten down by the heat. Only the stall that huddled under the protection of the long arcade was open.

Brunetti and Vianello stepped into the shadow of the arcade and waited. Penzo arrived quickly, carrying a briefcase.

'What did you show your colleague, Avvocato?' Vianello asked, then excused himself for his curiosity.

Penzo laughed out loud, an infectious sound. 'His client was claiming damages for whiplash he says he experienced in a road accident. My client was driving the other car. My colleague's client claimed he was incapacitated for months and couldn't work and because of that lost the chance of promotion at his job.'

Curious now, Brunetti asked, 'How much was he claiming?'

'Sixteen thousand Euros.'

'How long was he out of work?'

'Four months.'

'What did he do?' Vianello interrupted.

'Excuse me?' Penzo asked.

'What sort of work did he do?'

'A cook.'

'Four thousand a month,' Vianello said appreciatively. 'Not bad.'

The three men had begun walking towards Do Mori, automatically turning right and left and right again. Outside, Penzo halted, as if he wanted to conclude this part of their conversation before they went inside, and said, 'But his union saw that he was paid while he was out. This was damages for pain and suffering.'

'I see,' Brunetti said. Payment every week for pain and suffering. Far better than working. 'What did you show him?'

'A statement from two cooks who worked in a restaurant in Mira who said the man had worked with them for three of the four months he was claiming compensation.'

'How'd you find out?' Vianello asked impulsively, even though he knew this was something lawyers were always unwilling to divulge.

'His wife,' Penzo said with another loud laugh. 'She was separated from him at the time – they're divorced now – and he started being late with the child support. He used the accident as an excuse, but she knew him well enough to be suspicious, and so she had him followed when he went out to Mira. When she found out he was working there, she told me about it, and I went and spoke to the other cooks, got their statements.'

'If I might ask, Avvocato,' Brunetti began, 'how long ago did this happen?'

'Eight years,' Penzo answered in a cool voice, and none of them, each well versed in the workings of the law, found this in any way unusual.

'So he loses sixteen thousand Euros?' Vianello asked.

'He doesn't lose anything, Ispettore,' Penzo corrected him. 'He simply doesn't get the money he doesn't deserve.'

'And still has to pay his lawyer,' Brunetti observed.

'Yes, that's a lovely touch,' Penzo allowed himself to comment. That topic resolved, he waved them through the double doors that stood ajar and waited while Brunetti and Vianello went in ahead of him.

22

Some of the same people Brunetti had seen in the courtroom stood in front of the counter, wineglass in one hand, *tramezzino* in the other. A steady current of relatively cool air flowed from the open doors at both ends of the narrow bar: it was a relief to step inside, and not only because of the abundance of wonderful things on display in front of them. What kept Sergio and Bambola at the bar near the Questura from imitating what was on offer here? The *tramezzini* they made seemed, in contrast to these, pale representatives of the species. Looking at Vianello, Brunetti asked, 'Why couldn't the Questura be closer to here?'

'Because then you'd eat *tramezzini* every day, and never go home for lunch,' Vianello said and ordered a plate of artichoke hearts and bottoms, some fried olives, shrimp, and calamari, explaining, 'It's for all of us.' He also asked for an artichoke and ham *tramezzino* and a shrimp and tomato; Penzo chose bresaola and ruccola, Speck and Gorgonzola, and Speck and mushroom; Brunetti practised moderation and asked for bresaola and artichoke and Speck and mushroom.

They all chose Pinot Grigio, and large glasses of mineral water. They carried the glasses and plates to the small counter behind them, set them out, and handed round the sandwiches. When each had eaten his first *tramezzino*, Vianello raised his glass; the others joined him.

Penzo stuck a toothpick into one of the fried olives, bit off half of it, and asked, 'What client is it you want to ask me about?'

Before Brunetti could answer, a man passing by patted Penzo on the back and said, 'They feeding you or arresting you, Renato?' but it was said, and taken, as a joke, and Penzo returned his attention to finishing his olive. He tossed the toothpick on to the plate and picked up his wine.

'Zinka,' Brunetti said. He was about to explain how it was that he came to be curious about the woman when the flash of pain that shot across Penzo's face stopped him. The lawyer closed his eyes for an instant, then opened them again and took a sip of wine.

He set his glass down, picked up his second sandwich and turned to Brunetti. 'Zinka?' he inquired, voice light. 'Why would you be interested in her?'

Brunetti drank some of his water and reached for his second sandwich, as casually as if he had not noticed Penzo's reaction. 'We're not really interested in her but in something she said.'

'Really? What?' Penzo asked in a voice he had mastered and that sounded entirely calm. He raised the sandwich to his lips but set it back on the plate untasted.

Vianello glanced across at Brunetti and raised his eyebrows as he finished his glass of wine. 'Anyone want another?' he asked.

Brunetti nodded; Penzo said no.

Vianello went over to the bar. Brunetti put down his empty glass and said, 'She mentioned an argument her employer had had with one of his neighbours.'

Penzo looked at his sandwich and, keeping his eyes lowered, asked politely, 'Ah, did she?'

'With Araldo Fontana,' Brunetti said. By now, Penzo should have glanced up or looked at him, but he continued to study his sandwich, as though it, and not Brunetti, were speaking to him. 'And she said that Signor Fontana also had an argument with the man on the top floor.' Brunetti let some time pass and then said, 'Since the ground floor's empty, one could say that Signor Fontana argued with everyone in the building.'

Penzo did not reply. 'Yet Signora Zinka said – and she seems like a very sensible person –' Brunetti added, 'that Signor Fontana was a good man.' Brunetti glanced over to the counter, where Vianello stood, back to them, sipping at a glass of white wine.

If the normal number of clients had been there, Penzo's voice would have been drowned out, so softly did he say, 'He was.'

'I'm glad that's true,' Brunetti replied. 'It makes his death worse. But it makes his life better.'

Penzo raised his head slowly and looked at Brunetti. 'What did you say?' he asked.

'That his goodness must have made his life better,' Brunetti repeated.

'And his death worse?' Penzo asked.

'Yes,' Brunetti said. 'But that's not what counts, is it? It's the life that went before that's important. And what people will remember.'

'All people will remember,' Penzo said in a voice that was no less fierce for being so soft, almost a whisper, 'is that he was gay and was killed by some trick he brought back to his home for sex in the courtyard.'

'I beg your pardon,' Brunetti said, unable to disguise his astonishment. 'Where did you hear something like that?'

'In the Tribunale, in the offices, in the corridors. That's what people are saying. That he was a fag who liked dangerous sex and that he was killed by one of his anonymous tricks.'

'That's absurd,' Brunetti said.

'Of course it's absurd,' Penzo hissed. 'But that doesn't stop people from saying it, and it won't stop them from believing it.' There was rage in his voice but Penzo had returned his attention to his plate so Brunetti could not study his expression.

In other circumstances, hearing his tone, Brunetti would have been compelled to place a comforting hand on the arm of the speaker, but he stopped himself from making the gesture from some vague sense that it would be misunderstood. In a flash, Brunetti realized what that must mean and decided to risk any chance of trust on one word and said, 'You must have loved him very much.'

Penzo raised his head and stared at Brunetti like a man who has been shot. His face was blank, scrubbed of all expression by Brunetti's words. He tried to speak, and Brunetti read the history of years of denial that spurred him to look puzzled and ask whatever could Brunetti mean by saying such a thing: the habit of caution that had trained him to treat Fontana's name as though it were any other name, the man just like any other colleague.

'We met in *liceo*. That was almost forty years ago,' Penzo said and picked up his water. He put his head back and swallowed it all in four long gulps. Then, as if the water had restored his conversation with Brunetti to the most businesslike of events, he asked, 'What did you want to know about him, Commissario?'

Just as if he had not asked Penzo his previous question, Brunetti asked, 'Do you have any idea why Signor Fontana argued with his neighbours?'

Instead of answering, Penzo said, 'Could you get me another glass of water, please?' When Brunetti started to move towards the bar, Penzo added, 'You can bring the Inspector back with you.'

Brunetti did both things. When Penzo had drunk half of the water he set the glass down and said to Brunetti, 'Araldo told me that he thought the people who lived in those apartments – both of them – had got them in return for doing favours for the landlord.'

'Signor Puntera?' Brunetti asked.

'Yes.'

Penzo looked at the ground and said, 'It's very complicated.'

Brunetti lifted his chin in Vianello's direction, and the Inspector said, 'We're not in any hurry, Avvocato. Take all the time you need.'

Penzo, his lips tight, nodded. He looked at Brunetti and said, 'I'm not sure where to begin.'

'With his mother,' Brunetti suggested.

'Yes,' Penzo said with a bitter little shrug, 'with his mother.' He went on. 'She's a widow. If ever a woman had a profession, hers was widowhood. Araldo was only eighteen when his father died, and because he was the only child, he assumed that it was his responsibility to take care of his mother. His father had been a clerk; at first there was some money, but his mother quickly went through that. She spent it to keep up appearances. Araldo was supposed to go to university: we were both going to study law. But when the money was gone, he had to take a job, and his mother thought the safest thing was to become a civil servant, as his father had been.'

'So he became a clerk at the Tribunale?' supplied Brunetti.

'Yes. And worked and rose and was promoted and became – even he knew this – something of a joke for the seriousness with which he took his job. But there was never enough money, and then five years ago his mother got sick, or she thought she was sick. And then they needed more money for doctors and exams and tests and cures.

'It became difficult for him to pay her bills and still pay the rent. I offered to help, but he wouldn't let me. I knew he wouldn't, but I still wanted him to. So they moved, from Cannaregio down to a dark little apartment in Castello. And she got sicker and sicker, had more and more tests.'

'Was there anything wrong with her?' Vianello broke in to ask.

Penzo shrugged, quite an eloquent gesture. 'Something is wrong with her, but the tests found nothing.'

He stopped speaking for so long that Brunetti was finally moved to ask, 'What happened?'

'He went to his bank to try to borrow money to pay the bills. He knew enough people to be able to get to talk to the director, but he told Araldo it would be impossible to lend him any money since there was no guarantee that he could ever pay it back.'

'Was the bank director Signor Fulgoni?' Brunetti asked.

'Who else?' Penzo asked with a bitter laugh.

'I see,' Brunetti said. 'And then?'

'And then, one day, like Venus arising from the seas or descending on a cloud, Judge Coltellini appeared in Araldo's office – I think this was about three years ago – and told him she'd heard that he was looking for a new apartment.'

Penzo glanced at them to check that they had registered the significance of the name, then continued, 'Araldo told her that he was not looking, not at all, and she said how very disappointed she was because a friend of hers had an apartment on the Misericordia that he wanted to rent to what he called "decent people". She said he wasn't interested in the rent, that he simply wanted people in the apartment who were reliable, good people.'

Penzo gave them a look that asked if they had ever heard of such a thing. 'Before he spoke to me, Araldo made the mistake of talking to his mother about it.'

'She wanted to move?' Brunetti asked.

'Their apartment was fifty metres: two rooms, for two people, one of them a sick woman. The boiler was at least forty years old, and Araldo said they were never sure when there would be hot water,' Penzo said.

'Did you ever see it?' Vianello asked.

'I never saw any of their apartments,' Penzo answered in a voice that cut off discussion of that topic.

'The apartment on the Misericordia had a lower rent, and it had been restored two years before: new heating system, and the utilities were included. The way she presented it to them, she made it sound like they would be doing the landlord a favour. Which was exactly the right tack to take with Araldo's mother. She's always considered herself a cut above everyone else.' Penzo's voice took on a bitter edge when he said, 'Just the person to condescend to a landlord.'

'So he took it?' Brunetti asked.

'Once he told her about it,' Penzo said with a resigned shake of his head, 'he had no choice. She would have driven him mad if he hadn't taken it.'

'And when they'd moved?'

'She was happy with it, at least at the beginning.' Penzo looked at the sandwich he had abandoned. 'But she was never able to be happy for long.' He put one finger on the springy white bread and pressed down, then removed his finger. The bread remained compressed. He pushed the plate to the back of the counter and took a sip of water.

Brunetti and Vianello waited.

'After they had been living there for about six months, Judge Coltellini gave a file back to Araldo after a hearing. He took the file back to his office and checked through the documents to see that they were all there. I think he's the only one in the Tribunale who bothers – bothered – to do such a thing. A paper was missing, the deed to a house. So he took the file back to the judge and told her it was missing, and she said she knew nothing about it, that it had not been in the file when she read through it, or at least she had no memory of having seen it.'

'What was his reaction?'

'He believed her, of course. She was a judge, after all, and he had been raised to respect rank and authority.'

'And then?' prompted Vianello.

'A few months later, the judge postponed a hearing because the file on the case was missing,' he said and stopped.

'And where was it?' Brunetti asked.

'On her desk, buried under some others. Araldo found it when he went back in the afternoon to retrieve the case files.'

'Did he speak to her?'

'Yes. And she apologized and said she hadn't seen it there, that it must have been stuck inside one of the others.'

'And this time?' It was Vianello who asked.

'He still thought nothing of it. Or that's what he told me.'

'And then?' Brunetti asked.

'And then he stopped telling me about it.'

'How do you know there was anything to tell?'

'I told you, Commissario. We went to *liceo* together. Forty years. You learn to know what a person is thinking in that time, when something's bothering them.'

'Did you ask about it?' Brunetti asked.

'Yes, a few times.'

'And?'

'And he told me to leave him alone, that it was something at work and he didn't want to talk about it.' Penzo returned his attention to his abandoned sandwich. This time, he used his thumbnail to score an X in the lingering fingerprint, then returned to Brunetti.

'So I left the subject alone, and we tried to go on as if nothing were wrong.'

'But?'

Penzo took the tall glass and swirled the remaining water around a few times, then drank the last of it. 'You have to understand that Araldo was an honest man. A good man, and an honest man.'

'Meaning?' asked Brunetti.

'Meaning that the idea that a judge was lying to him or lying about something would upset him. And then anger him.'

'What would he do about it?' Brunetti asked.

Penzo gave a shrug. 'What could he do? He was in the honeytrap, wasn't he? His mother was as happy as she was capable of being. Would he want to take that away?'

'Was he sure they'd lose the apartment?'

Penzo did not bother to answer this.

'Was the apartment that important to her?'

'Yes,' Penzo answered instantly. 'Because she had the address and could invite her friends – the few she had – to come and visit her there and see how well she was doing, she and her son who was only a clerk. And not a lawyer.'

'And so?' Brunetti asked.

'And so he didn't talk about it. And I didn't ask about it.'

'And that was that?' Brunetti asked.

Penzo's glance was sudden and sober, as if he were deciding whether to be offended or not. 'Yes. That was that,' he said. In this heat, a light coating of perspiration lay upon everyone's face and arms, so Brunetti at first did not notice that tears had begun to run down Penzo's cheeks. He seemed not to notice them himself, certainly made no attempt to wipe them away. As Brunetti watched, they began to drip off his chin, splashing into invisibility on his white shirt.

'I will go to my grave wishing I'd done something. Made him talk. Made him tell me what he was doing.

What she was asking him to do,' Penzo said and wiped at the tears absently. 'I didn't want to cause trouble.'

'Did you see him that day?' Brunetti asked. 'Or speak to him?'

'You mean the day he was killed?'

'Yes.'

'No, I was in Belluno, seeing a client, and I didn't get back until the following morning.'

'Which hotel?' Vianello asked mildly.

Penzo's face froze, and it cost him an effort to turn to the Inspector. 'Hotel Pineta,' he said in a tight voice. He reached down and picked up his briefcase and walked out of the bar so quickly that neither Brunetti nor Vianello, had they had the will, would have had time to stop him.

23

Brunetti went over to the bar and was quickly back with two more glasses of white wine. He handed one to Vianello and drank some of his own.

'Well?' he asked Vianello.

The Inspector picked up the toothpick he had used to eat an artichoke and absently began to break it into small pieces, laying them one after the other on the plate beside Penzo's uneaten sandwich. 'Well,' he finally said, 'it looks like we have to examine his life.'

'Fontana's or Penzo's?'

Vianello glanced up quickly. 'Both, really, but we've already started with Fontana. First we find that he's gay, and then we have a tearful account of his sad life from someone who may well turn out – unless I'm misreading all the signs – to have been his lover. So it might be wise to find out where Penzo was the night Fontana was killed.'

'Does that mean you're not persuaded by his tearful story?' asked Brunetti in a tone more cynical than was his wont.

Breaking off another piece of toothpick, Vianello answered, 'I was, and am, persuaded by it. It's pretty obvious that he loved Fontana.'

'But?'

'People kill the people they love every day,' Vianello said.

'Exactly,' Brunetti affirmed.

'Does that mean we're treating him as a suspect?'

'It means we *have to* treat him as a suspect,' Brunetti said. He looked at the Inspector and asked, 'What do you think?'

'I told you I think Penzo loved him,' Vianello said, then paused a moment and went on in a voice that sounded almost disappointed, 'but I don't think he killed him.'

Brunetti was forced to agree with both propositions, but he finally gave voice to an uneasiness that had been created by their conversation with the lawyer. 'You think that means Penzo was his lover?'

'You heard the way he spoke,' Vianello insisted.

'Loving someone for forty years isn't the same as being his lover,' Brunetti said.

He saw Vianello's look of rigid opposition, and before the Ispettore could speak, Brunetti added, 'It's not the same thing, Lorenzo.' It came to Brunetti that he and Vianello surely loved one another, but this was not anything he could say, surely not to Vianello. Nor, he admitted, would he want Vianello to say it to him.

'You can see them as different, if you want,' Vianello said, sounding as if it were something he would choose not to do. 'If it turns out that he wasn't in Belluno that night, then what do we do?'

Brunetti could do nothing more than shrug off the possibility.

Back in his office, a wilted Brunetti stood by the window in search of any passing breeze and considered new connections and the possibilities they might create. Penzo and Fontana as loving friends: whatever that meant. Or as lovers: he did not exclude that possibility. Fontana and Judge Coltellini as adversaries over the whereabouts of legal documents. Fontana as the other side of two '*battaglie*' of words with his fellow tenants. And then Signor Puntera, wealthy businessman and owner of the *palazzo*, with a finger in this and that and therefore many reasons to want accommodating friends at the Courthouse.

He gave up on any hope of solace from the heat and went down to Signorina Elettra's office. Her door was closed. He knocked and, at a sound, entered. Into Paradise. It was cool, and it was dry, and he felt an automatic shiver, whether of cold or delight he did not know. She sat behind her computer wearing a light blue cardigan that appeared to be – could this be in August? – cashmere.

He stepped inside and quickly shut the door. 'How did he manage it?' he demanded. Then, unable to restrain his surprise, 'Did you help him?'

'Please, Commissario,' she said in an indignant voice. 'You know my feelings about air conditioning.' Indeed, he did. They had had a near falling-out over the subject, he maintaining that it was necessary for some people and in some circumstances – in which he silently included his own home in the months of July and August – while she argued that it was wasteful and thus immoral.

'What happened?'

'Lieutenant Scarpa,' she said with unveiled contempt, 'has a friend who rebuilds air conditioners; he had him bring one over here this morning and install it in the Vice-Questore's office.' Sitting up straighter, she added, 'I told him I had no need of one: enough cold air floods in here every time the door opens.'

At this, the door behind Signorina Elettra's desk slammed back against the wall and, instead of cold air, Patta erupted into the room. 'There you are. I've been calling your office for hours. Get in here.' He did not shout: he did not have to. The force of his anger almost reversed the effect of the air conditioning.

The Vice-Questore turned and started back into his office, but because the door had slammed shut from the force with which he had opened it, he had to open it again.

Brunetti had time to cast a glance at Signorina Elettra, but she raised her hands in an empty gesture and shook her head. Brunetti followed Patta into his office and closed the door.

'Are you out of your mind?' Patta demanded when he was standing behind his desk. He sat but did not wave Brunetti to a chair, which meant that things were bad and Patta was serious.

Brunetti drew closer to the desk, careful to keep his hands at his sides. 'What's wrong, sir?' he asked.

'What's wrong?' Patta repeated, then again, should anyone hiding behind his filing cabinet not have heard him the first time, repeated, 'What's wrong?' Then, sure that everyone had heard, he said, 'What's wrong is that

I've had two phone calls this morning, both of them reporting your all but criminal behaviour. That's what's wrong.'

'May I ask who called you, sir?' Brunetti asked, already fearing the worst.

'I was called by Signora Fulgoni's husband, who said his wife was much disturbed by the tenor of your interrogation.' Patta raised a hand to wave away any attempt Brunetti might make to explain or defend his behaviour. 'Worse, he told me that you dared to go downstairs and question a child.' The thought of the consequences of this pulled Patta up from his chair; he leaned over his desk and said, voice booming against the low hum of the air conditioner, 'A child, Brunetti. Do you know how much trouble this could cause me?'

'Who was the second call from, sir?' Brunetti asked.

'That's what I was about to tell you. From the Director of Social Services, saying she'd had a complaint about police harassment of a child and asking me what was going on.' Brunetti stifled the desire to ask who had filed the complaint, knowing that Patta would not tell him.

Patta lowered himself into his chair and said, voice calmer, 'Luckily, her husband is in the Lions Club with me, so I know them fairly well. I assured her that it was a complete misunderstanding, and she appeared to believe me. At least there will be no formal investigation.' His relief was palpable. 'That's one less thing to worry about.'

Brunetti stood still, deciding that the best tactic was to let the waves of Patta's anger break against him until the tide turned, and then to offer an explanation.

'Fulgoni is a bank director,' Patta said. 'Do you have any idea how influential a man like that can be? He's also a friend of the Questore's.' Patta paused to let the full enormity of this sink in and then said in a calmer voice, 'But I think I convinced him not to call and complain.'

Patta closed his eyes and took a deep breath, the better to demonstrate to Brunetti just how harshly tried was his forbearance by this most recent example of his inferior's rashness and irresponsibility, yet more evidence of how sorely tried he was by the perils of office.

'Very well,' Patta said tiredly. 'Stop standing there. Sit down and tell me your version of what happened.'

Brunetti did as told, careful to sit up straight with his legs together, hands on his knees: none of this passive-aggressive business of arms crossed over his chest. 'I did speak to Signora Fulgoni, Vice-Questore: according to Lieutenant Scarpa's report, she and her husband established the time before which the murder could not have taken place. I was curious as to whether they might have noticed anything unusual or out of place. I wanted to know about those four storerooms: someone could easily have hidden in there.'

'Fulgoni didn't say anything about that,' Patta said with the suspicion of a man accustomed to being lied to. 'He said you asked personal questions.'

Brunetti plastered a look of astonishment across his face, as if offended at such a suggestion, if only he had the right to be. 'No, sir. As soon as she answered my question about the time she and her husband arrived, I did nothing more than compliment her home and ask her if she was acquainted with the Fontanas. She said she was not, and Vianello and I left.'

'And went downstairs to interrogate that child,' Patta said with a full return to his former anger.

Brunetti raised his hands to ward off unwarranted criticism. 'That's either a misunderstanding or an exaggeration, sir. We went downstairs and rang the bell. A child spoke through the door and I asked to speak to her mother. When the door opened, I saw a woman standing in the back of the apartment' – he said, not finding it necessary to provide a physical description of the woman – 'and assumed it was her mother. So I went in, hoping to speak to her, but as soon as I realized the woman was not the girl's mother, Vianello and I left. Immediately, sir. Vianello can confirm this.'

'I'm sure he would,' Patta said with one of those flashes of sobriety that had for years kept Brunetti from being able to dismiss him as a complete fool.

'How are we going to present this?' Patta asked. 'I've seen the autopsy report,' he added. 'I doubt it will be very long before the press get hold of it.'

'Not from Rizzardi,' Brunetti said so hotly that Patta shot him a warning glance.

'Dottor Rizzardi is not the only person who works in the pathology laboratory, as you might recall, nor the only person to have access to the report,' Patta said. 'Once this is known, how do we play it?'

Brunetti studied the legs of Patta's desk, thinking about Signora Fontana and for how long she had kept herself from knowing certain things and how she had managed to do it. What did mothers dream of for their sons? And from their sons? A happy life? Grandchildren? Reasons to be proud of them? Brunetti knew women who wanted only that their sons stay free of drugs and out of jail; others who wanted them to marry a beautiful woman, make a fortune, and win social status; and some very few who simply wanted them to be happy. What had Signora Fontana permitted herself to want for her son?

'Well?' Patta's voice summoned back Brunetti's wandering thoughts.

'Rizzardi told me that it will be some time before the lab tests are back, sir,' Brunetti said.

'And so?'

'And so I think we should look for whoever might have wanted to kill . . .'

Before Brunetti could name Fontana, Patta cut him short, saying, 'He doesn't sound like the sort of man anyone would want to kill. This could have been a street crime.'

The temptation came to Brunetti to ask who, then, would so savagely have beaten the life out of him, but caution stayed the impulse and instead he said, 'So it would seem, Vice-Questore. But someone did want to kill him, and someone has.' He knew Patta well enough to know that he would now suggest that the police list the crime as a possible mugging, which Patta probably thought would tranquillize the people of the city. Consequently, Brunetti delivered a pre-emptive strike, saying, 'It might be rash to speak of street crime, Vice-Questore. No one wants to come to a city where people get killed in muggings.'

Though Patta was Sicilian, Brunetti knew the Vice-Questore had spent enough time among the politicians and what passed for high society in the city to have absorbed the Venetian faith in tourism. Sacrifice small children, round up the local population and sell them as slaves, slaughter all men of voting age, rape virgins on the altars of the gods: do all this, and more, but do not lay a hand upon a tourist or upon tourism. The sword of Mars was far less potent than their credit cards; their charges conquered all.

'. . . you paying attention to me, Brunetti?'

'Of course, Signore. I was trying to think of a way we could place this in the press.' Brunetti, too, had learned the language of accommodation.

Patta folded his arms across his chest and looked at the surface of his desk, as clear of papers as his mind of uncertainty. 'The results of the autopsy are going to be made public sooner or later, so I think what we have to say is that we are beginning to suspect that his death was linked to his private life.'

'Without any evidence?' Brunetti asked, his thoughts still on Fontana's mother.

'Of course there's evidence. There's the semen of another man.'

'That's not what killed him,' Brunetti shot back rashly.

Patta braced his elbows on the desk and pressed his lips against his folded hands, as if hoping to restrain whatever he wanted to say to Brunetti. The two men sat like that for some time, and then Patta asked, 'Do you want to place this story in the papers, or shall I ask Lieutenant Scarpa to do it?'

In his most moderate, reasonable voice, Brunetti said, 'I think it would be better if the Lieutenant did it, sir.'

'Are you sure you don't want to do it, Brunetti? After all, some of these reporters are your friends.'

'Thank you, sir, but if I ask them to print it, I'd have to tell them I don't believe it. The Lieutenant is far more at ease speaking to the press.' Brunetti smiled and rose from his chair. He went to the door, opened it, and closed it quietly, pulling on it to make sure it was securely closed: he didn't want too much of the cold air of the Vice-Questore's office to escape.

24

Leaving Patta's office, Brunetti took the course of wisdom and did not pause to talk to Signorina Elettra. He went up to his own office and called the farmhouse where Paola and the children were staying. Paola picked up on the seventh ring, answering with her name.

'It's hot and damp and the back canals stink,' he said by way of salutation, then, 'Why aren't you out walking?'

'We were out all day, Guido. I was out on the patio, reading.'

'Farmhouses aren't supposed to have patios,' Brunetti said grumpily.

'Would it help if I said it's the place where they used to slaughter pigs and the pavement slants down to a gutter where the blood was collected? And it still smells faintly of pigs' blood when the sun shines on it directly, making it impossible for me to devote my full critical expertise to the nuanced dialogues of *The Europeans*?'

'Are you lying?'

'Yes.'

'Why?'

'To make you feel better.' Then, the demands of sentimentality dispatched, Paola asked, 'How are things there?'

'Someone important whose wife I questioned complained to Patta, so I had to listen to a quarter-hour of his paranoia this afternoon.'

'What's Patta afraid of?' she asked.

'God knows. Not being invited to the Lions Club Ball, it sounds to me. If they have one. I don't understand him: he acts like he's still living at the court of the Bourbons, and the greatest achievement he could aspire to is to be recognized by a prince. If he ever had lunch with your father, he'd probably expire of joy.'

'My father's not a prince,' she observed.

'Well, counts are in the same line of business.'

'The monarchy was abolished in 1946,' she said with the asperity of a historian.

'You'd never know it from the bowing and scraping I've seen in my day,' Brunetti replied.

'What's going on?' she asked, uninterested in Brunetti's observations regarding the higher orders.

'The man who was killed was described by two reliable witnesses as a good man. He argued with his neighbours, had trouble with a judge, and was probably gay.'

'Rich and suggestive as that information is, I'm not sure it's enough to help me identify the killer, if that's why you called,' she said.

'No, it's not much for anyone to work on, is it?' Brunetti agreed. 'I really called to tell you I miss you and the kids with all my heart and wish I were there.'

'Get this settled and come up. We can always stay another week.'

'And spoil the children?' he asked with false horror.

'And have a vacation,' she corrected him. They exchanged further pleasantries and Brunetti set the phone down feeling refreshed.

He began to run over his conversation with Signora Fulgoni. He had asked her to confirm when she and her husband had returned, and she had given him a time defined by the sounding of the midnight bell: few answers could be more precise. Then he had asked her how long they had been in the building, and her answer had been equally precise. It was when he asked her how they had found out about the apartment that her demeanour had changed.

'Well, let's just find out about that, shall we?' he said out loud.

Vianello, whom Brunetti found in the squad room, assured him that it would be a relatively simple task to find information about the rental contract because he had recently learned how to access – in the use of that euphemism he betrayed Signorina Elettra as his teacher – the files of the Commune. Good as his word, and using the names of Puntera and the Fulgonis, he had the date of the contract within minutes as well as the number of the file at the Uffico di Registri where a copy of it could be found.

'Do we have to go over there to find out how much rent they're paying?' Brunetti asked.

Vianello started to speak, hesitated, gave quite an embarrassed look, and said, 'No, not really.'

'I'm assuming the amount of the rent's not in here,' Brunetti said, tapping the screen with his fingernail.

'No,' Vianello said, then immediately corrected himself and said, 'I mean yes.'

'Which is it, Lorenzo?' Brunetti asked.

'It's in the contract, certainly, but it wouldn't be in the computer files of the Uffico di Registri.'

'Then where would it be?'

'In Fulgoni's tax declarations.'

'They're in there, too?' Brunetti asked with a friendly nod in the direction of the computer, making it thus a metonym for information itself.

'Yes.'

'Well?' Brunetti said, waving an impatient hand at the screen.

'I don't know how to get to them,' Vianello confessed.

'Ah,' Brunetti said and went back to his office. In face of the likelihood that Patta was still in his office, Brunetti called Signorina Elettra and asked if she could check Puntera's tax records and see what rent he was being paid for the three apartments in the *palazzo* on the Misericordia.

'Nothing easier, Commissario,' she said. He replaced the phone, fighting to prevent the casualness of her response from lessening his regard for Vianello.

He stared at the wall for a few moments and then called her back. When she answered, he said, 'While you're having a look at that information, could you see if there's a list of his legal expenses and the names of any lawyers he's paid money to in the last few years? And any fines he might have paid for any of his companies. Or damages in a legal case. In fact, anything that connects him to lawyers or the courts.'

'Of course, Signore,' she said, and Brunetti gave silent thanks that the heavens had blessed him with this modern Mercury who so effortlessly carried messages between him and what he had come to think of over the years as Cyber-Heaven. A man of his age, with the prejudices of a person raised on paper, he was deeply unsettled by the idea that so much personal and private information was electronically available to any person able to find the way to it. Of course, he was perfectly willing to profit from Signorina Elettra's depredations, but that did not stop him from viewing her activities as just that: depredations.

Suddenly Brunetti was overcome by a wave of something approaching exhaustion. There was the heat, the solitude in which he was living, the need to defer to Patta in order to do what he thought right, and then there was the bloodstain on the pavement of the courtyard, the blood of that good man, Fontana.

He left the Questura without speaking to anyone, took the Number One to San Silvestro, where he went into Antico Panificio and ordered a take-out pizza with hot sausage, ruccola, hot pepper, onion and artichokes, then went home and sat on the terrace and ate it while drinking two beers and reading Tacitus, the bleakness of whose vision of politics was the only thing he could tolerate in his current state. Then he went to bed and slept deeply and well.

When he arrived at the Questura the following morning, the officer on duty told Brunetti that Ispettore Vianello wanted to speak to him. In the squad room, Vianello stood talking to Zucchero, but the young officer moved away when he saw Brunetti come in.

'What is it?' Brunetti asked when he reached Vianello's desk.

'I've been calling the Fontanas in the phone book and one of them, Giorgio, said the dead man was his cousin. When I asked if we could go and talk to him, he said he'd rather come here.'

'Did it sound like he had anything to tell us?'

Vianello made an open-handed gesture of uncertainty. 'That's all he said, that he'd come in now and talk to us.'

'What did you tell him?'

'That you'd be here by nine.'

'Good,' Brunetti said. 'Come up with me.' Vianello's phone rang, and at a nod from Brunetti, he answered it with his name. He listened a moment, then said, 'Good. Would you show him the way up to Commissario Brunetti's office, please.'

He hung up and said, 'He's here.'

Quickly, they went upstairs. Brunetti threw open the windows, but that made little difference; the room remained sultry with trapped heat and stale air. A few minutes later, Zucchero knocked on the door jamb and said, 'There's a visitor for you, Commissario: Signor Fontana.' He saluted neatly and stepped back.

Araldo Fontana had been described as a small, undistinguished man, as though he were a minor character in a dull novel. Brunetti had had a chance to see the real Fontana the day before, but cowardice – there is no better word for it – had kept him from asking Rizzardi to show him.

The man who came into Brunetti's office looked like a character who had tried, and failed, to free himself from the pages of the same novel. He was of medium height, medium build, and had hair that was neither light nor dark brown, nor was there much of it. He stopped inside the door, stepped away from it quickly when Zucchero closed it behind him, and asked, 'Commissario Brunetti?'

Brunetti walked over to shake his hand.

'Giorgio Fontana,' the man said. His grip was light and quickly gone. He looked at Vianello, then walked over and extended his hand to him. Vianello took it, saying, 'We spoke before. I'm Vianello, the Commissario's assistant.'

Vianello pointed to the chair beside his, then waited until the other man was seated before taking his own chair. Brunetti returned to his place behind his desk.

'I'm very glad you came to speak to us, Signor Fontana,' Brunetti said. 'We'd begun a search for your cousin's relatives, and you're the first we've managed to contact.' Brunetti spoke as though to suggest the police had already found the names, which was not the case. He gave what he hoped was a smile both grateful and gracious and said, 'You've saved us time by coming to talk to us.'

Fontana moved his lips in something that might have been a smile. 'I'm afraid I'm the only one,' he said. Seeing their glances, he went on, 'My father was Araldo's father's only brother, and I'm his only child. So I'm all the family you have to look for,' he concluded with a very small smile.

'I see,' said Brunetti. 'Thank you for telling us. We're grateful for any help you can give us.'

'What sort of help?' Fontana asked, almost as if he feared they were going to ask him for money.

'Telling us about your cousin, his life, his work, any friends of his. Anything you think it might be important for us to know.'

Fontana gave his nervous smile again, looked back and forth between them, at his shoes, and then, eyes still lowered, asked, 'Will this be in the papers?'

Brunetti and Vianello exchanged a quick glance; Vianello's lips tightened in the half-grimace one gives at the discovery of something that might prove interesting.

'Everything you tell us, Signore,' Brunetti said in his most official voice, the one he used when it served his purposes to assert something other than what he knew to be the truth, 'will be kept in strictest confidence.'

His reassurances caused no visible signs of relaxation in Fontana, and Brunetti began to suspect this was a man who did not know how to relax or, if he did, would not be capable of doing it in the presence of another person.

Fontana cleared his throat but said nothing.

'I've spoken to your aunt, but in this painful time, it seemed unkind to ask her to speak about her son.' Effortlessly, he transformed those things he had neglected to do into reality and said, 'This afternoon, we have appointments with some of his friends.'

'Friends?' Fontana asked, as if uncertain about the meaning of the word.

'The people who worked with him,' Brunetti clarified.

'Oh,' Fontana said, averting his eyes.

'Do you think colleagues would be a more accurate word, Signore?' Vianello interrupted to ask.

'Perhaps,' Fontana finally said.

Brunetti asked, 'Did he talk about the people he worked with?' When Fontana did not answer the question, he said, 'I'm afraid I have no idea how close you were to your cousin, Signor Fontana.'

'Close enough,' was the only response he got.

'Did he talk about work with you, Signore?' Brunetti asked.

'No, not much.'

'Could I ask you,' Brunetti began with an easy smile, 'what you did talk about, then?'

'Oh, things, family things,' was his sparse reply.

'His family or yours?' Vianello asked in a soft voice.

'They're the same family,' Fontana said with some asperity.

Vianello leaned forward and smiled in Fontana's direction. 'Of course, of course. I meant did you talk about your side of the family or his?'

'Both.'

'Did he talk about your aunt, his mother?' Brunetti asked, puzzled that they could have spent so much time talking about so small a family.

'Seldom,' Fontana said. His eyes moved back and forth between them, and he always looked at the person who asked him a question, attentive to him while he answered, as if he had been taught this as a child and it was the only way he knew how to behave.

'Did he ever talk about himself?' Brunetti asked in a voice he worked at keeping low and steady and warm with interest.

Fontana looked at Brunetti for a long time, as if searching for the trap or the trick that was sure to come. 'Sometimes,' he finally answered.

If they kept at it this way, Brunetti realized, they would still be here for the first snow, and Fontana would still be looking back and forth between them. 'Were you close?' he finally asked.

'Close?' he repeated, as if he had already forgotten being asked this question.

'In the way of friendship,' Brunetti explained with no end of patience. 'Could you talk openly to one another?'

At first Fontana stared at him, as if puzzled at this

novel way for two men to interact. But after some thought he said, in a lower voice, 'Yes.'

'Did he talk about his private life with you?' Brunetti asked, imitating the voice of the priest who had heard his first confession, decades ago. He thought he saw Fontana relax minimally and said, 'Signor Fontana, we want to find who did this.' Fontana nodded a few times, and Brunetti repeated, 'Did he talk about his life?'

Fontana looked from Brunetti to Vianello and then he looked at his knees. 'Yes,' he said in a voice that was barely audible.

'Is that why you've come to talk to us, Signor Fontana?' Brunetti asked, wishing he had thought to ask this earlier.

Eyes still lowered, Fontana said, 'Yes.'

Brunetti had no idea which part of Fontana's life, personal or professional, could have caused his death, but no trace of this uncertainty was audible in his voice when he said, 'Good. I think the reason for his death might be there.'

This was enough to encourage Fontana to remove his attention from his knees. He looked at Brunetti, who was struck by the sadness in his eyes. Fontana said, 'So do I.'

'Could you tell us about him, then, Signore?' Brunetti asked.

'He was a good man,' Fontana began, surprising Brunetti by using the same words as Signora Zinka. 'My uncle was a good man, and he raised Araldo that way.' If Brunetti found it strange that Fontana did not mention his cousin's mother, he kept it to himself.

'We were always close when we were kids, maybe less so as we got older, but I guess that's normal.' It was said as a statement, but Brunetti sensed that it was really a question. Fontana took a breath and went on. 'But then I married and had children. And things changed.' Brunetti smiled at this and did not glance in Vianello's direction. 'I had less time for Araldo then.'

'Did you still see him?'

'Oh, of course. He's the godfather of both of my children, and he took it seriously.' Fontana paused and looked away from them, out the window at the roof of the Casa di Cura across the canal. It seemed to Brunetti that the mention of his children had strengthened Fontana; it had certainly strengthened his voice. Brunetti made no attempt to call his attention back.

They waited and, after some time, Fontana said, 'He was homosexual, Araldo.'

Brunetti nodded, a nod that both acknowledged the remark and declared that the police already knew this.

Fontana reached into his pocket and brought out a cotton handkerchief. He wiped his face and put the handkerchief back. 'He told me years ago, perhaps fifteen, perhaps more than that.'

'Were you surprised?' Brunetti asked.

'I think I wasn't,' Fontana said. Absently, he glanced down at his lap and pinched the crease in his trousers, ran his fingers back and forth along it, though the gesture made no difference against the weight of humidity in the room, in the city. 'No, I wasn't. Not really,' he corrected. 'I'd thought for years that he was. Not that it mattered to me.'

'Did it matter to his parents, do you think?' Vianello asked. 'Were they surprised?'

'His father was dead when he told me.'

'And his mother?' the Inspector asked.

'I don't know,' Fontana said. 'She's a great deal smarter than she lets on. She might have known. Or suspected.'

'Would it have bothered her?' Vianello asked.

Fontana shrugged, started to say something, stopped, then went on, speaking quickly, 'So long as no one knew about it and he paid the rent, she wouldn't care, not really.'

Brunetti interrupted to remark, 'That's an unusual thing to say about a man's mother.'

'She's an unusual woman,' Fontana said, giving him a sharp look.

A silence fell. Interesting as a discussion of Signora Fontana might be, Brunetti thought it was of little use to them. It was time to get back to Fontana's death, so he asked, 'Did your cousin ever say anything about his private life?'

'Do you mean sex?' Fontana asked.

'Yes.'

Fontana tried again to help the crease in his trousers, but again the humidity won. 'He told me,' he began and stopped to clear his throat a few times. 'He told me once that he envied me.' He stopped.

'Envied you what, Signor Fontana?' Brunetti was finally forced to ask him.

'That I love my wife.' He looked away from Brunetti after he said this.

'And why was that?' Brunetti asked.

Again Fontana cleared his throat, gave a few coughs, and said, not looking at him, 'Because – this is what he said – he never managed to make love with anyone he really loved.'

25

Brunetti nodded again, suggesting that he was already in possession of this information. In his most sympathetic voice he said, 'That must have made his life very difficult.'

Fontana gave the phantom of a shrug and said, 'In a way, but not really.'

'I'm afraid I don't understand,' Brunetti said, though, thinking of Fontana's mother, perhaps he did.

'That way, he could separate his emotional life from his sexual life. He loved me and his mother and his friend Renato, but we were already – what's the right way to say this? – out of bounds sexually.' He paused, as if considering what he had just heard himself say, then went on. 'Well, Renato isn't, I suppose. But I think Araldo couldn't stand confusion of any sort in his life. So by separating them, those two things, then he didn't have confusion. Or he thought he didn't.' Again, that shrug,

230

and Fontana said, 'I don't know how to explain this, but it makes sense to me. Knowing him, I mean. How he is. Was.'

'You said a moment ago, Signore, that you think this might have had something to do with his death,' Brunetti said. 'Could you explain that to us, please?'

Fontana folded his hands primly on his lap and said, speaking to Brunetti, 'By keeping things separate, he was free – if that's the word – to have anonymous sex. When we were younger . . . that sort of thing was all right, I suppose. And then I, well, I changed. But Araldo didn't.'

After the silence had grown long, Brunetti asked, 'Did he tell you this?'

Fontana tilted his head to one side. 'Sort of.'

'Excuse me,' Brunetti said. 'I'm not sure I understand.' He probably did, but he wanted to hear from Fontana what the other man had in mind.

'He'd tell me things, answer questions, sort of hint at things,' Fontana said, abruptly getting to his feet. But all he did was pull his trousers away from the back of his thighs and take a few steps on the spot to let them fall free from his body. He sat down again and said, 'I knew what he meant to say, even if he didn't say it.'

'Did he tell you where this took place?' Brunetti asked.

'Here and there. In other people's homes.'

'Not in his?'

Fontana gave Brunetti a severe look and asked, 'Have you met his mother?'

'Of course,' Brunetti said, glancing at the surface of his desk and then back at Fontana.

As if as a form of apology for the sharpness of his last remark, Fontana offered this: 'Once, when I went to visit them, the speaker phone and door latch were broken, so I had to call Araldo on my *telefonino*, and he came down to let me in. As we were crossing the courtyard, he stopped and looked around. Then he said something about it being his little love nest.'

'What did you say?' Vianello broke in to ask.

'I was embarrassed, so I ignored him and pretended he hadn't said anything.' A moment passed and he said, 'I didn't know what to say. We'd been so close as kids, and then he'd say something like this. I didn't understand.'

'Maybe he was embarrassed, as well,' Brunetti suggested. Then, more appositely, 'Did he ever mention anyone by name or make a remark that would allow you to identify one of his . . .' Brunetti struggled to find the right word: 'lovers' seemed wildly wrong, given what Fontana had been telling him. '. . . partners?'

Fontana shook his head. 'No. Nothing. Araldo would have thought that was wrong.' He waited for them to ask him about that, and when they did not, he continued. 'It was all right for him to talk about his own life, but he never said anything about anyone else: no names, not even ages. Nothing.'

'Just that he couldn't love them?' asked Vianello in a sad voice.

Fontana nodded, then whispered, 'Or shouldn't.'

After that, the information Fontana provided was routine: his cousin had never introduced him to anyone who was other than a friend from school or a colleague at work, nor had he ever spoken with particular affection of anyone except Renato Penzo, whom he had praised as a good friend. He had always gone on vacation with his mother and had once joked that it was more work than going to work.

In recent months he had seemed nervous and pre-occupied, and when Giorgio commented on this, his cousin had told him only that he was having trouble at work and at home.

'Many of the people I've spoken to,' Brunetti began, 'have told me he was a good man. And you used the term yourself. Could you tell me what you mean by it?'

A look of real confusion spread across Fontana's face. 'But everyone knows what that means.' He looked towards Vianello for confirmation, but the Inspector remained silent.

Finally Brunetti allowed himself to say it. 'There are many people who would not think he was good once they learned he was homosexual.'

'But that's ridiculous,' Fontana snapped. 'I told you: he was a good man. For the last year he'd been collecting clothing for that woman – that servant – what's her name?'

'Zinka?' Brunetti suggested.

'Yes. He'd been collecting clothing for her family in Romania and mailing it to them. And I know his friend Penzo is trying to get her a *permesso di soggiorno*. And he had the patience of a saint with his mother. He'd have done anything to keep her happy. And he really was incapable of dishonesty. Of any sort.' Then, as the memory came back, he said, 'Ah, I'd forgotten. He told me, about two months ago, that he was thinking about moving, but he couldn't bear the thought of how much it would upset his mother.'

'Did he say why?'

Fontana shook his head. 'Nothing I could understand. Something about work and its not being right that they lived in that *palazzo*. But he didn't really explain it.'

'Do you think he would have moved?' Brunetti asked.

Fontana closed his eyes and raised his eyebrows. When he opened his eyes, he met Brunetti's gaze and said, 'If it meant disturbing his mother . . .' before his voice trailed away.

'You really think that apartment is so important to her?' Brunetti asked with surprise he could not hide.

'You've spoken to my aunt?'

'Yes.'

'You saw her little red cheeks and her stylish hair?'

'Yes.'

Fontana leaned forward so quickly in his chair that Vianello moved aside hurriedly to get away from him. 'My aunt is a harpy,' Fontana said with a violence that astonished Brunetti and left Vianello with his mouth ajar. 'If she doesn't get what she wants, other people have to pay for it, and she wants that apartment. Like she has never wanted anything in her life.'

No one in the room found the proper thing to say for some time, until Brunetti asked, 'And was that enough to stop your cousin from doing what he wanted to do?'

'I don't know, but when I think about it now, I think that's what made him so nervous the last few times I saw him or spoke to him.'

'Did your cousin ever mention a Judge Coltellini?' Brunetti asked suddenly.

Fontana could not disguise his surprise. 'Yes. He did. For the last few years, well, maybe two. He was very taken with her. She was always very pleasant to him, seemed to appreciate his work.' Fontana paused and then added, 'Araldo would get crushes on women every once in a while, especially women where he worked who had more power or responsibility than he did.'

'What would happen with these women?'

'Oh, he got tired of them, sooner or later. Or they'd do something he didn't approve of, and then they'd sink back under the waves and be treated just like anyone else.'

'Did that happen with Judge Coltellini?' As he asked the question, Brunetti was aware of how much this man, and their dealings with him, had changed since he had come into his office. The meekness was gone; so was the timidity. In place of the appearance of uncertainty, Brunetti saw both intelligence and sensitivity. His initial nervousness, then, could be attributed to the fear that any involvement with the forces of order brought to the average citizen.

Brunetti tuned into Fontana's answer in mid-sentence. '. . . that made things change. When he didn't talk about her – I noticed the change because he had been so taken with her – I asked about her, and he said he had been mistaken about her. And that was that. He refused to say anything else.'

'Have you seen your aunt since his death?'

Fontana shook his head. He sat quietly for a while, and then said, 'The funeral's tomorrow. I'll see her there. Then I hope I never have to see her again. Ever.'

Brunetti and Vianello waited.

'She ruined his life. He should have gone to live with Renato when he had the chance.'

'When was that?' Brunetti asked.

When Fontana looked at him, Brunetti saw that his eyes had grown sadder still. 'It doesn't matter, does it? He could have, and should have, but he didn't, and now he's dead.'

Fontana got to his feet, reached across the desk and

shook Brunetti's hand, then Vianello's. He didn't bother to say anything else but walked to the door and let himself out of the office.

26

The silence in the room remained after Fontana left, neither Brunetti nor Vianello willing to disturb it. After some time, Brunetti got up from his desk and went over to the window, but he found no puff of air to ward off the sodden weight of the day or of Fontana's words. 'My family is sleeping under eiderdowns, and we have to go to a funeral tomorrow,' he said, looking out the window.

'Nothing better for me to do with Nadia and the kids gone,' Vianello said wistfully. 'I'll probably start talking to myself soon. Or eating at McDonald's.'

'Probably less harmful to talk to yourself,' Brunetti observed. Then, more seriously, 'You listen while I talk, all right?'

Vianello folded his arms across his chest, and slid down in his chair with his feet stuck out in front of him, crossed at the ankles.

Brunetti leaned back against the windowsill, propped

his hands beside him, and said, 'The DNA sample that Rizzardi took from Fontana's body's no use unless we can match it to someone. Penzo and Fontana weren't lovers, for whatever that's worth. The mother may have known he was gay, but she seems to have cared more about keeping the apartment. Fontana had some sort of crush on Judge Coltellini, and then it ended for reasons yet to be discovered. Fontana liked anonymous sex. Someone at the Tribunale is saying he liked dangerous sex. He argued with both neighbours; we don't know about what. Some cases brought before Judge Coltellini have had inordinately long delays. Fontana wouldn't talk about her. He wanted to move out of the apartment but probably lacked the courage to do it.'

Vianello crossed his ankles the other way. Brunetti went back to his desk and sat. 'It's a jigsaw puzzle: we've got lots of pieces, but we don't have any idea how they fit together.'

'Maybe they don't,' observed Vianello.

'What?'

'Maybe they don't fit together. Maybe he picked someone up and brought him back to the courtyard. And things got out of control.'

Brunetti propped his head on one hand and said, 'I'm hoping this suggestion doesn't result from some idea that gay sex always has to be dangerous.' His voice was neutral, but his intention was not.

'Guido,' Vianello said in an exasperated way, 'give me some credit, all right? We've got lots of little facts and even more inferences, but we also have someone whose head was bashed against a marble statue three times, and that's not something that happens to a good man, not unless he's doing something very rash.'

'Or dealing with a man who is not good and who *is* rash,' Brunetti added quickly.

'I think we . . .' Vianello began but was interrupted by Pucetti, who catapulted through the door, his momentum carrying him almost up against Vianello's chair. 'The Ospedale,' he managed to blurt out, then leaned over to take two deep breaths. 'We had a call,' he said, but even as he spoke, Brunetti's phone rang.

'Commissario,' a voice Brunetti did not recognize said, 'the Ospedale called. Something's going on in the lab.'

'What?'

'It sounds like a hostage situation, sir.'

'A *what*?' Brunetti asked, wondering if everyone there had been watching too much television.

'It sounds like there's someone locked in the lab, making threats.'

'Who called you?' Brunetti demanded.

'The *portiere*. He said people escaped from the lab. One of them called him.'

'What do you mean, "escaped"?' Brunetti demanded. He covered the mouthpiece and told Vianello, 'Go down and get Foa. I want a launch.' Vianello nodded and was gone. Pucetti went out with him.

Brunetti returned his attention to the phone just in time to hear the explanation. 'The *portiere* said that's what the person who called him told him.'

'What else did he say, the person who called him?'

'I don't know, sir. The *portiere* called 113, but there was no answer, so he called us. That's all.'

'Call him back and tell him we're on the way,' Brunetti said.

Outside, as he crossed the pavement to get to the launch, Brunetti realized he had left his jacket in his office, and thus his sunglasses. The morning light stunned him, and he jumped on to the boat half-blind. Vianello grabbed his arm to steady him and led him down into the cabin to escape the light. Even though they left the doors open, and Vianello slid open the windows, the heat battered them.

Foa did a three-point turn and took them up towards Rio di Santa Marina. He flicked the siren on and off to warn approaching boats that a police boat was coming the wrong way. He slowed to turn into Rio dei Mendicanti and pulled them up at the ambulance landing of the Ospedale. Brunetti and Vianello jumped on to the dock, Brunetti turned to Foa to tell him to wait for them, and they walked quickly into the Ospedale, trying to look like men in a hurry for medical reasons. The trip couldn't have taken them five minutes.

Brunetti led the way, along the side of the cloister, then to the left and up the stairs towards the laboratory. The door to the lab stood at the end of a corridor, and in front of the door to the corridor stood five people, three of them wearing white lab jackets and two the blue uniforms of guards. Brunetti recognized one of Rizzardi's assistants, Comei.

'What's going on?' Brunetti asked him.

The young man's staring blue eyes stood out alarmingly in his bronzed face. Vacation time was over.

It took him a moment to recognize Brunetti, but when he did, some of the tension disappeared from his face. 'Ah, Commissario.' He clutched Brunetti's arm as if he were drowning and only Brunetti could save him.

'What happened, Comei?' Brunetti said, hoping to calm him with his voice.

'I was in there, and suddenly she started to shout, and

then she threw something. Then she knocked everything off her desk: there was glass and chemicals and blood samples. All over the place.' He stared down at his feet, grabbed Brunetti's arm, and said, '*Oddio*. Look, look what she did.'

Brunetti followed his pointing finger and saw a red stain on the front of the technician's green plastic clog.

'She's gone mad,' Comei said, and a sudden scream that carried down the corridor from the lab gave evidence of that.

'Who is it?' Brunetti asked.

'Elvira, the technician.'

'Montini?' asked Brunetti.

Comei nodded absently, as if the name did not matter, and bent down. Gingerly, holding the cloth at the knee, he lifted the cuff of his trousers and exposed his ankle and the top of his naked foot. Four long splashes of blood trailed across the arch of his foot.

The technician leaned heavily against Brunetti. '*Oddio, oddio*,' he whispered, then he pulled himself away from Brunetti and stood motionless, eyes still on the blood.

Brunetti was about to say something when Comei turned and walked quickly towards the central part of the hospital.

Another noise, of something heavy being dropped, came down the corridor.

A woman in a white jacket approached Brunetti. 'You're the police?' she asked them.

Brunetti nodded. 'Can you tell us what happened?'

She was tall and slender and had an air of competence. 'I'm Dottoressa Zeno,' she said, not bothering to extend her hand. 'I'm in charge of the lab.'

Again Brunetti nodded.

'About half an hour ago, I asked Signora Montini about a blood sample she tested last week. The results didn't correspond with results from the same tests done in the hospital in Mestre three days ago, and the patient's doctor called to find out if the first test had been done correctly because the sudden difference didn't make any sense to him.'

She paused, then continued.

'I checked our lists and saw that Signora Montini had done the original test.' She looked from Brunetti to Vianello. 'This isn't the first time something like this has happened or that I've had to ask her about it.'

Brunetti tried to look as if he understood.

'I went to speak to her, but as soon as I told her about it . . .' Her voice lost some of its control as she went on. 'She grabbed the list of new results from me and ripped it up, then she knocked some things off her desk: vials and a microscope. Comei works beside her.'

Brunetti asked, 'And then, Dottoressa?'

'She pushed me away and started screaming.' As if hearing herself say that, she quickly amended it. 'Not really pushed me, just sort of put her hands on my arms and turned me away from her. She didn't hurt me.'

'Then what, Signora?'

'Then she picked up one of those cutters we use to open boxes with and started waving it around. She told us to get out. All of us. When I tried to talk to her, she held the cutter up.'

'Did she threaten you, Dottoressa?'

'No, no,' she said in notes that descended into pain. 'She held it over her wrist and said she'd cut it if we didn't get out.'

She took a breath and then another one. 'We all came

out here. I called security and someone went down to tell the *portiere*. Then someone said you were on your way, so we stayed out here, all of us.' He thought she was finished, but then she said, 'I called Dottor Rizzardi at home. She always worked very well with him.'

'Is he coming?'

'Yes.'

Brunetti exchanged a look with Vianello, told the five people to remain where they were, and pushed open the door to the corridor. It closed softly behind them, trapping them in the clinging heat of the corridor. They could hear some sort of low noise from the lab, like the buzz of a machine left running in a distant room.

'Do we wait for Rizzardi?' Vianello asked.

Brunetti pointed towards the door to the lab, a white wooden panel with a single porthole. 'I want to take a look inside first, see what she's doing.'

They walked down the corridor as quietly as they could, but as they got closer to the door of the lab the noise grew loud enough to cover any footsteps. Brunetti approached the window slowly, aware that any sudden motion might be seen from inside. A step, another, and then he was there, with a clear view into the room.

He saw the usual ordered clutter: vials held upright in wooden racks; dark apothecary jars pushed against the wall; scales and computers at every work station; books and notebooks to the left of the computers. One table in the centre of the room held no equipment. On the floor surrounding it, like wreckage from a sunken ship, a computer monitor, pieces of broken glass and papers lay in small red puddles.

His eyes followed his ears to the noise. A woman in a white lab coat leaned into one of those deep sinks, her back to him. The noise and steam came from the torrent of running water that must be spilling over whatever she held in her hands. He thought of his children, the Water Police, and how they would reprove the waste of all that hot water and the energy necessary to produce it.

He stepped aside and let Vianello take his place. Though the water made it possible for him to speak in his normal voice, Vianello whispered when he asked, 'Why's she washing her hands?'

Like the noble Romans, Brunetti thought as he shoved past Vianello and pushed open the door. As he ran by one of the desks, he ripped the receiver from a phone, and then yanked the cord from it. Just as he reached her, the woman slumped forward over the edge of the sink, and he saw the red – pink, really – swirling down into the drain.

He grabbed her, pulled her back and laid her on the floor, then used the phone cord as a tourniquet around her right arm. Vianello knelt beside him with another piece of phone cord, and tied off the left.

The face of the woman on the floor was pale, her hair shoulder length and more white than brown. She wore no makeup, but little could have been done to alleviate the plainness of those heavy features and pocked skin.

'Get someone,' Brunetti said, and Vianello was gone. He looked at her wrists: the cuts were deep, but they were horizontal, rather than vertical, which left some room for hope. The tourniquets had stopped the bleeding, though some blood had seeped on to the floor.

Her eyes opened. Her lashes and eyebrows were sparse, the eyes a dusty brown. 'I didn't want to do it,' she said. The continuing rush of the water made it difficult to hear her.

Brunetti nodded, as if he understood. 'We all do things we regret, Signora.'

'But he asked me,' she said and closed her eyes for so long that Brunetti feared she was gone. But then she opened them again and said, 'And I was afraid he'd . . . he'd leave me if I didn't do it.'

'Don't worry about that now, Signora. Lie quietly. Someone will be here soon.' They were in the middle of a hospital: why was it taking so long?

He heard footsteps, looked up, and saw Rizzardi. The doctor came over and knelt on the other side of the woman. He sighed, almost moaned, when he saw her there. 'Elvira,' he said, 'what have you done?' Brunetti noted that he used the familiar '*Tu*' when speaking to her. He sounded like a parent, disappointed in a child who has failed at something.

'Dottore,' she said and opened her eyes. She smiled. 'I didn't want to cause trouble.'

Rizzardi leaned down and placed one of his hands over hers. 'You've never caused a moment's trouble, Elvira. Quite the opposite. The only reason I have any faith in this lab is because you're here.'

She closed her eyes again and tears trickled from the outer edges. They spurred Rizzardi to say, 'Don't cry, Elvira. Nothing's going to happen. You'll be all right.'

'He'll leave me,' she said, eyes still closed and tears running into her ears.

'No, once he knows what you've done, he'll want to help you,' Rizzardi said, then glanced at Brunetti, as if to ask if he were saying the right lines.

'He won't be able to use the lab results now,' she said. 'People won't believe he helps them.' She closed her eyes for a moment, then looked up at Rizzardi. 'But he does,

Dottore. He really does.' She smiled, and for an instant her face was transformed into something approaching beauty. 'He helped me.'

There was a great deal of noise behind them. Brunetti looked up and saw three green-jacketed aides blocking the door with a wheeled stretcher. They banged it repeatedly against the sides of the door until one slipped around to the front and guided it through. Two of them came quickly over to the woman on the floor and the men kneeling beside her, forcing them aside with the press of their bodies.

Brunetti and Rizzardi got to their feet. Almost maddened by its sound, Brunetti took two steps to the sink and turned off the water. Vianello, who had come in with the attendants, went to stand beside Rizzardi. The third aide came over, pushing the stretcher. He did something with a lever and the stretcher sank almost to the ground, then he joined his colleagues and together they lifted the woman on to it. Another motion of the switch raised her slowly to waist height. The first one took a tube running from a bottle of clear liquid hanging above the stretcher and inserted the needle into a vein in her arm.

Rizzardi stepped forward then and wrapped his fingers around her wrist, holding it for some time, either to take her pulse or to convey whatever reassurance he could. 'Get her to emergency,' he said.

One of the attendants started to say something, but the first one, who seemed to be in charge, said, 'He's a doctor.'

As Rizzardi started to unwrap his fingers from her wrist she opened her eyes again and said, 'Will you come with me, Dottore?'

Rizzardi smiled at her, and Brunetti realized how seldom he had seen the doctor smile in all the years he had known him. 'Of course,' he said, and the attendants started towards the door.

27

Brunetti's first thought was the Contessa. He didn't know exactly how Gorini had profited from the lab tests Signorina Montini must have altered, but he knew she had done it to his profit, and for love, so that he would not leave her. If Gorini was capable of this, then Brunetti wanted to keep his mother-in-law away from him.

'I can't let Paola's mother see him.' Vianello, who knew of Brunetti's conversation, understood. Brunetti took out his *telefonino*, found the number for Palazzo Falier and was quickly put through to her.

'Ah, Guido, how lovely to hear your voice. How are Paola and the kids?' she asked, as if she did not speak to her daughter at least twice a day.

'Fine, fine. But I'm calling about that other thing.'

After the briefest of pauses, she said, 'Oh, you mean that Gorini man?'

'Yes. Have you done anything about contacting him?'

'Only indirectly. As it turns out, a friend of mine, Nuria Santo, has been going to him for months, and she says she'd be happy to introduce me to him. She's convinced he saved her husband.'

'Oh, how?' Brunetti inquired, speaking in his mildest voice and allowing signs of only the most modest curiosity.

'Something about his cholesterol. She said it doesn't make any sense: Piero eats like a bird, never eats cheese, doesn't like meat, but his bad cholesterol – I think there's a bad one and a good one . . .' The Contessa paused and then added, 'Isn't it strange that nature should be so Manichaean?' Brunetti ignored the remark, told himself to be patient and listen, and she continued, 'Whatever it is they count, it was up near the stars, and the good one was no help at all. Nuria told me that during one of his consultations Gorini recommended some herbal tea – it costs the earth – that he guaranteed would bring it down, and it did, so now she's convinced he's a saint and she's spreading the word among all of our friends.'

'Do you have an appointment with him?' Brunetti asked in what he hoped was a conversational tone.

'Next Tuesday,' she said and laughed. 'He's a clever devil, isn't he? Makes people wait a week before he'll talk to them.'

'Donatella, I'd like you not to go.'

Warned, perhaps, by the change in his voice as much as by his words, the Contessa asked, 'Is this something I should tell Nuria?'

How to warn off this other woman without frightening his prey? 'Maybe you could suggest she cancel her appointment.'

The Contessa was silent for some time, and then she asked, 'Can you tell me about it?'

'Not now. But I will.' He realized how quickly he was speaking, hastening her to go.

'Good. I'll tell her. Thank you, Guido,' she said and replaced the phone.

Looking at Vianello, Brunetti asked, 'You didn't hear any of it, did you?'

It took the Inspector a moment to sort out which conversation Brunetti was referring to, and when he did, he said, 'No, nothing. I came in too late.'

'She did it because she loves him,' Brunetti told him, oppressed by the sadness of the words.

'Did what?' Vianello asked impatiently.

'She said he – Gorini, I'm sure – was using the lab results – I think this is what it's got to mean – to convince people he could cure them. She said if he couldn't use the results then people wouldn't believe he could help them any more. And then he'd leave her.' Brunetti raised a hand in a vague gesture of incomprehension or acceptance. 'So she changed them.' Vianello had not heard her tell Rizzardi that she had not wanted to cause any trouble, but Brunetti didn't know if he could bear to repeat that.

Vianello looked around the lab, at the vials of different-coloured fluids still standing upright in the wooden stands, the various machines that had perhaps been too heavy for Signora Montini to try to destroy, and the jars and bottles only a professional could understand the use of. Brunetti could almost hear the Inspector thinking it all out. To aid him, Brunetti said, 'All he needed was to convince one person that he had worked a cure, and the word would spread.' He waited, then added, tapping the pocket where he had put his *telefonino*, 'My mother-in-law told me a friend of hers is convinced he saved her husband by giving him some herbal tea that gets rid of cholesterol.'

'It becomes a contest, doesn't it, once people find someone they think can help them?' Vianello asked.

'My doctor's better than your doctor,' Brunetti said. 'Just convince one person you've cured them, and soon all their friends will be at your door, and soon you'll have to beat them off with a boathook.'

'But the tests?' Vianello objected. 'How could he be sure Montini would get to do them?' Before Brunetti could begin to speculate on that, they were disturbed by a noise at the door. Dottoressa Zeno took a half-step into the lab. 'Can we come back in?' she asked.

'Yes, yes, of course,' Brunetti said and started walking towards her. 'I'd like to talk to you, Dottoressa.'

They soon had a clear idea of how Signora Montini could have done it. Everyone at the lab had worked together for so long that the choice of who would do which tests was often left to choice: usually the first people who came to work in the morning selected the first sample that had been delivered to the lab or the ones they wanted to do, and the others took what was left. Since Signorina Montini was usually the first to get there, she took first choice.

It soon became obvious to Dottoressa Zeno what sort of possibility they were considering, and she told them she could easily check for any tests done by Signora Montini where very bad results had improved over a short time.

The results took her only minutes to find in the computer, and when she printed them out for Brunetti, they were remarkable: among the people whose exams Signora Montini had performed during the last two years, there were more than thirty – all of them well over the age of sixty – whose cholesterol level had spiked suddenly, then after a period of about two months had gradually begun to sink back towards normal levels. The same pattern showed for numerous cases of what might have been adult-onset diabetes, with suddenly spiking glucose levels that descended to normal in a period of a few months.

'Oh, the clever bastard,' Vianello exclaimed when the pattern became obvious. Then, more practically, 'Why didn't anyone see it?'

Signora Zeno pushed a few keys, and the number 73,461 came up on the screen.

'What's that?' Vianello asked.

'The number of separate tests we did last month,' she answered coolly. Then, driving in the nails, she added, 'That's only the ones from patients in the hospitals in the city, not those we're sent by doctors who take their own samples.' She smiled and asked the Inspector, 'Would you like to see that number?'

Vianello put up his hands like a man about to be shot. 'You win, Dottoressa. I had no idea.'

Gracious in victory, she said, 'Most people don't, even people who work in the hospital.'

Brunetti heard a noise and noticed that two of the technicians were looking towards the door. He turned and saw Rizzardi. Brunetti had no idea how it had happened, but the normally dapper pathologist looked haggard and rumpled, as if he had slept in his clothing. He took a few steps into the room and raised his right hand in a half circle, ending with his hand upside down and his fingers outstretched, pointing out nothing and nothingness.

'They bandaged her wrists and set up a transfusion, but then the nurse was called to another room,' he began, looking across at Brunetti. He took out his handkerchief, wiped his face and forehead, and then his hands. 'She tore off the bandages while the nurse was gone, and took out the drip.' He shook his head.

Brunetti's thoughts fled to Cato, that noblest of noble Republicans. When life proved intolerable, he cut open his stomach, and when his friends tried to save him, he ripped out his viscera because death was preferable to a life without honour.

'I'm going home,' Rizzardi said. 'I won't do it.' And then he was gone.

Dottoressa Zeno left them and went over to talk to the technicians. 'Won't do what?' Vianello asked.

'The autopsy, I assume,' Brunetti said, wishing Vianello had not asked.

That stopped Vianello in his tracks.

'This means the case is . . .' Brunetti began but could not bring himself to use the word 'dead'. 'It's over,' he said. Without the testimony of Signorina Montini – and there was never any reason to believe she would have testified – there was no evidence against Gorini. Mistakes happen, all sorts of errors abound in the hospitals: people suffer and die as a result.

'We don't know if it was only the cholesterol tests she was changing.'

'You think she'd put people in danger?'

No, Brunetti did not, but that was hardly a secure enough protection for the people whose lab work she had handled. 'They'll have to redo all the tests she did,'

Brunetti said, thinking that this was an order only Patta, or perhaps the director of the hospital, could give. As to making any move against Gorini, that was impossible. Signorina Montini's death had removed any risk he ran, and it was unlikely she would have kept a written record of what she was doing. Certainly she would not keep such a document in the home she shared with Gorini, nor at work, the place where she was betraying her honour.

'The only thing we can do is call the police in Aversa and Naples,' Brunetti said resignedly, 'and tell them he's here.'

28

As Brunetti had both known and feared, it proved impossible to persuade Vice-Questore Patta that the laboratory tests performed by Signorina Montini should be repeated. His superior had already dismissed the idea of investigating Signor Gorini or his dealings with his clients. The man – Patta had this on good authority – had been very helpful in treating the wife of a member of the city council, and thus the idea of causing him trouble – in the face of a complete absence of evidence – was unthinkable.

When Brunetti refused to abandon the idea of redoing the tests, Patta demanded, 'Do you have any idea how much money ULSS loses every year?' When Brunetti did not answer, Patta said, 'And you want to add to it because of some wild theory you have that a faith healer corrupted this woman into falsifying medical reports?'

'A faith healer with a long criminal record, Dottore,' Brunetti added.

'A long history of accusation of crime,' Patta corrected. 'I don't think you, of all people, Commissario, should have to be reminded that they are not the same thing.' Patta gave a friendly smile here, as if this were a joke with an old friend who had never understood the difference.

Brunetti was having none of it. 'If this woman was tampering with test results, Vice-Questore, then the tests have to be redone.'

Patta gave another smile, but there was no humour in his voice when he said, 'In the absence of any evidence that this woman was involved in criminal behaviour – regardless of what you suspect, Commissario – I think it would be irresponsible on our part to spread needless alarm among the people whose tests she might have performed.' He paused in reflection and then added, 'Or to weaken in any way the public's faith in government institutions.'

As so often happened when Brunetti dealt with Patta, he was forced to admire the skill with which his superior could transmute his own worst failings – in this case blind ambition and an absolute refusal to perform any action that did not benefit him directly – into the appearance of probity.

Not bothering to explain or prepare for the change in subject, Brunetti said, 'I'm going to Fontana's funeral tomorrow morning, sir.'

The temptation proved too strong for Patta, who asked, 'In hopes of seeing the murderer there?' He smiled, inviting Brunetti to share the joke.

'No, sir,' Brunetti said soberly. 'So that his death isn't treated as something insignificant.' Good sense and the instinct of survival stopped Brunetti from adding, 'too' to his sentence. He got to his feet, said something polite to the Vice-Questore, went upstairs and made two disappointing calls to his colleagues in Aversa and Naples, and then went home and spent the rest of the day and evening reading the *Meditations* of Marcus Aurelius, a pleasure he had not permitted himself for some years.

The funeral took place in the church of Madonna dell'Orto, the parish into which Fontana's mother had been born and which had always been the spiritual centre of her life. Brunetti and Vianello arrived ten minutes before the Mass began and took seats in the twelfth row. Vianello wore a dark blue suit and Brunetti dark grey linen. He was glad of the jacket, for this was the first place he had felt cool since stepping into the house where he had found Lucia and Zinka.

The heat of the day had kept at bay the morbidly curious and the habitual attenders of funerals, so there were only about fifty people present, seated sparsely and in sad separation in the rows in front of them. After doing his rough count of those present, Brunetti realized they averaged only one person for each year of Fontana's life.

Brunetti and Vianello were too far back to see who sat in the first rows, reserved for family and close friends, but they would soon file from the church after the coffin and reveal themselves.

The music began: some sort of dreary organ theme that would have suited an elevator in a very respectable, if not necessarily wealthy, neighbourhood. Noise from behind slipped under the sound of the organ; Brunetti and Vianello stood and turned to face it.

A flower-draped coffin on a wheeled bier came down

the aisle, pulled along by four black-suited men who looked extraneous to any emotional weight this scene might have. Would the mother have hired mutes if they had been available, Brunetti wondered? When the coffin stopped in front of the altar, everyone in the church sat and the Mass began. Brunetti was attentive for the first minutes, but the ceremony was duller now than it had been when he, as a boy, had attended the funerals of his grandparents and his aunts and uncles. The words were spoken in Italian: he missed the magical incantation of the Latin. Suddenly aware of the silence, he wondered if the absence of the tolling of the death bell during the Mass, the sound that had accompanied so many members of his family to their last resting place, most recently his mother, was also planned in this modern – and banal – ceremony.

As he stood and sat, knelt briefly only to rise to his feet again, moved on the tides of memory, Brunetti reflected on this strange death. Signorina Elettra had 'accessed' the files of the Tribunale and had managed to trace Signor Puntera's legal history. Both the case of the contested warehouses and the injured worker had been assigned to Judge Coltellini, and in both cases long delays had resulted from the absence or temporary misplacing of files and pertinent documents. Further, other cases that had been assigned to the judge's docket had experienced similar delays. In all of them, Signorina Elettra's researches had ascertained, one party in the cause stood to profit from these delays. The judge, however, owned her own home, which she had bought three years ago, though not from Signor Puntera.

The bank of which Signor Fulgoni was the director, it turned out, had granted a loan to Signor Puntera at very favourable rates, and Signor Marsano was a lawyer in a firm that had once represented a client in a case brought, unsuccessfully, against Signor Puntera. Signor Puntera's tax return listed the rent he received from each of their apartments, as well as that occupied by the Fontanas, at four hundred and fifty Euros a month or about 20 per cent of the rent they might be expected to pay.

The priest circled the coffin, dipping his aspergillum repeatedly into the holy water and sprinkling it across the surface. Brunetti saw how perfectly the rituals of pre-Christian Rome – priests mumbling incantations that put evil spirits to flight, searching for the future in the organs of sacrificed animals – blended with those of the new Italy – evil spirits kept at bay by magic *tisana*, the future revealed in the turn of a card. We pass through centuries, and we learn nothing.

Puntera, too, had adapted to the new order: nothing he had done was in any way unusual in these modern times, and it was unlikely that anything could be proven against Judge Coltellini for her various accommodations in his favour. With bitter cynicism, Brunetti had to admit they had been in no danger from any revelations Fontana might have chosen to make. There was the risk of temporary embarrassment for Puntera and Coltellini, but if embarrassment were a bar to advancement, then there would be no government and no Church.

The return of the organ's rumbling put an end to Brunetti's reflections and signalled the end of the Mass; Brunetti and Vianello got to their feet and turned to face the aisle.

The four men wheeled the coffin slowly towards the door of the church; first behind it came Signora Fontana, her head covered by a black veil that blended into the long-sleeved black dress she wore. A man Brunetti did not recognize walked close beside her, supporting her by her right arm. Two steps behind them walked her nephew, who nodded to Brunetti as he passed. Brunetti recognized a few faces, people who worked at the Tribunale; he was surprised to see Judge Coltellini among them. The people filing out kept their eyes straight ahead or on the pavement in front of them.

A youngish couple walked arm in arm, and close behind them came Signora Zinka, bulky and overheated in a black dress that was too long and too tight. Her face was damp and swollen, not because of the heat, Brunetti thought. An arm's length to her right walked Penzo, looking as though he were somewhere else, or wanted to be.

Seeing the next couple, Brunetti realized he had been wrong in believing the habitual frequenters of funerals had been deterred by the heat. Maresciallo Derutti and his wife were well known in the city, omnipresent at funerals, to which he insisted on wearing the dress uniform of the Carabinieri, whose ranks he had left more than two decades before. Seeing the Maresciallo walk by, Brunetti decided the funeral was over and stepped into the aisle, Vianello close behind.

Slowed by the solemnity of motion the situation imposed, it took them some time to reach the door of the church. From inside the church, Brunetti saw the coffin being wheeled, untolled, towards a boat moored by the *riva*. He and Vianello stepped outside; the marble pavement caught the light and hurled it back into Brunetti's eyes, momentarily blinding him. He turned towards the church and, protected by his own shadow, fumbled in his pocket for his sunglasses. He felt them in his right pocket, but they were caught in his handkerchief; he pulled, but they would not come free. He opened his eyes to narrow slits to see what was wrong, but before he could look down, he noticed Signora Fulgoni emerging from the church into the dazzling light on the arm of another woman, one even taller, though not as slender, as she. Both wore wide-shouldered trouser suits, and both of them paused to put on their sunglasses.

He gave another tug and pulled the glasses free from his pocket. He slipped them on and looked back at Signora Fulgoni, only to see that the person holding her arm was actually a man who wore identical sunglasses to the woman; taller, though with the same feminine look and carefully cut short hair. Together, they descended the steps of the church and followed the other people to the water.

'And the scales fell from his eyes,' Brunetti whispered, wondering even as he spoke at his need, always, to be such a clever boots.

'What?' Vianello turned to ask him.

'Patta joked that the murderer always comes to the funeral,' Brunetti answered.

Confused, Vianello, eyes safe behind his own sunglasses, looked across the open space in front of the church, towards the people clustered around the boat that would take Fontana's coffin to San Michele. He saw what Brunetti saw: the mother of the deceased, climbing now into the boat that would take her son away from her, Penzo's rigid form next to the squat cylinder that was Zinka, the Maresciallo, arm raised in a long-held salute, and two tall people standing to his left.

Seeing the Inspector's perplexity, Brunetti said only, 'Wait until those two turn around.'

Brunetti and Vianello waited, both suddenly unaware of the sun or the heat. The man who had accompanied Signora Fontana to the boat followed her on board and down into the cabin. Someone on shore cast off the mooring rope, and the boat started to move slowly away from the *riva*. The people on the embankment remained motionless as the sound of the motor diminished until it was gone, leaving only silence behind. Then, as if they had all heard the same command at the same time, the people standing in front of the church turned to right or left and began to take themselves away from the place of grief.

Penzo, Brunetti noticed, went in the opposite direction from Signora Zinka, who joined the two young people. They started towards the Misericordia, and Zinka fell into step behind them.

Signora Fulgoni appeared to be keeping an eye on the other couple, for she stood still, clinging to the arm of the person with her, until the others had climbed the bridge and disappeared down the *calle* on the other side. She raised her head and spoke to her companion. They turned and started to walk in the same direction as the other two; Signora Fulgoni's companion was nearest to them and thus was visible in profile.

It was a man walking beside Signora Fulgoni. Nothing strange in that. She said something to him, and he stopped and turned to her. They exchanged words, apparently not kind words, and then the man pulled his arm free of hers and waved a hand at her, as if to chase her away. Was it the way his wrist moved, finishing in a sharp angle, fingers pointing at the pavement, that made Vianello see? Was it the sudden twist of his head, a motion that was unconscious of itself as a violent parody of anger?

' "My husband is a bank director",' said Vianello.

The sun blasted down on them from its highest point, nailing them to the pavement, and they were again aware of its weight. Brunetti looked at his watch just as the sound of the bells of some other church rolled across the city and over them. Amazed, he looked up at the bell tower of La Madonna dell'Orto and saw the bells hanging there, lifeless. 'The bells aren't ringing,' he said, marvelling.

29

As Brunetti had both known and feared, Patta proved resistant to the idea of questioning Signor and Signora Fulgoni – separately – about their movements on the night of Fontana's death. Patta also pointed out that there was no way to constrain a person to submit a DNA sample for 'purposes of elimination'. Nor, indeed, for any reason.

Brunetti still winced at the memory of his superior's response to his explanation of why he wanted to question the Fulgonis. 'You want *me* to jeopardize my position because you *think* he might be gay?' Even though the Vice-Questore was no friend of homosexuals, the force of his anger had pulled him up from his chair and halfway across his desk. 'The man is a bank director. Have you any idea of the trouble this would cause?'

Thus the workings of Patta's mind. Those of the mechanism controlling the bells of Madonna dell'Orto were no less strange, they having ceased to work two weeks before. The *parocco*, when Brunetti spoke to him, explained that it was impossible, during the long holiday, to find anyone who would come to fix them, and so they tolled neither the passing hours nor the passing of life.

Prompted by his curiosity about why one of the Fulgonis should lie, Brunetti began to wonder about the other. Banks must be like any other business, he reflected, different only because their product was money, not pencils or garden forks. This similarity dictated that employees would gossip and that the reputations of the people in power would be coloured – if not entirely fashioned – by that gossip. It was common knowledge at the Questura that Signorina Elettra – for reasons that she had never fully explained and that no one had ever fathomed – had left her job at the Banca d'Italia to come and work at the Questura, so Brunetti asked her to check among her friends who still worked in that sector to see what rumours existed about bank director Lucio Fulgoni.

Signorina Elettra came up to his office on the afternoon of the day he had made his request. He waved her to a chair. 'I take it you've discovered something, Signorina?'

'Not much, and nothing definite, I'm afraid,' she said, sitting opposite him.

'What does that mean?' he asked.

'That there is a certain amount of talk about him.'

He did not interrupt to ask what sort of talk: even if the man was a bank director, gossip would most likely centre on his sexual life.

'What speculation exists – at least this is what two people have told me – concerns his sexual preference.' Before Brunetti could comment, she added, 'Both of these people told me they'd heard others say they thought he was gay, but no one seems able to provide any evidence of this.' She shrugged, as if to suggest how common this situation was.

'Then why is there talk?' Brunetti asked.

'There's always talk,' she answered immediately. 'All a man has to do is behave a certain way, make a particular remark, and someone will start to talk about him. And once it starts, it can only get worse.' She looked across at him. 'The fact that there are no children is used as evidence.'

Brunetti closed his eyes for a moment, then asked, 'Has he ever approached anyone at the bank?'

'No. Never, at least not that my friends have heard about.' She thought for a moment and then added, 'If anything had actually happened, everyone would know about it. You have no idea how conservative bankers are.'

Brunetti steepled his fingers and pressed his lips against them. 'The wife?' he asked.

'Rich, socially ambitious, and generally disliked.'

Brunetti decided to keep to himself the observation that this would describe the wives of many of the men he dealt with.

'One gets the sense, listening to people,' she permitted herself to say, 'that the third would be true of her, even without the first two.'

'Have you met her?' he asked.

She shook the question away and said, 'But you have.'

'Yes,' Brunetti answered. 'I can see why people might not like her.'

Signorina Elettra did not bother to ask for an explanation.

'Maybe we're asking the wrong people for information about him,' Brunetti finally said, giving in to the temptation that had nagged at him since his conversation with Patta.

'And we should be asking rent boys, instead of bankers?'

'No. We should be asking the Fulgonis directly.' He realized, as he said it, that his soul was tired of backstairs gossip, tired of listening from the eaves and consorting with informers. Ask them directly and have done with it.

Brunetti, as a kind of anticipatory punishment for going against Patta's direct warning not to persecute the Fulgonis, submitted himself to the flagellation of the sun as he walked to their apartment. As he passed the wall relief of the Moor leading his camel, Brunetti was tempted to consult with him on how best to treat the Fulgonis, but all the Moor had wanted to do for centuries was to lead his pack-laden beast off that *palazzo* wall in Venice and back to his home in the East, so Brunetti resisted the impulse.

He announced himself to Signora Fulgoni, who buzzed him into the courtyard without question or protest. Before starting towards the stairs, Brunetti made a half-circle of the courtyard; the chalked outline of Fontana's body had long since been washed away, leaving behind only a wispy grey trail that ran off into the small drain holes in the middle of the courtyard. The scene of crime tape had disappeared, but the heavy chains still sealed closed the storerooms.

As she had the last time, Signora Fulgoni awaited him at the door to the apartment, and again she made no attempt to take his outstretched hand. Seeing her, hair perfectly brushed into place, looking even more like a caryatid with pink lipstick, Brunetti wondered if she had perhaps found a way to keep herself vacuum packed for days at a time. He followed her down the corridor and into the same room, which conveyed the same impression of being for display rather than for use.

'Signora,' he said, when they were seated opposite one another, 'I'd like to ask you a few further questions about the evening of Signor Fontana's death. I'm not sure we've understood everything you told us.' He did not waste a smile after saying this.

She looked surprised, almost offended. How could a policeman have misunderstood what she said? And how could anyone, regardless of his rank, think of questioning the accuracy of her statements? But she would not ask: she would wait him out.

'You said that, just as you and your husband turned off Strada Nuova, while you were taking a walk to escape the heat of the evening, you heard the bells of La Madonna dell'Orto ringing midnight. Are you sure it was midnight, Signora, and not, perhaps, the half-hour or perhaps even as much as an hour later?' Brunetti's smile was even blander than the question.

As the mistress of the dacha would gaze at the serf who questioned her word about the proper spoons to use for tea, Signora Fulgoni stared at Brunetti for long seconds. 'Those bells have been ringing for generations,' she said with indignation she was too polite to make fully manifest. 'Are you suggesting I would not recognize them or that I would not understand the time they were ringing?'

'Certainly not, Signora,' he said with a self-effacing smile. 'Perhaps you mistook the bells of some other church that are less accurate?'

She allowed small cracks to appear in the wall of her

patience. 'I *am* a member of this parish, Commissario. Please permit me to recognize the bells of my own church.'

'Of course, of course,' Brunetti said neutrally, surprising her, perhaps, by the fact that her last words had not caused him to fall off his chair and crawl towards the door. 'You said, Signora, that you and your husband had no familiarity with the dead man.'

'That is correct,' she said primly, folding her hands on her knees to enforce the words.

'Then how can it be,' he began, deciding to take a stab, 'that traces of both Signor Fontana and your husband were found in the same place in the courtyard?'

Had he really stabbed her, Brunetti could have caused no greater shock. Her mouth opened, and she raised a hand to cover it. She stared at him as if seeing him for the first time and not liking what she saw. But in an instant she had gained control and wiped away all sign of surprise.

'I've no idea how that could be possible, Commissario.' She devoted some moments to this mystery and then volunteered, 'Of course, my husband might have met Signor Fontana in the courtyard and not thought it important enough to mention it to me. Helped him move something, perhaps.'

It was not in Brunetti's experience that bank directors aided with the moving of heavy objects, but he let her remark pass with a pleasant nod suggestive of belief.

'And your husband didn't leave the apartment without you that evening, Signora? Perhaps to get some fresh air? Or to get some wine from your storeroom?'

She sat up straighter and said, voice tight, 'Are you suggesting that my husband had something to do with that man's death?'

'Of course not, Signora,' Brunetti – who was suggesting exactly that – said calmly. 'But he might have seen something unusual or something out of place, and mentioned it to you and then perhaps forgot about it himself: memory is a very strange thing.' He watched this idea work its way into her mind.

She looked at one of the paintings on the far wall, studied it long enough to memorize its strict horizontality, and then looked back at him. She pressed her lips together and looked down, then up at him with a look of embarrassed surprise. 'There was one thing . . .'

'Yes, Signora?'

'The sweater,' she said, as though she expected Brunetti to understand what she was talking about.

'Which sweater, Signora?' he asked.

'Ah,' she said, as if suddenly coming back to the room and recalling the circumstances of the conversation. 'Of course. The light green sweater. It was a Jaeger he bought years ago, a V-neck. He bought it when we were in London on vacation. And he had the habit of putting it over his shoulders whenever we went out for a walk.' Then, before Brunetti could ask, 'Yes, even in this heat.' Her voice grown suddenly softer, she went on, 'It had become a sort of talisman for him, well, for both of us when we went out in the evening.'

'And what happened with the sweater, Signora?'

'When we got back here that night, my husband realized it wasn't over his shoulders.' She crossed her arms and put her hands on her own shoulders and found no sweater there. 'So he went downstairs immediately to look for it. There hadn't been many people on the street, so if it had fallen off, he thought it might still be wherever he dropped it.'

'I see,' Brunetti said. 'Did he find it?'

'Yes. Yes. When he came back, he said it was on the ground just at the foot of Ponte Santa Caterina. Almost at the Gesuiti.'

'So he retraced the route of your walk, Signora?' Brunetti asked, after calculating the distance between their home and the bridge.

'He must have. I was in bed by then, so all I asked was whether he had found the sweater, and when he told me he had, I'm afraid I went right to sleep.'

'I see, I see,' Brunetti said. 'It's surprising he said nothing about this in the statement he gave to Lieutenant Scarpa.'

'As you said, Commissario, memory is a strange thing.' Then, before he could say it, she continued, 'It's strange, as well, that I didn't remember this until now.' As if to emphasize just how odd all of this really was, she put a hand to her forehead and gave him a vague look.

'How long do you think he was gone, Signora?' Brunetti asked.

She did that familiar Venetian thing of gazing off while memory walked the distance. 'It would take about fifteen minutes to get to the bridge, I suppose, because he would have been walking slowly. So twice that,' she said, then, as if uncertain that he could work out the maths unaided, she supplied the sum: 'Half an hour at most.'

'Thank you, Signora,' Brunetti said and got to his feet.

By the time Brunetti got to Signor Fulgoni's bank, his jacket was plastered to his back, and his trousers bunched together uncomfortably between his legs at every step. He stepped into the air-conditioned foyer and paused to wipe his face and neck with his handkerchief. Luckily, the created temperature was mild, rather than arctic, and Brunetti soon adjusted to it. He crossed the marble-floored lobby and approached a desk behind which sat a crisp-suited young woman. She glanced up and must have seen a dishevelled man in a wrinkled blue jacket, for she asked with badly disguised disdain, 'May I help you, Signore?' She spoke in Italian but with an undisguised Veneto cadence.

Brunetti took out his wallet and showed his warrant card. 'I'd like to speak to Signor Fulgoni,' he said, careful to speak Veneziano. Then, imitating the thick accent of the friends with whom his father had played cards in the *osterie* of Brunetti's youth, he added, 'I want to talk to him about a murder.'

The young woman got to her feet with a speed that, had there been no air conditioning, would have brought sweat to her brow. She looked at Brunetti, off to the left, and then picked up the phone and dialled a number.

'There's someone here who would like to speak to Dottor Fulgoni,' she said; then, after listening for a moment, added, 'He's a policeman.' She looked at Brunetti with a placating smile, said '*Sì*,' said it again, and set down the phone.

'I'll take you there,' she said, careful not to get too close to Brunetti. She turned and started to walk towards the back of the bank.

Brunetti had once read an article in a publication he could no longer recall that discussed the location of the various rooms in a house in terms of atavistic memories of danger. The rooms where people were at their weakest were invariably placed – or so the article maintained – farthest from the point of entry, the place where danger would burst into the house. Thus bedrooms were on the second floor or at the back of the house, forcing the invader, it was suggested, to fight his way through less well-defended positions with his sword or club, thus alerting the owner and giving ample time to prepare for escape or defence.

Brunetti had no doubt that Signora Fulgoni would have phoned her husband by now, perhaps hoping to give him enough time to slip out a back window or to start sharpening his axe.

Two desks stood on either side of a door at the back of the bank, as though they were bookends and the door some rare piece of incunabula. Another young woman stood in front of one desk; the other was empty.

The first woman stopped and said, raising a hand in Brunetti's direction, 'This is the policeman.'

Brunetti fought down the impulse to growl and wave his hands in their faces, but then he remembered that, in the land where money was god, policemen were not meant to enter the places of worship. Instead, he smiled amiably at the second young woman, who turned and opened the central door without bothering to knock. There was to be no surprising Dottor Fulgoni.

The man was already moving towards Brunetti. He was dressed in a sober dark grey suit. His tie was maroon, with some sort of fine pattern on it, and he had a maroon handkerchief in his breast pocket. As the man approached, Brunetti hunted for the signs of femininity he had noticed at the funeral and, seeking, found none.

His steps were precise, his hair and features well cut, and his eyebrows pointed arches over his eyes. 'I'm sorry, Commissario; they didn't give me your name,' Fulgoni said in a voice that was reassuringly deep. He shook

Brunetti's hand and led him to a sofa that sat on one side of the office.

Brunetti introduced himself as they crossed the room and chose to seat himself in the leather chair that stood in front of the sofa; Fulgoni took the sofa. He had sharply defined cheekbones and a long nose. 'May I offer you something, Commissario?' Fulgoni asked. He had an attractive voice, very musical, and he spoke Italian from which had been erased all sign of Veneto accent or cadence.

'Thank you, Dottore,' Brunetti said. 'Perhaps later.'

Fulgoni smiled and thanked the young woman, who left the office.

'My wife called me and told me about your visit,' Fulgoni said. 'She said there was some confusion about the time we got back to our home the night Signor Fontana was killed.'

'Yes,' Brunetti said, 'among other things.'

Fulgoni did not pretend to be surprised by this. 'I assume my wife has clarified the time we got home.'

'Yes, and she told me about your sweater, and your going out to look for it,' Brunetti said.

Fulgoni did not respond but sat quietly, studying Brunetti's face while allowing his own to be studied. Finally he said, 'Ah, yes. The sweater.' The way Fulgoni pronounced that last word told Brunetti that it had enormous significance for him, but Brunetti had no idea what the significance might be.

'She said you realized, when you got back from your walk, that you had lost a green sweater. She said the sweater was important to you – I think "talisman" was the word she used – so you went back outside to look for it.'

'Did she tell you that I found it?'

'Yes, and that you told her you had when you came back.'

'And then?'

'And then, she said, she went to sleep.'

'Did she tell you, by any chance, how long I was out? Looking for the sweater?'

'She wasn't sure, but she said it was about half an hour.'

'I see,' Fulgoni said. He pushed himself back in the sofa, sitting up a bit higher. He met Brunetti's gaze for a moment but then glanced away and fixed his eyes on the far wall. Brunetti did not interrupt his reflections.

A minute passed before Fulgoni said, 'My wife told me that you – the police – have found traces of me and Signor Fontana in the courtyard. In the same place in the courtyard, to be exact.'

'That's true.'

'What traces?' he asked, cleared his throat, and then added, 'And where?'

Trapped in his own lie, Brunetti waited some time before answering the question. Fulgoni glanced at him but then looked away, and Brunetti decided to risk saying, 'I think you know the answers to both those questions, Dottore.'

Only a man with the habit of honesty or one sufficiently ingenuous to be deceived by Brunetti's air of certainty would have found that a satisfactory answer to his questions.

'Ah,' escaped Fulgoni's lips in a single long breath, the sort of noise a swimmer makes when hauling himself out of the pool at the far end, race over. 'Would you tell me again what my wife said?' he asked in a voice he struggled to keep calm.

'That you went out for a walk with her to escape the heat in your apartment, and that when you came back, you realized you had dropped your sweater, and that you then went out for about half an hour and came back with it.'

'I see,' Fulgoni said. Looking directly at Brunetti, he asked, 'And do you think this would have been enough time for me to go downstairs and kill Fontana? To have beaten his head in against that statue?'

With no hesitation, Brunetti said, 'Yes,' and added, 'There would have been time enough.'

'But that doesn't mean I did it?' Fulgoni asked.

'Until there is a motive, your killing him would make no sense,' Brunetti answered.

'Of course,' Fulgoni said, 'and how – what's the English word, "sporting" of you to tell me.'

Brunetti was more surprised by the sentiment than by Fulgoni's use of the word.

'Would those samples you say you've found supply a motive?' Fulgoni asked.

'Yes, they would,' Brunetti answered, intensely conscious of Fulgoni's phrasing: 'you say you've found'.

Fulgoni startled Brunetti by getting suddenly to his feet. 'I think I don't want to be in the bank any more, Commissario.'

Brunetti rose but remained silent.

'Why don't we go to my home and have a look, then?' Fulgoni suggested.

'If you think that will help things,' Brunetti said, though he had no idea, not really, of what he meant by that.

Fulgoni reached for his phone and asked that a taxi be called for him.

The two men stood side by side on the deck, not speaking, as the taxi carried them up the Grand Canal and under the Rialto. The day was sun-bright, but the breeze on the water kept them from feeling the heat. In Brunetti's experience, tension drove most people to talk, and the tension that filled Fulgoni was easily read in the white of his knuckles as he grasped the taxi's railing. But anger just as often kept them silent as they used their energy to run over the past, perhaps seeking the place or time where things went wrong or flew out of control.

The taxi pulled up at the same place Foa had used the day the body was discovered. Fulgoni paid the driver and added a generous tip, then stepped on to the embankment. He turned to see if Brunetti needed a hand, but he was already beside him.

Still not speaking, they walked down the embankment and over the bridge. They stopped at the *portone* and Brunetti waited while Fulgoni pulled out his keys and opened the door.

Fulgoni led the way to the storeroom that held the birdcages and drew up sharp in front of the padlocked chain. 'I assume it's there that you found your samples?' he asked, pointing inside.

Brunetti had thought to get the keys from the evidence room and pulled them from his pocket. He fitted the various keys in the lock until he found the right one, removed the lock and opened the door. It was almost noon, so the sun beat down squarely upon them and cast no light into the storeroom. Fulgoni reached inside and switched on the light.

Ignoring the birdcages, he walked straight to the boxes piled beside them. Brunetti watched as he read the labels, though his body blocked Brunetti from reading them. At last he reached up and slid one out, creating a small avalanche as the boxes above it collapsed to fill the space. He placed it on a small round table with a scratched surface that Brunetti had overlooked. Fulgoni picked at the tape, dry and difficult to remove, that sealed the box and pulled it loose in a single long strip. Turning to Brunetti, he said, 'Perhaps you'd like to open it, Commissario.'

He moved past Fulgoni and pulled back the first flaps, then the next two. A grey turtleneck sweater lay on the top.

'I think you have to look deeper, Commissario,' Fulgoni said and then gave a dry laugh in which there was no humour whatsoever.

Brunetti folded back the sweater; beneath it was a thick blue sweater with a zipper. And beneath that was a light green V-neck sweater. 'Yes, look at the label,' Fulgoni said at the same instant Brunetti's eyes fell upon the Jaeger tag.

Brunetti let the other sweaters fall back into place and closed the flaps of the box. He turned to Fulgoni and said, 'Does this mean you did not go out in search of your sweater?'

'This box was packed at the end of winter, Commissario,' Fulgoni said. 'So, no, I wasn't wearing it, and I did not drop it. And so I did not go out in search of it.' He placed the sweater carelessly on top of the pile of boxes, then bent to pick up the dry strip of tape from the floor.

Keeping his eyes on the brown tape as he wrapped it around two fingers, he said, 'My wife doesn't like mess. Or disorder.' He slipped the paper cylinder into his pocket, looked at Brunetti and said, 'I've always tried to respect her wishes.' He nodded towards the birdcages and said, 'That's proof that I did, I suppose. We didn't have children, so one year she decided that she wanted birds. She filled the house with them.' He waved a magician's arm over the empty cages. 'But they died or they grew sick, so we gave them away. Well, the ones that weren't sick.'

'And those that were?' Brunetti asked, as he felt he was being asked to do.

'My wife disposed of them when they died,' Fulgoni said. He turned to Brunetti. 'I've always been far more sentimental than my wife, so I wanted to bury them over on the other side of the courtyard, under the palms.' He made a vague gesture beyond the door of the storeroom. 'But she put them in plastic bags and had the garbage man take them away.'

'But you kept the cages?' Brunetti said.

Fulgoni ran his eye over the stacks of wooden bird houses and said, puzzled by it, 'Yes, we did, didn't we? I wonder why that was?'

Brunetti knew this was a question not in search of an answer.

'Maybe my wife likes cages,' Fulgoni said with a desolate smile. 'I'd never thought of it that way.' He walked over and pulled the grated door of the storeroom towards them until it closed and then stood for a moment with his hands holding two of the upright bars, looking out at the courtyard. Then he turned to face Brunetti and asked, 'But which side is the cage, do you think, Commissario? In here or out there?'

Brunetti was a man of infinite patience, so simply stood and waited for Fulgoni to speak again. He had seen this moment many times before and had come to think of it as a kind of unravelling or unhinging, when a person decides that things have to be made clear, if only to himself.

Fulgoni put the tips of the fingers of his right hand on his lips, as if to give evidence of how deep in thought he was. When he removed his fingers, his lips and the area around them were stained a dark brown; Brunetti's eyes fled to Fulgoni's hands, but he saw there only the rust from the bars, not Fontana's blood.

Brunetti closed his eyes, suddenly aware of the heat of this cage in which the two of them were trapped.

'I'd like to show you something, Commissario,' Fulgoni said in an entirely normal voice. When Brunetti looked at him, he saw that the banker was wiping his hands with the handkerchief from his jacket pocket. Brunetti was struck by the way his hands grew cleaner without making the handkerchief darker.

Fulgoni moved past Brunetti and returned to where the cages were stacked. He studied them for a moment, then leaned down to examine one on the bottom row. He bent and put his hands on either side of it and started to wiggle it back and forth, working it free from the other cages trapping it.

He yanked it out, and the cages imitated the boxes by collapsing into the space where it had been, landing askew.

Fulgoni carried the cage to the table and set it beside the box. 'Have a look, Commissario,' he said, stepping back to remove his shadow, which the light cast across the cage.

Brunetti bent to study it: he saw a wooden birdcage, thin ribs of bamboo, the classic 'Made in China' construction. On the bottom, instead of newspaper, lay a piece of red cloth. It seemed to be woven of light cotton, and near the back Brunetti could see a separate piece: could it be a sleeve? Yes, that was it, a sleeve, and there was the collar, right at the back. A sweater then, a red cotton sweater, summer weight. Fulgoni stood beside him, motionless and silent, so Brunetti returned his attention to the cloth, puzzled that the other man should want him to look at it. Just below the neck there appeared a figure, or at least a change in colour. Darker than the rest of the sweater, it was amorphous: a flower, perhaps? One of those big things like a peony? An anemone?

There, on the top of the sleeve, was another flower, this one smaller and darker. Drier.

Brunetti reached to open the door of the cage but before he could, Fulgoni put a hand on his arm, saying, 'Don't touch it, Commissario. I don't think you want to contaminate the evidence.' There was no trace of sarcasm in his voice, only concern.

Brunetti looked at the sweater for a long time before he asked, 'How careful were you when you put it in there?'

'I picked it up with my handkerchief after she went back upstairs. I didn't know what would happen, but I wanted there to be some . . .'

'Some what?' Brunetti asked.

'Something that would show what had happened.'

'Would you tell me what that was?'

Fulgoni moved closer to the door, perhaps in search of cooler air. Both of them were sweating heavily, and the birdcages, since being disturbed by Fulgoni, emanated a foul, dusty odour.

'Araldo and I had use of one another. I suppose you could say it that way. He seemed to like things to be quick and anonymous, and I had no choice but to settle for that.'

Fulgoni sighed, and in the process must have drawn in some of the air disturbed by the cages, for he started to cough. The force of it bent him forward, and he covered his mouth with his hand, smearing the rust stains further.

When the coughing stopped, he stood upright and continued. 'We would meet here. Araldo called it,' he said with conscious melodrama and a wave of his arm at the low ceiling, the dust-tinged beams, 'our own little love nest.' He pulled out his handkerchief and wiped at his face, spreading the rust, but lighter now, across his forehead. 'My wife knew, I suppose. My mistake was to think she didn't care.'

He said nothing more for so long a time that Brunetti asked, 'And that night?'

'It was almost as my wife told you, except that it was her sweater that was dropped. A red cotton sweater. I said I'd go out and look for it. It wasn't as far as Santa Caterina, but just on the other side of the first bridge. When I went out, I saw that the door to Fontana's mailbox was open: that was the signal we used. If I saw it when my wife and I came home together, I'd make some excuse about going out for a walk, and I'd come downstairs and ring his doorbell from out in the *calle*, so he'd have an excuse to go out. And when he came down, we would retreat to our bower of love.'

'Is that what happened?'

'Yes. I put the sweater on the railing of the staircase, where it would be safe. And then Araldo came down. It never took long. Araldo didn't want to waste time on talk or anything like that. When we were finished, he always went out first: we were careful about that.'

'But not always?' Brunetti asked.

'Signor Marsano, you mean?'

'Yes.'

Fulgoni shook his head at the memory. 'We were in the courtyard one time when he opened the door. It's not that we were doing anything, but it must have been obvious to him.' Fulgoni shrugged. 'It was another reason we were careful. After that, I mean.'

'And that night?'

'Araldo left first and was crossing the courtyard, when I heard her voice. The light was out in here, so I thought if I just stayed quiet maybe everything would be all right. And then I'd stop. I always wanted to stop,' he said, voice wistful. 'But I knew I wouldn't.'

Fulgoni wiped his face again, and Brunetti was about to suggest they go out into the courtyard when the other man continued. 'So I stayed in here, trapped, and listened to them argue. I'd never heard her talk like that before, never heard her lose control.' Fulgoni turned and started to nudge the birdcages into line. As they fell or slipped into place, dust rose from them and he started coughing again.

When the coughing stopped, he went on. 'Then I heard a noise. Not a voice, but a noise, and then more noises and then a voice, but very short, and then more noises. And then I didn't hear anything more.'

Fulgoni pointed to the sofa. 'I was there, lying there with my pants down around my ankles, so it took me time to go and see what had happened.' Then, in a voice he forced to be stronger, he said, 'No, that's not the reason. I was afraid of what I would find.

'I heard footsteps going up the staircase, but I still waited. When I finally got to the door . . . there,' he said, pointing to the door that still closed them off from the courtyard, 'the light was on and I saw him on the ground.

But the light's on a timer and it went out. So I had to walk back to the switch and turn it on again, walking through the dark, knowing he was there, on the ground.' He stopped for what seemed a long time.

'When I came back, I saw what she had done. She must have seen the sweater on the railing when she came down, so she knew I was here. And then she saw him coming out, and it was . . .'

'And the sweater?'

'It was lying beside him. She must have had it in her hands when she . . .' For a moment, Fulgoni looked as though he would be sick, but that passed and he went on. 'I took out my handkerchief. I'd realized how things would look or could look. I didn't want anything to happen to her.' Then, like a man discovering honesty, or courage, he added, 'Or to me.'

He took two deep breaths after saying that, then said, 'So I wrapped my hand in my handkerchief and brought the sweater back in here and put it in the cage. I moved it around to flatten it out a little.'

'What did you do then, Signore?' Brunetti asked.

'I locked up this room and went back upstairs and went to bed.'

30

Paola, who did not have the legitimacy conferred by the possession of a driver's licence but who did have the security conferred by a husband who was a commissario of police, drove down to the railway station in Malles to pick Brunetti up, risking not only her own life to do so, but that of their children, as well. They went directly to La Posta in Glorenza, where the children gave evidence of having spent most of the day walking in the mountains by devouring a platter of Speck the size of an inner tube, tagliatelle with fresh *finferli*, and apricot strudel with vanilla cream.

Both Raffi and Chiara were comatose by the time they drove up to the farmhouse and had to be prodded out of the car and into the house, where they disappeared into their rooms, though Chiara did drape her arms around him and mumble something about being happy to see her father.

Later, stretched in front of the open fire, Brunetti sipped at a whisper of Marillen schnapps while Paola disappeared to get them sweaters. When she came back, she put it over his shoulders, but he insisted on standing to pull it on.

'Tell me,' she said, sitting down beside him.

He did. His glass remained untouched as he described the events of that morning, the funeral of Signora Montini, attended by himself, Vianello and Doctor Rizzardi, as well as two or three people who had worked with her in the lab.

Paola asked no questions, hoping the momentum of his story would carry him along.

'They held it at San Polo, though she went to church at the Frari. The pastor there didn't want to say Mass over her.' He turned and leaned against the arm of the sofa, the better to see her. 'It was miserable. We sent flowers, but the rest of the church was bare. The priest looked at his watch twice during the Mass, and he spoke a bit faster after he did.' And Brunetti, sitting in the church, hot and exhausted from a sleepless night, could not keep his thoughts from returning to the scene, less than two weeks before, when he stood in the *campo* not far from the church, waiting for Vianello's aunt to emerge from this woman's house.

He saw the plain coffin, the three wreaths, smelled the incense. 'But at least it was short,' he told Paola. 'Then they took her to San Michele.'

'And you came up here?' she asked.

Brunetti hesitated for some time and then said, 'I did a favour for Vianello first.'

'What?'

'I talked to his aunt.'

Paola could not hide her surprise. 'But I thought she was away for two weeks with her son.'

Brunetti got up and tossed a log on to the fire, poked it into place with the end of another one, and went back to the sofa. 'Why do we love fires so much?' he asked.

'Atavistic. We can't help it. Caves. Mammoths. Tell me about Vianello's aunt,' Paola said, drink forgotten in her hand.

'His cousin called him the night before and told him she'd gone back to Venice, so we went by to see her after the funeral.'

'As if the funeral weren't enough, eh?' she asked, patting his knee.

Brunetti said, 'It was better, really. Lorenzo's talked about me, so she had an idea of who I am. And I think she trusted me. No matter how angry she was with her son or with him, she still listened to me.'

'What did you tell her?'

'Everything we learned about Gorini,' Brunetti said. 'I took along the police reports.'

'Thus violating the law on privacy?' she inquired.

'I suppose so.'

'Good. What did she say?'

'She read them all. She asked me about some of them; what the different branches of the police did and whether the documents were believable.'

'You told her?'

'Yes.'

'Where was Vianello during all of this?'

'Sitting on a chair, pretending to be invisible.'

'And? Did she believe you?'

'In the end, she really had no choice,' Brunetti said. The vigorous woman he had so recently followed down Via

Garibaldi had sat between him and Vianello, face tear-stained, silent and tense; one wrinkled hand clutching at the papers, as if she could somehow squeeze the truth from them.

'What happened?'

'It took her some time, and then she told us,' Brunetti said, not describing the way the old woman had let the papers fall to the ground as she searched for a hand-kerchief to wipe her face and eyes, 'that she'd been buying special *tisane* for her husband after his lab results said he had the beginnings of diabetes.' He uncorked the bottle and added some schnapps to his glass, then slapped the cork back in with his palm.

'Then she told Vianello she'd been a fool,' he said, his voice lightening with the word, 'and wanted to call her son and apologize.'

'What did Vianello do?'

'He told her not to be a fool herself and that he'd take her back to her family to finish her vacation.'

'And you?' she asked.

'I got on the train to come up here,' he said, not mentioning his irritation with what he suspected were histrionics on the part of Vianello's aunt. During his career, Brunetti had seen and heard so many timely tears that it was difficult for him to be easily convinced of their sincerity.

'What about Gorini?' Paola asked.

He shrugged. 'Who knows? He's gone. We went to Montini's home after she was dead, but there was no sign of him. Nothing.' He swirled the liqueur in his glass but drank none.

'What will happen?' Paola asked.

'To him? Nothing, probably. He'll move somewhere

else and find some other gullible woman, and then he'll find more gullible people.'

'Like Vianello's aunt?'

'I suppose so,' he said. 'Or people like her.'

Abandoning Vianello's aunt and people like her to their beliefs, Paola asked, 'And the Fulgonis?'

Brunetti made a puffing noise and took a small sip of the schnapps. 'She says she came down and found Fontana on the ground and pulled off her sweater to try to stop the bleeding. Then her husband came out of the storeroom, and she understood what had been going on and what had happened. She says she ran back upstairs but couldn't bring herself to call the police.'

'And her story about hearing the church bells? Why would she tell that unless she wanted it to sound as if he was murdered later that night?'

'She said it was her husband's idea to tell me, so that it would seem as though Fontana had been murdered after they went upstairs. If there was no body when they came in, and it was already after midnight, then the obvious conclusion would be that Fontana was killed after they went upstairs.'

'Then why did she tell you about the sweater in the first place?'

Brunetti had thought about that during the long train ride from Venice. 'Who knows? Maybe she thought someone had seen her husband outside, and she thought it would be best to tell the police he had gone out. That way, we might believe the rest.'

'Was she trying to protect him, do you think?' she asked.

'Maybe. At the beginning,' Brunetti said.

'Then why lie and say it was his sweater?'

Brunetti shrugged. 'Surprise? Or she instinctively wanted to distance herself from the crime, or she wanted suspicion to fall on him. Or maybe she's just a bad liar.'

'How will it end?' she asked.

Brunetti leaned forward and set his empty glass on the table, then sat back and sank even deeper into the sofa. 'Until one of them confesses, it will all lead to nothing.'

'And if neither one does?'

'Then the case will churn on for ever, and the lawyers will pick their bones clean,' Brunetti explained.

'Isn't there enough to convict either one of them?' Paola asked, confusion and irritation fighting for dominance in her voice.

Brunetti, if only to keep himself from sinking into sleep, pushed himself up and went over to the fire again, but only to feel its warmth. How strange, yet how delicious, the feel of heat on his legs. He looked out of the window that gave to the north and pointed towards a slant of white that glistened in the light of the moon. He could form no clear idea of the distance: it was far away, yet it seemed very close. 'Is that the Ortler?' he asked.

'Yes.'

He moved away from the heat but returned to her question. 'There's enough evidence to convict either one of them, but the real problem is that there's enough evidence to convict both of them.' He thought with disgust of the media spectacle that was sure to ensue: blood and death and illicit sex among the birdcages. It had everything, and more, that an avid public could devour. 'But that's not likely.'

'Do you believe him?' Paola asked.

After some time, Brunetti said, 'I'd like to.' Then, after a longer pause, he added, 'I'm afraid of that.'

Paola waited until she was sure he was finished, and said, 'Let's go to bed.'

Later, Brunetti lay awake, looking off at the Ortler, visible from their bed: gleaming bright, beaming in the absence of men.

'My talisman,' Brunetti said, took his wife in his arms, and slept.

DRAWING CONCLUSIONS

The new Commissario Brunetti novel by Donna Leon is now available from William Heinemann.

Turn over for an exciting new extract.

1

Because she had worked for decades as a translator of fiction and non-fiction from English and German to Italian, Anna Maria Giusti was familiar with a wide range of subjects. Her most recent translation had been an American self-help book about how to deal with conflicting emotions. Though the superficial idiocies she had encountered – which had always sounded sillier when she put them into Italian – had occasionally reduced her to giggles, some of the text returned to her now, as she climbed the stairs to her apartment.

'It is possible to feel two conflicting emotions about the same person at the same time.' So it had proven with her feelings towards her lover, whose family she had just returned from visiting in Palermo. 'Even people we know well can surprise us when they are placed in different surroundings.' 'Different' seemed an inadequate word to describe Palermo and what she had found there. 'Alien', 'exotic', 'foreign': not even these words did justice to what she had experienced, yet how explain it? Did they not all carry *telefonini*? Was not everyone she met exquisitely well dressed and equally well mannered? Nor was it a question of language, for they all spoke an Italian more elegant than anything she heard from her Veneto-cadenced family and friends. Nor financial, for the wealth of Nico's family was on view at every turn.

She had gone to Palermo in order to meet his family, believing he would take her to stay with them, yet she had spent her five nights in a hotel, one with more stars awarded it than her own translator's earnings would have permitted her, had the hotel accepted her insistence that she be allowed to pay the bill.

'No, Dottoressa,' the smiling hotel director had told her, 'L'Avvocato has seen to it.' Nico's father. 'L'Avvocato.' She had started by calling him 'Dottore', which honorific he had dismissed with a wave of his hand, as though her attempt at deference had been a fly. 'Avvocato' had refused to fall from her lips, and so she had settled on 'Lei' and had used the formal pronoun, after that, for everyone in his family.

Nico had warned her that it would not be easy, but he had not prepared her for what she was to experience during the week. He was deferential to his parents: had she seen this behaviour in anyone other than the man she thought she loved, she would have described it as fawning. He kissed his mother's hand when she came into the room and got to his feet when his father entered.

One night, she had refused to attend the family dinner; he had taken her back to the hotel after their own nervous meal together, kissed her in the lobby, and waited while she got into the elevator before going meekly back to sleep in his parents' *palazzo*. When she demanded the next day to know what was going on, he had replied that he was the product of where he lived, and this was the way people behaved. That afternoon, when he drove her back to the hotel and said he'd pick her up at eight for dinner, she had smiled and said goodbye to him at the hotel entrance, gone inside and told the young man at the desk that she was checking out. She went to her room, packed, called for a taxi, and left a note for Nico with the concierge. The only seat on the evening plane to Venice was in business class, but she was happy to pay it, thinking it took the place of at least part of the hotel bill she had not been allowed to pay.

Her bag was heavy and made a loud noise when she set it down on the first landing. Giorgio Bruscutti, the older son of her neighbours, had left his sports shoes on the landing, but tonight she was almost happy to see them: proof that she was home. She lifted the bag and carried it up to the second landing, where she found, as she had expected, neatly tied bundles of *Famiglia cristiana* and *Il Giornale*. Signor Volpe, who had become an ardent ecologist in his old age, always left their paper for recycling outside the door on Sunday evening, even though there was no need to take it out until Tuesday morning. So pleased was she to see this sign of normal life that she forgot to pass her automatic judgement that the garbage was the best place for both of those publications.

The third landing was empty, as was the table to the left of the door. This was a disappointment to Anna Maria: it meant either that nothing had arrived in the mail for her during the last week – which she could not believe – or that Signora Altavilla had forgotten to leave Anna Maria's post for her to find when she got back.

She looked at her watch and saw that it was almost ten. She knew the older woman stayed up late: they had once each confessed to the other that the greatest joy of living alone was the freedom to stay up reading in bed for as long as they pleased. She stepped back from the door to Signora Altavilla's apartment and looked to see if light filtered from beneath the door, but the landing light made it impossible to detect. She approached the door and placed her ear against it, hoping to hear some sound from within: even the television would indicate that Signora Altavilla was still awake.

Disappointed at the silence, she picked up her bag and set it down loudly on the tiles. She listened, but no sound from inside followed it. She picked it up again and started up the steps, careful to let the edge of the bag bang against the back of the first step, louder this time. Up the stairs she went, making so much noise with the bag that, had she heard someone else do it, she would have made some passing reflection on human thoughtlessness or stuck her head out of the door to see what was wrong.

At the top of the steps she set the bag down again. She found her key and opened the door to her own apartment, and as it opened, she felt herself flooded with peace and certainty. Everything inside was hers, and in these rooms she decided what she would do and when and how. She had no one's rules to obey and no one's hand to kiss, and at that thought all doubt ended, and she was certain she had done the right thing in leaving Palermo, leaving Nico, and ending the affair.

She switched on the light, looked automatically across the room at the sofa, where the military precision of the cushions assured her that her cleaning lady had been there in her absence. She brought her suitcase inside, closed the door, and let the silence drift across and into her. Home.

Anna Maria walked across the room and opened the window and the shutters. Across the *campo* stood the church of San Giacomo dell'Orio: if its rounded apse had been the prow of a sailing ship, it would have been aimed at her windows, and would soon have been upon her.

She moved through the apartment, opening all the windows and pushing back and latching the shutters. She carried her suitcase into the guest room and hoisted it on to the bed, then moved back through the apartment, closing the windows against the chill of the October night.

On the dining room table, Anna Maria found a piece of paper with one of Luba's curiously worded notes and, beside it, the distinctive buff notice that indicated the attempted delivery of a registered letter. 'For you came,' the note read. She studied the receipt: it had been left four days before. She had no idea who could have sent her a registered letter: the address given for '*mittente*' was illegible. Her first thought was a vague fear that some government agency had discovered an irregularity and was informing her that she was under investigation for having done, or failed to do, something or other.

The second notice, she knew, would have come two days after this one. Its absence meant that Signora Altavilla, who over the years had become the custodian of her post and deliveries, had signed for the letter and had it downstairs. Curiosity overcame her. She set the receipt on the table and went to her study. From memory, she dialled Signora Altavilla's number. Better to disturb her this way than to fret until morning about the letter that would turn out, she told herself, to be something innocuous.

The phone rang four times without being picked up. She stepped aside and opened the window, leaned out and heard the ringing below. Where could she be at this hour? A film? Occasionally she went with friends, and sometimes she went to babysit her grandchildren, though sometimes the oldest spent the night with her.

Anna Maria hung up the phone and returned to the living room. Over the years and even though separated in age by almost two generations, she and the woman downstairs had become good neighbours. Perhaps not good friends: they had never had a meal together, but now and then they met on the street and had a coffee, and there had been many conversations on the stairs. Anna Maria was sometimes called to work as a simultaneous translator at conferences and thus would be away for days, sometimes weeks, at a time. And because Signora Altavilla went to the mountains with her son and his family each July, Anna Maria had her keys, in order to water the plants and, as Signora Altavilla had said when she gave her them, 'just in case'. There was a clear understanding that Anna Maria could – indeed, should – go in to get her post whenever she returned from a trip and Signora Altavilla was not at home.

She took the keys from the second drawer in the kitchen and, propping her own door open with her handbag, switched on the light and went down the stairs.

Though she was certain no one was home, Anna Maria rang the bell. Taboo? Respect for privacy? When there was no answer, she put the key in the lock, but, as often happened with this door, it would not easily turn. She tried again, pulling the door towards her as she turned the key. The pressure of her hand moved the handle down, and when she gave the sudden pull and push the recalcitrant door proved to be unlocked and opened without resistance, pulling her a step forward into the room.

Her first thought was to try to recall Costanza's age: why was she forgetting to lock her door? Why had she never changed it and got *una porta blindata* that locked automatically when it closed? 'Costanza?' she called. *'Ci sei?'* She stood and listened, but there was no answering call. Without thinking, Anna Maria approached the table opposite the doorway, drawn by the small pile of letters, no more than four or five, and that week's *Espresso*. Reading the title of the magazine, it struck her that the light in the hallway was on and that more light was coming down the corridor from the half-open door to the living room, as well as, closer to her, from the open door of the larger bedroom.

Signora Altavilla had grown up in post-war Italy, and though marriage had made her both happy and prosperous, she had never unlearned the habits of frugality. Anna Maria, who had grown up in a wealthy family in booming, prosperous Italy, had never learned them. Thus the younger woman had always found quaint the older's habit of turning off lights whenever she left a room, of wearing two sweaters in the winter, and of expressing real satisfaction when she found a bargain at Billa.

'Costanza?' she called again, more to stop her own thoughts than because she believed there would be an answer. In an unconscious attempt to free her hands, she set the keys on top of the letters and stood silent, eyes drawn to the light coming from the open door at the end of the corridor.

She took a breath, and then she took a step, and then another and another. She stopped then, and found she could go no farther. Telling herself not to be foolish, she forced herself to lean forward and take a look around the half-open door. 'Costan . . .' she began but slapped her mouth closed with one of her hands when she saw another hand on the floor. And then the arm, and the shoulder, and then the head, or at least the back of the head. And the short white hair. Anna Maria had for years wanted to ask the older woman whether her refusal to have her hair dyed the obligatory red of women her age was another manifestation of her learned frugality or simply acceptance of how her white hair softened the lines of her face, adding to their dignity.

She looked down at the motionless woman, at the hand, the arm, the head. And she realized she would never get to ask her now.

2

Guido Brunetti, Commissario di Polizia of the city of Venice, sat at dinner across from his immediate superior, Vice-Questore Giuseppe Patta, and prayed for the end of the world. He would have settled for being abducted by aliens or perhaps for the violent irruption of bearded terrorists, shooting their way into the restaurant, bloodlust in their eyes. The resulting chaos would have permitted Brunetti, who was, as usual, not wearing his own gun, to wrest one from a passing terrorist and use it to shoot and kill both the Vice-Questore and his assistant, Lieutenant Scarpa, who, seated to the left of the Vice-Questore, was at this very moment passing his measured – negative – judgement on the grappa that had been offered at the end of the meal.

'You people in the North,' the Lieutenant said with a condescending nod in Brunetti's direction, 'don't understand what it is to make wine, so why should you know about making anything else?' He drank the rest of his grappa, made a small moue of distaste – the gesture so carefully manufactured as to allow Brunetti to distinguish easily between distaste and disgust – and set his glass on the table. He gave Brunetti an open-faced glance, as if inviting him to make a contribution to oenological frankness, but Brunetti refused to play and contented himself with finishing his own grappa. However much this dinner with Patta and Scarpa might have driven Brunetti to long for a second grappa – or the second coming – the realization that acceptance would prolong the meal led him to resist the waiter's offer, just as good sense led him to resist the bait offered to him by Scarpa.

Brunetti's refusal to engage spurred the Lieutenant, or perhaps it was the grappa – his second – for he began, 'I don't understand why Friuli wines are . . .' but Brunetti's attention was called away from whatever deficiency the Lieutenant was about to reveal by the sound of his *telefonino*. Whenever he was forced into social occasions he could not avoid – as with Patta's invitation to dinner to discuss candidates for promotion – Brunetti was careful to carry his *telefonino* and was often saved by a generous Paola, calling with an invented urgent reason for him to leave immediately.

'*Sì*,' he answered, disappointed at having seen it was the central number of the Questura.

'Good evening, Commissario,' said a voice he thought must be Ruffolo's. 'We just had a call from a woman in Santa Croce. She's found a dead woman in her apartment. There was blood, so she called us.'

'Whose apartment?' Brunetti asked, not that it mattered that he know this now, but because he disliked lack of clarity.

'She said she was in her own apartment. The dead woman, that is. It's downstairs from hers.'

'Where in Santa Croce?'

'Giacomo dell'Orio, sir. She lives just opposite the church. One seven two six.'

'Who's gone?' Brunetti asked.

'No one, sir. I called you first.'

Brunetti looked at his watch. It was almost eleven, long

after he had thought and hoped this dinner would end. 'See if you can find Rizzardi and have him go. And call Vianello – he should be at home. Send a boat to pick him up and take him there. And get a crime scene team together.'

'What about you, sir?'

Brunetti had already consulted the map of the city imprinted in his genes. 'It's faster for me to walk. I'll meet them there.' Then, as an afterthought, 'If there's a patrol anywhere near, call them and tell them to go over. And call the woman and tell her not to touch anything in the apartment.'

'She went back to her own, sir, to make the call. I told her to stay there.'

'Good. What's her name?'

'Giusti, sir.'

'If you speak to the patrol, tell them I'll be there in ten minutes.'

'Yes, sir,' the officer said and hung up.

Vice-Questore Patta looked across at Brunetti with open curiosity. 'Trouble, Commissario?' he asked in a tone that made Brunetti aware of how different curiosity was from interest.

'Yes, sir. A woman's been found dead in Santa Croce.'

'And they called you?' interrupted Scarpa, placing just the least hint of polite suspicion on the last word.

'Griffoni's not back from vacation yet, and I live closest,' Brunetti answered with practised blandness.

'Of course,' Scarpa said, turning aside to say something to the waiter.

To Patta, Brunetti said, 'I'll go and have a look, Vice-Questore.' He put on his face the look of a beleaguered bureaucrat, reluctantly pulled away from what he wanted to do by what he had to do; he pushed back his chair and got to his feet. He gave Patta the chance to make a comment, but the moment passed in silence.

Outside the restaurant, Brunetti left the business of getting there to memory and pulled out his *telefonino*. He dialled his home number.

'Are you calling for moral support?' Paola asked when she picked up the phone.

'Scarpa has just told me we northerners don't know anything about making wine,' he said.

There was a pause before she said, 'That's what your words say, but it sounds as if something else is wrong.'

'I've been called in. There's a dead woman in Santa Croce, over by San Giacomo.'

'Why did they call you?'

'They probably didn't want to call Patta or Scarpa.'

'So they called you when you were with them? Wonderful.'

'They didn't know where I was. Besides, it was a way for me to get away from them. I'll go over to see what happened. I live the closest, anyway.'

'Do you want me to wait up?'

'No. I have no idea how long it will take.'

'I'll wake up when you come in,' she said. 'If I don't, just give me a shove.'

Brunetti smiled at the thought but confined himself to a noise of agreement.

'I have been known not to sleep through the night,' she said with false indignation, her aural radar having caught the precise nuance of his noise.

The last time, Brunetti recalled, was the night the Fenice burned down, when the sound of the helicopter repeatedly passing overhead had finally summoned her from the deep abyss to which she repaired each evening.

In a more conciliatory tone, she said, 'I hope it's not awful.'

He thanked her, then said goodbye and put the phone in his pocket. He called his attention back to where he was walking. The streets were brightly lit: more largesse from the profligate bureaucrats in Brussels. If he had chosen to do so, Brunetti could have read a newspaper in the light from the street lamps. Light still poured from many shop windows: he thought of the satellite photos he had seen of the glowing night-time planet as measured from above. Only Darkest Africa remained so.

At the end of Scaleter Ca' Bernardo, he turned left and passed the tower of San Boldo, then walked down from the bridge and into Calle del Tintor and went past the pizzeria. Next to it a shop selling cheap purses was still open; behind the counter sat a young Chinese girl, reading a Chinese newspaper. He had no idea what the current laws were about how late a shop could stay open, but some atavistic voice whispered to him about the unseemliness of engaging in commercial activity at this hour.

A few weeks ago he had had dinner with a commander of the Frontier Police, who had told him, among other things, that their own best estimate of the number of Chinese currently living in Italy was between 500,000 and five million. After saying this, he sat back, the better to enjoy Brunetti's astonishment. In the face of it, he had added, 'If the Chinese in Europe were all wearing uniforms, we'd be forced to see it as the invasion it is.' He had then returned his attention to his grilled calamari.

Two doors down he found another shop, with still another young Chinese girl behind the cash register. More light spilled into the street from a bar; in front of it four or five young people stood, smoking and drinking. He noticed that three of them drank Coca-Cola: so much for the nightlife of Venice.

He came out into the *campo*; it too was flooded with light. Years ago, just when he had been transferred back from Naples, this *campo* had been infamous as a place to buy drugs. He remembered the stories he'd heard about the abandoned needles that had to be swept up every morning, had a vague memory of some young person who had been found dead, overdosed, on one of the benches. But gentrification had swept it clean; that or the shift to designer drugs that had rendered needles obsolete.

He glanced at the buildings on his right, just opposite the apse. The shadowy form of a woman stood outlined in the light from a window on the fourth floor of one of them. Resisting the impulse to raise his hand to her, Brunetti went over to the building. The number was nowhere evident on the façade, but her name was on the top bell.

He rang it and the door snapped open almost immediately, suggesting that she had gone to the door at the sight of a man walking into the *campo*. Brunetti had been the solitary walker at this hour, tourists apparently evaporated, everyone else at home and in bed, so the odd man out had to be the policeman.

He walked up the steps, past the shoes and the papers: to a Venetian, this amoeba-like tendency to expand one's territory beyond the confines of the walls of an apartment seemed so entirely natural as barely to merit notice.

As he turned into the last ramp of stairs, he heard a woman's voice ask from above him, 'Are you the police?'

'*Sì*, Signora,' he said, reaching for his warrant card and stifling the impulse to tell her she should be more prudent about whom she let into the building. When he reached the landing, she took a half-step forward and put out her hand.

'Anna Maria Giusti,' she said.

'Brunetti,' he answered, taking her hand. He showed her the card, but she gave it the barest glance. He estimated she was in her early thirties, tall and lanky, with an aristocratic nose and dark brown eyes. Her face was stiff with tension or tiredness; he guessed that, in repose, it would soften into something approaching beauty. She drew him towards her and into the apartment, then dropped his hand and took a step back from him. 'Thank you for coming,' she said. She looked around and behind him to verify that no one else had come.

'My assistant and the others are on their way, Signora,' Brunetti said, making no attempt to advance farther into the apartment. 'While we wait for them, could you tell me what happened?'

'I don't know,' she said, bringing her hands together just at her waist in a visual cliché of confusion, the sort of gesture women made in the movies of the fifties to show their distress. 'I got home from vacation about an hour ago, and when I went down to Signora Altavilla's apartment, I found her there. She was dead.'

'You're sure?' Brunetti asking, thinking it might upset her less if he asked it that way rather than asking her to describe what she had seen.

'I touched the back of her hand. It was cold,' she said. She pressed her lips together. Looking at the floor, she went on. 'I put my fingers under her wrist. To feel her pulse. But there was nothing.'

'Signora, when you called, you said there was blood.'

'On the floor near her head. When I saw it, I came up here to call you.'

'Anything else, Signora?'

She raised a hand and waved it towards the staircase behind him, as if pointing to things in the one below. 'The front door was open.' Seeing his surprise, she quickly clarified this by saying, 'Unlocked, that is. Closed, but unlocked.'

'I see,' Brunetti said. He was silent for some time and then asked, 'Could you tell me how long you've been away, Signora?'

'Five days. I went to Palermo on Wednesday, last week, and just got home tonight.'

'Thank you,' Brunetti said, then asked solicitously, 'Were you with friends, Signora?'

The look she shot him showed just how bright she was and how much the question offended her.

'I want to exclude things, Signora,' he said in his normal voice.

Her own voice was a bit louder, her pronunciation clearer, when she said, 'I stayed in a hotel, the Villa Igiea. You can check their records.' She looked away from him in what Brunetti thought might be embarrassment. 'Someone else paid the bill, but I was registered there.'

Brunetti knew this could be easily checked and so asked only, 'You went into Signora Altavilla's apartment to . . .?'

'To get my post.' She turned and walked into the room behind her, a large open space with a peaked ceiling that indicated the room had – how many centuries before? – originally been an attic. Brunetti, following her in, glanced up at the twin skylights, hoping to see the stars beyond them, but all he saw was the light reflected from below.

At a table she picked up a piece of paper. Brunetti took it from her outstretched hand: he recognized the beige receipt for a registered letter. 'I had no idea what it could be and thought it might be something important,' she said. 'I didn't want to wait until tomorrow to find out, so I went down to see if the letter was there.'

In response to Brunetti's inquisitive glance, she continued. 'If I'm away, she gets my post, and then leaves it out when I come home, or I go down and get it from her.'

'And if she's not there when you get home?' Brunetti asked.

'She gave me the keys, and I go in to get it.' She turned to face the windows, beyond which Brunetti saw the illuminated apse of the church. 'So I went down and let myself in. And the letters were where she always put them: on a table in the entrance.' She ran out of things to say, but Brunetti waited.

'And then I went and looked in the front room. No reason, really – but there was a light on – she always turns them out when she leaves a room – and I thought maybe she hadn't

309

heard me. Though that doesn't make any sense, does it? And I saw her. And touched her hand. And saw the blood. And then I came back up here and called you.'

'Would you like to sit down, Signora?' Brunetti asked, indicating a wooden chair that stood against the nearest wall.

She shook her head, but at the same time took a step towards it. She sat down heavily, then gave in to weakness and leaned against the back. 'It's terrible. How could anyone . . .'

Before she could finish her question, the doorbell rang. He went to the speaker phone and heard Vianello announce himself, saying he was with Dottor Rizzardi. Brunetti pushed the button to release the downstairs door and replaced the phone. To the seated woman he said, 'The others are here, Signora.' Then, because he had to ask, he said, 'Is the door locked?'

She looked up at him, confusion spread across her face. 'What?'

'The door downstairs. To the apartment. Is it locked?'

She shook her head two, three times and seemed so unconscious of the gesture that he was relieved when she stopped it. 'I don't know. I had the keys.' She searched the pockets of her jacket but found no keys. She looked at him, confused. 'I must have left them downstairs, on top of the post.' She closed her eyes, then, after a moment, said, 'But you can go in. The door doesn't lock on its own.' Then she raised a hand to catch his attention. 'She was a good neighbour,' she said.

Brunetti thanked her and went downstairs to find the others.